HIDDEN SECRETS: A THRILLER
Copyright © 2024 by S.F. Baumgartner

ISBN: 979-8-9911287-0-4
Library of Congress Control Number: 2024916482

Edited by Brilliant Cut Editing and Represent Publishing

Book Cover Design by 100Covers

HIDDEN SECRETS

HIDDEN SECRETS

A THRILLER

S.F. BAUMGARTNER

FB PUBLISHING

AUTHOR'S NOTE

To all readers, especially residents and those familiar with the state of Florida, I wish to clarify that the town of Marian and the Mirror Estate are purely fictional creations for this series.

All characters and events depicted in this novel are born from my imagination. Any resemblance to actual people, living or dead, or to real-life events is entirely coincidental.

RECAPS

BURIED SECRETS - WHERE IT ALL BEGINS, BOOK 1

Twenty-five-year-old Dylan Roche barely has time to mourn his mom before an attorney appears with an invitation to his long-lost maternal grandmother's opulent estate. Eager to learn about the family he believed dead, and armed with a mysterious key his mom gave him before her death, he's ready to uncover what he believes are buried family secrets.

After a lifetime of scraping by with his mom, he's shocked she grew up wealthy. But, while the estate is lavish, something's off, and he can't shake the haunting feeling that he's being watched. As he delves deeper, he unearths his family's dark history tied to organized crime. His focus, however, remains unshaken, latched onto what the mysterious key unlocks.

At last, he locates the buried box the key opens. Then, along with those buried secrets, he discovers that the ever-present, sinister aura he's been sensing is his mother's twin sister, believed to have died shortly after birth. Very much alive, this ghost is now a criminal mastermind out to kill him. Although he dodges her murder attempt, he's left questioning everything he thought he knew about family, trust, and his past.

LIVING SECRETS, BOOK 2

Twenty-two-year-old hotel worker Lily Tso has grown up in Hong Kong believing she's an orphan. Then her mother, Olivia, who's alive and working for the US government—possibly as a spy—entrusts Lily with a mission. Lily is to deliver an antidote for an experimental biological weapon to her father, US Senator Simon Roth.

FBI Special Agent Kyle Peters is assigned to get Lily safely to the US and to her father. Posing as her boyfriend, he works with Dylan Roche, a young tycoon asked to assist them. But the trio soon finds themselves pursued by mysterious assailants in a harrowing life-or-death chase.

Undercover Agent Olivia Tso, code-named Phoenix, has infiltrated the organization run by the Ghost (Dylan's aunt) and thinks she can stay in the background during this operation. But when Kyle's shot, Dylan injured, and Lily kidnapped, Olivia must join forces with Simon, her former lover and Lily's father, and an FBI task force led by Ron Peters, Kyle's father.

Symptoms of the bioweapon soon start to appear among the population. After multiple setbacks, the team locates Lily. They deliver the antidote and other critical information to Simon. While a few casualties occur due to the virus, global catastrophe is ultimately contained.

Now, Lily's reunited with her long-lost parents, but a new world of familial connections and covert operations awaits this fast-becoming tight-knit group.

FORGOTTEN SECRET, BOOK 3

In Forgotten Secret, Clara Khoury, a magazine writer who lost her memories two decades ago, faces a turning point when a TV news report about a grisly discovery triggers a fragment of her past. Married to Dr. Michael Khoury and mother to Faith and Jason, Clara's led a stable life until this moment.

Driven to investigate the murder for a magazine article, Clara embarks on a journey, but each step leads her closer to her forgotten history. As her investigation unearths troubling hints about her past, her persistence attracts attention, including attempts on her life.

Despite mounting evidence and suspicion, Clara refuses to believe her husband, who once saved her, could be involved. Then their daughter, Faith, is abducted. Concurrently, a criminal mastermind known as the Ghost seeks to live on Mirror Estate and, in exchange for the privilege, provides a lead to a man named Ray Ho.

Eva, operating undercover to uncover the truth about her aunt Clara, whom she believed was tracked, stumbles upon Faith instead. Unaware that Faith is her cousin, Eva rescues her with the help of a task force.

The climax reveals a harrowing past event: At a party, Clara witnessed her friend's ex-boyfriend assault and kill her. Then Ray Ho's men, called in to clean up, took both women. While Clara's friend's body was left in the building where her remains were eventually found, Clara was intended to be sold. However, Clara recognized Ray Ho from her part-time job at the foundation and became a liability. Unable to risk being exposed, Ray Ho shot Clara, leading to the traumatic amnesia that defined her life for the next two decades. This revelation ties Clara's fragmented past with the present, culminating in a dramatic and poignant conclusion.

TANGLED SECRETS, BOOK 4

Grace Benson, a young schoolteacher, lives a quiet life until a disturbing note shatters her sense of normalcy. Meanwhile, wedding planner Sheila Mitchell suspects her current husband,

Doug, of being a spy. Seeking help, she turns to her ex-husband, FBI agent Ron, and their son, Kyle. Initially, they dismiss Doug's behavior as infidelity, but their assumptions change dramatically when Sheila returns home to find Doug murdered. Sheila is knocked unconscious and awakens with the murder weapon in her hand, making her the prime suspect.

At the Marino Hotel, Lily takes charge of the Private Select Program and uncovers irregularities in an account, prompting her own investigation. Olivia, determined to root out a mole leaking classified information, faces growing danger. As Grace and Kyle become targets of a kill order, they are placed in protective custody. Lily's investigation leads to her mysterious disappearance, prompting Dylan to embark on a perilous search to find her.

Olivia eventually uncovers the mole, who meets an unexpected end. During the investigation into Doug's death, his secret double life is revealed. A SWAT team, led by Ana, successfully rescues Grace and Kyle from imminent danger. Meanwhile, Lily is taken into protective custody by an undercover spy, and Dylan is captured by a drug cartel during his search for her. In a dramatic turn of events, the undercover spy ultimately rescues Dylan, bringing the intense saga to a close.

Relationship Chart

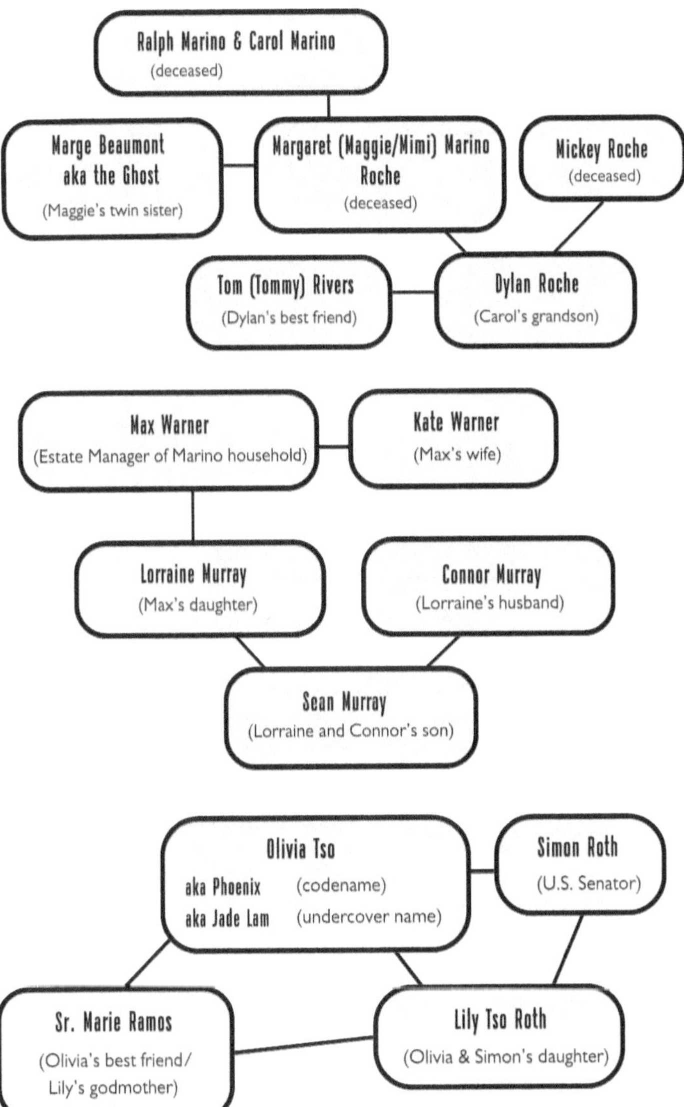

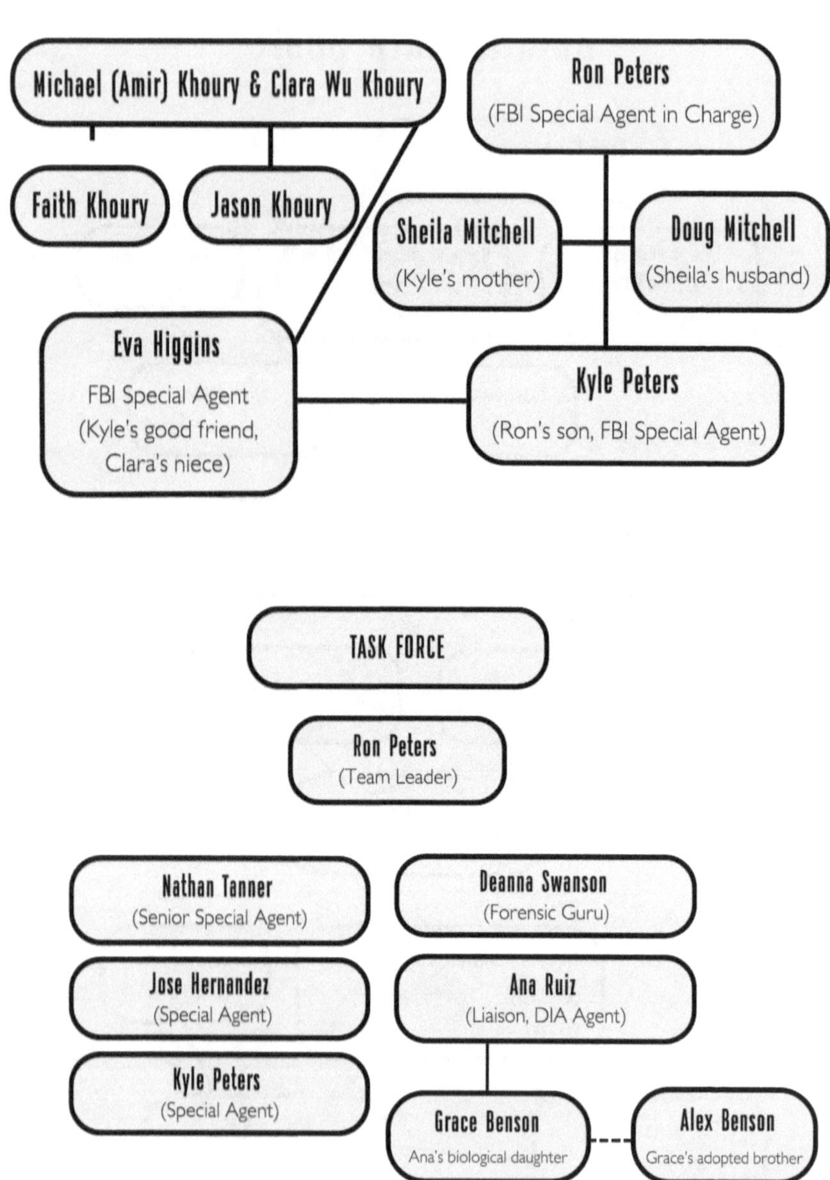

Michael (Amir) Khoury & Clara Wu Khoury
Faith Khoury
Jason Khoury
Ron Peters
(FBI Special Agent in Charge)
Sheila Mitchell
(Kyle's mother)
Doug Mitchell
(Sheila's husband)
Eva Higgins
FBI Special Agent
(Kyle's good friend, Clara's niece)
Kyle Peters
(Ron's son, FBI Special Agent)
TASK FORCE
Ron Peters
(Team Leader)
Nathan Tanner
(Senior Special Agent)
Deanna Swanson
(Forensic Guru)
Jose Hernandez
(Special Agent)
Ana Ruiz
(Liaison, DIA Agent)
Kyle Peters
(Special Agent)
Grace Benson
Ana's biological daughter
Alex Benson
Grace's adopted brother

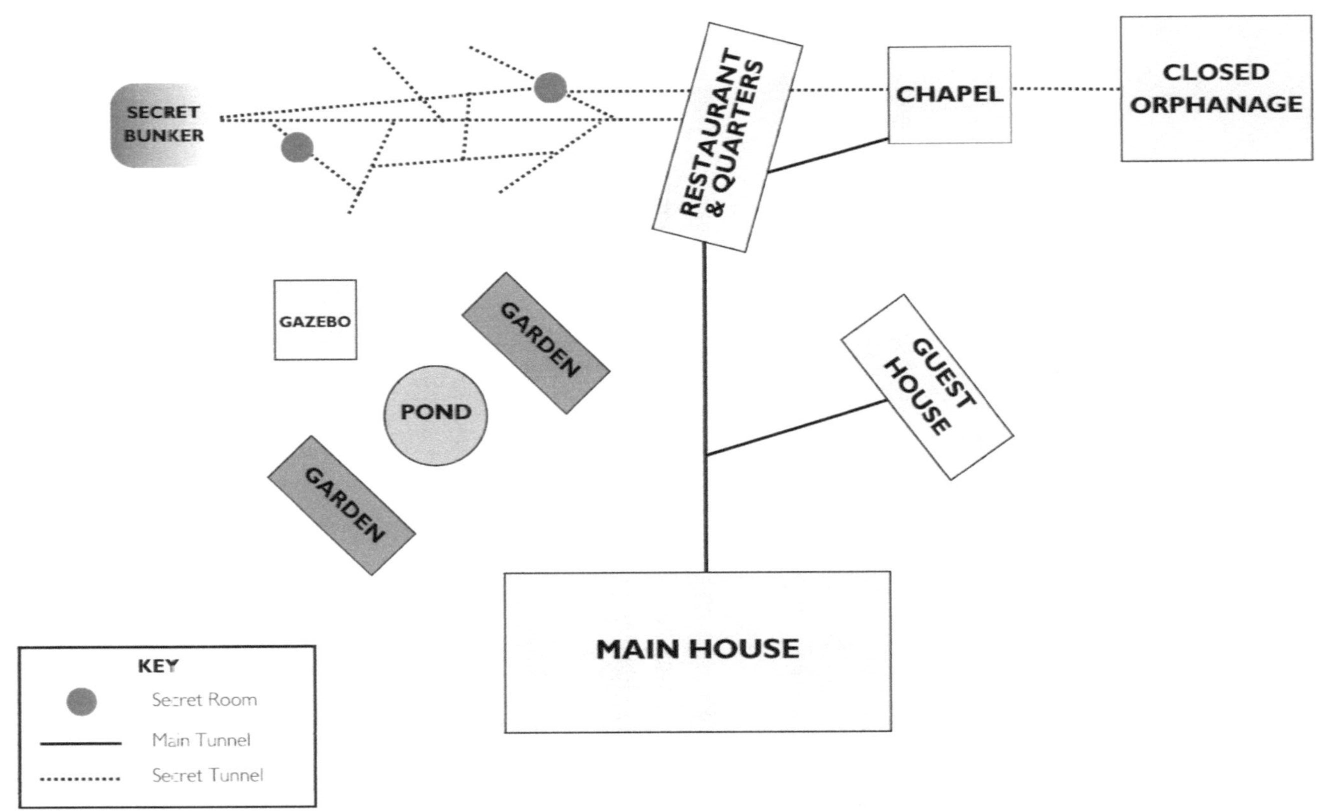

SECRET BUNKER
RESTAURANT & QUARTERS
CHAPEL
CLOSED ORPHANAGE
GAZEBO
GARDEN
POND
GARDEN
GUEST HOUSE
MAIN HOUSE
KEY
Secret Room
Main Tunnel
Secret Tunnel

PRAISE FOR BURIED SECRETS - WHERE IT ALL BEGINS: BOOK 1

I felt that the author wove a story that had twists and turns with unexpected moments sprinkled here and there.

— DELPHIA, GOODREADS

They say that dynamite comes in small packages. This one was definitely loaded with plenty of information that will blow your mind.

— TAMMY, GOODREADS

What a great story! This had enough thrill and mystery to draw me in even though it was a short novella.

— MEGAN, GOODREADS

PRAISE FOR LIVING SECRETS: BOOK 2

A great crime novel! Loved that it picked up right where the prequel left off. Loved all the chasing of Lily and who was after her. Loved the cliffhanger and can't wait to read the next one!!

— KRYSTA, GOODREADS

The book is one you will not want to put down, and if you read it at night, you will jump at every noise and check the locks on your doors and windows. Highly recommend.

— BARBARA, GOODREADS

Edge of your seat reading that keeps you guessing until the end. Plenty of drama with twists and turns that keeps you going until the end. Great characters to follow along on this adventure. Good read.

— RHONDA, GOODREADS

PRAISE FOR FORGOTTEN SECRET: BOOK 3

I am exhausted!!! This is an absolute whirlwind and it kept me guessing from the very beginning. I loved Living Secrets and I can safely say, this is even better! I'm not even going to say it's a "one more chapter" book, it's an "I read it in a day book." An amazing plot, great characters, and so many twists and turns your head will spin. I'm loving this series, if you like your fast paced psychological suspense books, give this a go!

— VICKIE, GOODREADS

WOW, TALK ABOUT NEEDING A SCORE CARD TO KEEP TRACK!! I enjoyed Clara's story, and I thought I knew who the culprit was, but I was wrong given all of the players involved! I SURE HOPE THERE'S ANOTHER BOOK IN THE WORKS!!!

— BECKY, GOODREADS

AWESOME BOOK !!! This is a great psychological suspense thriller that I would recommend to anyone.

— MICHELLE, GOODREADS

PRAISE FOR TANGLED SECRETS: BOOK 4

These books are so addicting—I don't want to do anything else except for finishing the book! The suspense and anticipation was awesome. Getting reacquainted with all of the characters—Olivia, Dylan, Lilly, Ron, Grace, etc. were all great.

— LAURA, GOODREADS

The book has infinite layers, the plot is intriguing and secrets are way too deep. The world is dangerous. The book is filled with twists and turns. The ending shook me.

— RUDRASHREE, GOODREADS

This book had amazing characters, many with secrets that seem to connect them all together. The storyline is intriguing & mysterious. I was always wondering who the person was that had their hands in both sides of the game. The ending left me shocked and ready for the story to continue.

— LUNAWOLFWY, GOODREADS

PRAISE FOR HIDDEN SECRETS: BOOK 5

If there's one thing Baumgartner knows it's suspense. If you haven't already read the first three books of this series, I'd do that. There's a wrap-up/summary of the books at the beginning, which I appreciated, but you'll get a better look at the whole picture and story if you read all of the books in order. Another great story and I can't wait to see what comes next!

— LENA, GOODREADS

What a thrilling ride into this fourth book of the series. The twist and turns keep coming and the secrets keep being revealed. I can't wait to see what is going to happen next as I know there has to be more secrets!! if you enjoy fast paced, being on the edge of your seat reading you will enjoy this series.

— CAROLYN, GOODREADS

I love how fast paced this book is! Once I started it I couldn't put it down. I HAD to know what was going to happen! Between the kidnapping and murders everything was great about this book. There were twists everywhere!

— KRYSTA, GOODREADS

"Men make counterfeit money; in many more cases,
money makes counterfeit men."
— Sydney J. Harris

CHAPTER 1

LORRAINE'S KITCHEN, MIRROR ESTATE

CONNOR

As usual, Connor Murray went downstairs to the restaurant to help his wife, Lorraine, set up for the day bright and early. Lorraine's Kitchen didn't open until 10 a.m., but they needed to do a lot of prep work first. He'd made sure Sean, their ten-year-old son, was up and ready for school before heading downstairs. His family, along with his in-laws, Max and Kate Warner, all lived in the quarters above the restaurant, a perk of being part of the Marino household. Of course, they weren't related to the Marinos, but Max had been with the family for decades as the majordomo. Max's father had also been the Marinos' head butler.

"Morning, Connor." Kate joined them in the kitchen. Max had likely gone over to the main house to start his day. Kate always helped out, either in the kitchen or out front.

"Morning, Kate." Connor flashed her a smile as he began chopping vegetables while Lorraine bustled around, organizing the ingredients and ensuring everything was in its place.

"Here, Sean, your lunch." Lorraine held out his lunch pack.

The boy grabbed it and dashed off with a quick "Thanks, Mom!"

His chest swelling, Connor watched his son walk out the door. Turning back to his task, he focused on the steady rhythm of chopping, the sound oddly soothing.

While prepping her kitchen, Lorraine asked, "What do you think of the new priest?"

"Fr. Jeremy? He's young, but he seems nice." Kate handed Connor a bowl of freshly washed tomatoes.

Fr. Jeremy seemed about Connor's age, late thirties or early forties, but then Kate still called them kids. "Does that mean Fr. Phil is finally retiring? He's talked about it for a while."

"Seems like it." Lorraine arranged the tomatoes on a platter. "Fr. Jeremy's homily was good, though. Fresh perspective."

Connor nodded, thinking about last Sunday Mass. "Yeah, he is good. Brings a different energy."

He headed out to the dining room to set the tables. The morning light streamed through the windows, casting a warm glow over the neatly arranged room. This quiet time before the rush, the calm before the storm, was always a blessing.

"Hey, you guys open yet?" A voice hollered from outside the side door.

This happened once in a while. People didn't want to go out front to check the opening hours. Connor headed to the side door and peered out. The person he saw brought him back to that fateful day.

Dad looked him in the eye through the mirror and mouthed, "Run!"

The man turned and looked into his eyes.

In an instant, his heart raced, his hands clammy. He managed to mutter, "We're open at ten."

CHAPTER 2

MARINO HOTEL BAR

SIMON

In the dimly lit hotel bar, shadows seemed to dance along with the low hum of conversation and the clinking of glasses. Simon Roth spotted Javier Jimenez on a barstool. Javier's presence was unmistakable, even from a distance. His frame, usually poised and commanding, slumped slightly over the counter, a clear sign of the weight he carried on his shoulders. The haphazard state of his hair and the absence of his customary tie painted a picture of a man unmoored, adrift in thoughts that offered little solace.

"Hey, Javier. How's it going?" Simon's voice broke through the ambient noise, a beacon of familiarity in the semidarkness.

"Simon! Good to see you, man." His smile didn't quite reach his eyes, which flickered with relief and something else—was it apprehension?

"How's the fam?" Simon nodded his thanks to the bartender who placed his drink in front of him. Scotch, neat, just the way he liked it.

Javier raised his glass. "Here's hoping Tyler stays clean this time." He took a sip of his bourbon. "I told Liz I won't bail him out again."

Simon's chest tightened. Javier had spoken of his stepson's drug addiction. Now that Simon had a daughter, a grown daughter, he could relate to Javier's concern about his kid. No matter the age, parents always worry.

"Enough about me. Now, tell me about your new fiancée and your newfound daughter." Javier raised his glass to Simon.

He displayed photos on his phone. "Olivia is doing some consulting with the FBI, and Lily actually works here. She's in charge of the Private Select Program."

Javier leaned in to look at the photos. "Oh, I met your daughter. She checked me in and escorted me to my suite. I was so tired that I didn't even connect her to you." He swallowed and lowered his voice. "I've heard rumors about Olivia. Is she really with the Bureau? Or is she still a spook?"

Simon swirled his Scotch to consider his answer. "I can neither confirm—"

"Or deny it." Javier finished the sentence. "The standard answer. Pretty much tells me she's still attached to Langley."

"Why the sudden interest? What rumors have you heard?"

Olivia recently uncovered the mole. Everyone believed that was the end of it. Or did someone finally find out she was Phoenix?

Javier shrugged. "Just curious is all. The task force 629 you guys are consulting with is mysterious."

Simon wiped away a ring someone's glass must've left on the bar. He didn't even know they assigned a number to Ron's task force. He always thought of it as the Ghost task force. "Classified stuff is always mysterious. If it's an open book, it wouldn't be classified. So, tell me about Liz. Still trying to get you to lose weight?"

Javier laughed. "Always." They chitchatted in this vein until Javier clattered his glass back onto the counter. His scowl returned before whispered words rushed out. "I don't know what to do."

"About?" Simon's concern deepened at the shift in Javier's tone.

"The story about me growing up in a foster home was a lie." Javier kept his scowl fixed on the bar's worn surface.

Simon blinked. "Okay, why? You and your folks don't get along?"

Javier hung his head, a gesture heavy with more than just denial. "It's worse. The business, uh, I can't get involved in the business."

Simon puzzled over this. Sure, it wasn't uncommon for children to shy away from a family business, but to fabricate a story of foster care? That was a drastic step. Most didn't lie about it.

"My mother agreed not to spill the beans. But now..." Javier rubbed his eyes. "I don't know what to do."

Not knowing the whole situation, Simon didn't comment.

Javier sighed again, a sound heavy with unsaid words. "I may follow your footsteps."

Simon's resignation from his senatorial position months earlier had been a decision born of necessity, a path chosen amid a thicket of complexities. While Javier wasn't a senator, he was a US congressman. Was he facing a similar crossroads?

"You're thinking about resigning?" Simon kept his voice steady but his heart not quite so.

"I can't see another way out."

"What's the problem? Anything I can do?"

Javier turned, and an inner conflict twisted his features before they slacked into resignation. He opened his mouth, perhaps ready to unveil the storm within, but then he paused. A sudden movement, a glance that darted toward the lobby, and the moment shattered.

His friend stood, throwing some cash onto the bar with a haste that spoke volumes. "I'll see you Friday. Need to go."

Simon followed Javier's gaze to a man lounging in the lobby. The Hispanic man, engrossed in his phone, seemed harmless, but the tension in Javier's posture suggested otherwise. Who was he? A threat? A reminder of whatever storm Javier was navigating?

But before Simon could piece together the puzzle, Javier was gone, slipping away into the night as if trying to outrun his own shadow. Left at the bar, a witness to a friend's turmoil, Simon stiffened under the weight of unanswered questions. What was Javier involved in? Was it political, personal, or something sinister? The man in the lobby, now looking up from his phone, seemed to hold a piece of the puzzle, yet his role in this enigmatic evening remained a mystery.

CHAPTER 3

CHAPEL, MIRROR ESTATE

FR. PHIL

The chapel was steeped in shadows as the evening sun's last rays filtered through the stained glass windows, casting a kaleidoscope of colors across the cool stone floor. Fr. Phil stood alone, his hands clasped behind his back, his gaze lingering on the empty pews. This week was significant. Fr. Jeremy Holmes's arrival as the new parochial vicar marked a new chapter for their small parish. This must be God's answer to his prayer for a man to take over.

Fr. Phil had followed Jeremy's journey since the young man had entered the seminary. Something was compelling about him —not just his intellect and his faith but also his past as a marine. How could Fr. Phil, with his own Navy SEAL background, not appreciate such a rare blend of skills and experiences? He often mused that the skills learned in such demanding service were seldom relevant to pastoral care, yet life had a way of surprising you. The Marino family, who wielded considerable influence within the parish, was a testament to that. The complexities of their dealings required a delicate touch and perhaps, at times, the strategic finesse of a military mind.

But the impending arrival of the Ghost—Ms. Carol's long-lost daughter, spirited away at birth and now a notorious criminal—heralded an unwelcome complication. Letting her live on the estate brought peril to the grounds, a reality now weighing on Fr. Phil's conscience. Were they inviting danger too great to manage?

Lord, please give me the wisdom to do the right thing!

He had prayed long and hard for what he was about to do. This was the only way to keep the promise he made and the secret he shielded without breaking his vows to God.

"Father!" The voice echoed through the stillness, jarring him from his thoughts.

Fr. Phil pivoted, his eyes adjusting. Connor, breathless and visibly upset, rushed to him, his apron from Lorraine's Kitchen still draped over his clothes. Why did he come running over here? Especially during the dinner rush in his restaurant?

"Yes, Connor?" Fr. Phil maintained his calm, a stark contrast to the young man's flustered demeanor.

Connor's gaze darted around the chapel as if he feared being overheard. He leaned in, his voice barely above a whisper. "I saw him this morning at the restaurant."

Despite the warm evening, a chill swept over Fr. Phil. Almost twenty years had passed since a US marshal deposited a frightened teenager, still adapting to his new name, at the rectory. The very thought that those dark elements had returned to disrupt the peace raised unsettling shivers over his arms.

"Are you sure?" Fr. Phil guided Connor toward the rectory. "You were only fifteen or sixteen then."

They stopped before the large crucifix hanging in the hallway, under which so many confessions and revelations had been shared. Connor lifted his gaze to the figure of Christ. His eyes dimmed, glazing with an age-old pain, even as his squared shoulders and stiffening spine displayed his certainty. "You don't forget the man who killed your parents."

CHAPTER 4
FEDERAL DETENTION CENTER

OLIVIA

The Federal Detention Center's visiting room where Olivia and Dylan now sat with the Ghost was as grim as one would expect, surrounded by thick glass and cold steel. The Ghost, Marge Beaumont, was still confined here, her permanent incarceration residence at the Mirror Estate yet to be completed. The room buzzed faintly with the low hum of monitored conversations and the watchful eyes of security cameras.

The Ghost sat across from them, seemingly undisturbed by her surroundings. Her posture was relaxed, her hands folded neatly on the table, her gaze sharp and assessing as it rested on Dylan. "How are you feeling, Dylan? I heard you had an unfortunate encounter with the cartel."

Olivia kept her expression neutral while remaining alert, scrutinizing Beaumont's every move.

Dylan replied with a nod and a steady voice. "I'm okay. In case you didn't know, they were either arrested or killed."

Enough of this. Olivia leaned forward, eager to extract the

information that prompted this meeting. "So, you called me. You have a name?"

Beaumont's lips twitched into a slight smile. "Always to the point, Olivia. Yes, I do. Moneyman."

Moneyman. It rang a bell—the shadowy figure rumored to be the financial backbone for several underground operations. If this was who this Moneyman was, then his capture could lead to major disruptions in criminal financial flows. "Do you know his name?"

"I never dealt with him directly. His main business is counterfeit currency. I don't deal with counterfeit. Check with your Secret Service. They'll share what they have with your FBI buddies, if you ask nicely. After all, counterfeit currency is their jurisdiction, no?"

"What else do you know about him?"

She shrugged. "Not much. Rumors have it that he has some kind of connection to the Perez family. Jorge Perez. The truth is that family is not in my league, so I can't help you. Don't know much about them. By the way, are you sure you never worked with Phoenix? You were on all those classified ops. Never even met him? Or her?" Her gaze, intense and probing, locked onto Olivia's.

Heartbeat elevated, Olivia breathed in to remain calm. She wouldn't allow the Ghost to rattle her. And she'd never let the Ghost know she was Phoenix. Still, the way Beaumont said "Or her?" got Olivia's mind thinking. Did Beaumont figure it out? No, Olivia was just being paranoid. "Anything else?"

"I've answered your questions. Now, I'd like to talk to my nephew alone."

Fine with that, Olivia stood up. "All right, five minutes."

DYLAN

"So, have you decided?"

The Ghost's voice, now softer, held an edge of something indefinable as she addressed him. Dylan folded his hands on the cold table. "I'm still thinking. But let me be very clear—I won't help you escape or do anything illegal. And if that's what you want, no."

The Ghost leaned in, her expression softening. "Come on. I know you have a pure heart. I wouldn't dream of corrupting you. We can work together to locate the treasures. Your parents left you something, right?"

He couldn't let on that he and Tommy had uncovered some mementos from the past. The map would be a crucial part of locating the rumored treasure, but without the map's other half or the key to decipher its symbols, it remained useless. Out loud, he said, "It's a rumor. If something is buried on Mirror Estate grounds, don't you think it'd have been found by now?"

She sighed, a gesture of frustration or perhaps resignation. "That's why you need me to help you. There are things of the past you don't know." Then she turned serious. "A little birdie told me some other people might be onto the treasures. I suggest you increase security. Don't forget there are all kinds of hidden paths in the estate."

"What other people? Who else knows about this?"

"Oh, people."

He frowned. Was she playing him? Or was she orchestrating something behind the scenes again? "I already sealed off the tunnels, except for the main ones. And we've added locks to those doors. It's secured."

"There's another—"

The conversation ended as Olivia returned. Dylan shifted in his chair, left to wonder what his aunt meant. Another what?

CHAPTER 5

MIRROR ESTATE

DYLAN

After work, Dylan Roche took Lily Roth to the Mirror Estate. Tommy, currently finishing up a report, would meet them there. Now that Dylan and Lily were officially a couple, Dylan decided to let her in on what he and Tommy had dug up a while ago.

The gate opened once the duty guard saw him on the monitor. He drove up the lengthy driveway and meandered to the garage. After parking, he got out and started to go around to open the passenger door only to see Lily get out by herself.

"Dylan, I told you. I can get out by myself." She walked toward him.

"I know, but my mom drilled it into my head to do that."

"Your mom didn't go to finishing school, did she?"

"I doubt it." He opened the door to the estate. To get to the estate proper, they had to walk the length of a football field. Max had told him repeatedly to leave the car in front and Duke, the chauffeur, would take care of it. But it wasn't Dylan's style. "She ran off and eloped with my dad when she was a high school senior."

"But I bet she went to a lot of high society events in her day."

As they approached the mansion, his phone beeped. He glanced at it. "Tommy is here. I'm telling him to head to my room." He texted while he talked.

"Watch out!"

A small figure dashed out from somewhere and almost collided with him.

"Oh, sorry, Dylan." Ten-year-old Sean stopped himself just in time.

"It's all right. What are you up to?"

The boy gestured for him to bend, then, hand to his mouth, whispered, "Exploring. I found another one."

Sean must be referring to hidden passageways. Before Dylan visited the estate for the first time the previous year, he'd only seen concealed doors on TV or in movies. He'd never have believed real-life people had them. How wrong he'd been! The estate housed so many secret tunnels and entries he doubted anyone knew them all. He thought he had all of them sealed. Evidently, Sean the explorer had located yet another one. And that arrested his attention. Could this be what the Ghost meant?

He grabbed the boy's arm. "I thought I closed all of them. Where is it?"

Sean's eyes grew wider, and he bounced from foot to foot. "There's a hidden door in the tunnel. I haven't walked all the way through, so I don't know where it goes yet. But it's long. I'll let you know."

"SEAN!"

Sean almost jumped when Max's booming voice yelled out his name. "Coming!" And he dashed off.

Minutes later, they were gathered in Dylan's suite. A corner of his spacious room was filled with the items from inside the container he and Tommy discovered: old photos, half of a worn map, and other memorabilia.

"Wow! This looks like a time capsule." Lily perused the photos and other items. "Is there a key? If the treasures are hidden in a box, don't you think there'd be a key?"

"Well, we think the key is the map or shown on the map." Tommy picked up the map. "Unfortunately, we only have half of it."

"And, according to Fr. Phil, we'd need a cipher to decode these symbols." Dylan rubbed the back of his neck. "And of course, we need the other half."

She tipped one photo to the light. "He looks a bit like you. Your grandfather?"

His neck muscles tensed beneath his fingers. "I don't know. I guess. I'm gonna ask Fr. Phil or Grandma one of these days."

A frown creased her delicate forehead. "Why haven't you asked your grandma? She might know about the treasures."

The thought occurred to him many times. "I have a feeling she might not know about it. I mean, I thought she'd have mentioned it to me. My grandfather would probably have known about it. But, Grandma, I'm not so sure. Anyway..." He spread out the photos. "You see, I looked online, and I was able to identify a few of them. They were all on my mother's side. Their criminal past. And, uh, something—well, I don't know how to explain this. Let me show you." He slid out his phone, tapped the camera, and zoomed in on the photo. "You see, this is my grandfather's arm. My father's father. I don't know who this woman is, but I kind of doubt she is my grandmother."

Tommy and Lily both stared. Then Tommy cuffed Dylan's arm. "This is new. You didn't tell me."

"I just did."

"So, you're saying this woman was with your mother's side of the family. And you suspect your paternal grandfather and this woman might be an item?" Lily asked.

"I don't know what to think. His arm appears to be on her back—"

"Right, on the small of her back." Tommy elaborated. "It does suggest some familiarity, if not intimacy."

That was what was bothering Dylan. Fr. Phil said Dylan's grandfather had been a decorated police officer. So, what was he doing with the criminals? And he appeared to be friendly with them? Was he in an undercover sting? Dylan would have to ask Fr. Phil.

A pause hung in the air, filled with the soft rustling of leaves in the gentle evening breeze. Then Lily stepped back from the table. "And what about your aunt's request? How did it go this morning?"

Dylan couldn't help but shrug, and a wry smile flickered across his lips. "I didn't commit. It's weird. She said something about other people wanting the treasures too. I didn't think anyone else would know about it. If anyone knew, they'd have to be connected to the Ghost."

"You said she wanted you to help her find the treasures." Lily touched the map. "You know, have you thought about the possibility that she has something, like maybe the other half of the map, and needs you to give her what you have so she can find the treasures?"

A realization passed between Dylan and Tommy, a possibility neither had entertained before now tangibly dawning on them. Tommy raised his eyebrows. "But you're not seriously suggesting he join forces with the Ghost?"

Lily shook her head, her gaze fixed on Dylan with an intensity that demanded consideration. "No, but he can pretend. You know, like an undercover operation. But you should tell my mom."

"I'll consider it."

CHAPTER 6
CHAPEL, MIRROR ESTATE

FR. PHIL

Evening light spilled through the chapel's stained glass windows, painting the stone floor with hues of ruby and sapphire. Fr. Phil sat in one of the pews, his hands clasped, and his eyes cast downward in prayer.

As the heavy chapel door creaked open, the sound echoing through the hall, he looked up. FBI Special Agent Ron Peters stepped into the muted lighting, his face shadowed and serious. The priest rose to greet him, offering a reassuring smile.

"Evening, Ron." Fr. Phil's voice reverberated in the vast space.

"Hey, Phil." Ron nodded, scanning the chapel. He then joined the priest and settled into the pew, his expression grim. "What's so important that you didn't go through channels?"

"Eva would have to go through all kinds of encryption protocols. And it takes time." Fr. Phil looked around to ensure no one was within earshot. "Connor came to me last night, quite shaken. He believes he's seen Doyle again."

Ron's brow furrowed deeply. "Doyle? As in Liam Doyle?"

His fingers pressed at those tight furrows, almost ironing them away as his skeptical tones dismissed the possibility. "If I remember correctly, Doyle runs with the Irishman Gang. They're not active here. Could he just be visiting?"

The priest shrugged, the fabric of his pants rustling. "It very well could be. And it's been what, twenty years now? If Doyle was looking for Connor, he'd have found him sooner, don't you think?"

Ron's fingers slid down to rub the bridge of his nose. "I don't know, Phil. The marshals are great at what they do. As far as I know, his identity is safe. I haven't heard otherwise. But you should ask for tighter security, just in case. And if he spots him again, he needs to stay out of sight and let me know. I promised Frankie I'd watch out for Connor."

Fr. Phil dipped his head, a somber weight pressing on him. "I will. Wasn't Frankie the marshal who brought him here?"

"Yes," Ron said. "He passed several years ago. His one regret was this case. It never went to trial. He held out hope Doyle would be brought to justice someday."

Right, it had been Frankie—Connor's neighbor at the time—whom Connor had run to for help on that fateful day.

A beat later, Fr. Phil ventured another topic to lighten the mood. "You heard about Ortiz?"

Ron looked to the side, his gaze distant. "Why does the name sound familiar?"

"Dante Ortiz. Former FDLE agent. He's the new chief of security here."

"Right, right. I remember now." Ron snapped his fingers. "He was undercover and almost died saving Dylan and Lily last year. He retired from FDLE?"

"Medical retirement, I think. He's still fit."

"Good, he should be great. Let him know to beef up security." Ron stood and adjusted his coat. "Keep me posted, Phil."

"I will. And thank you for coming."

CHAPTER 7

TASK FORCE OFFICE

RON

Ron stepped into the task force office as the sun began to rise, its early light casting long shadows across the room. The office buzzed with the low hum of computers and the distant clatter of keyboards, a familiar symphony to start another day on edge. His mind was already racing with the details Olivia relayed the night before. Their new target was Moneyman with ties to the Perez family, and according to the Ghost, the Secret Service was already circling the waters.

With a steaming cup of coffee in hand, he approached the large digital screen in the squad room. As he sipped the bitter brew, the door swung open and Nathan Tanner, his senior agent whose rugged look and wary eyes betrayed years of fighting bad guys, walked in with a stranger.

"Guys, this is Agent Flo Davis, Secret Service." Tanner gestured toward the new face—a matronly Black woman with medium-length, frizzy hair, who carried herself with an unspoken authority.

One by one, José Hernandez, Kyle Peters, and Ana Ruiz

exchanged greetings, each offering a handshake and a smile. Ron, observing the formalities, gave a nod toward the absent figure. "Our tech guru, Deanna Swanson, is in the lab now. Thanks for helping out."

"Glad to be here," Davis replied, her voice steady, her eyes scanning the room.

Ron then turned his attention back to the team. "Our new target is Moneyman. Agent Davis, would you like to get us up to speed?"

"Certainly." Davis, with her hawklike gaze and aura of unspoken authority, didn't waste a moment. "As you're aware, we've been tracking a significant uptick in counterfeit operations. Uh, let me back up a bit. Moneyman is, uh, a title of sorts. For a long time, Diego Morales served as the Moneyman. But since he stepped down a few years ago, a new person has taken his place. Unfortunately, the identity of the new Moneyman remains a mystery."

"Can you elaborate? How does one become the Moneyman?" Ron asked.

"According to our intel, a consortium of criminal figures, like the Japanese yakuza, appoints someone to act as the Moneyman." Davis continued. "We've heard rumblings that the Perez family might be extending their reach into this arena. It's still conjecture at this point, without concrete evidence, but given their history, it's a lead we cannot ignore."

"Well, that is exactly what we heard too," Ron said. It would jibe with what Olivia heard from the Ghost.

"An undercover agent alerted us to a deal being made. Once I have the details, I'll share."

"Thank you!" Ron said. "Tanner—"

"I'll look into the Perez family." Ana tucked wisps of her curly brown bob back behind her ears.

Davis scoffed. "I don't think you can even get close to the Perez family. We tried."

"I still have some contacts," Ana muttered.

Ron frowned. Something was off with her this morning. Although her poised shoulders and alert posture remained intact, she didn't offer any opinion or ask any questions about the Perez family or the Morales. And now, she said she had contacts. Anyhow, he nodded, accepting her offer, and continued to assign tasks for the others.

"Ana, walk with me." He beckoned as he headed back to his office. "What's going on?"

"I had some dealings with the Perez family."

There must be more to it, what with her being especially tight-lipped today. "Oh?"

CHAPTER 8

MIRROR ESTATE

FR. PHIL

In the morning's soothing silence, Fr. Phil lingered at the lectern, putting away his notes for the weekend's homily. Today, Connor occupied his thoughts. In a way, Fr. Phil felt responsible for the young man. Years ago, he pulled Connor out of his depression after his parents' murders and encouraged him to finish high school.

Though he told Connor these individuals might simply be passing by, deep down Fr. Phil doubted his own words. He needed to be proactive. After folding his reading glasses into his pocket, he made his way across the quiet, leaf-strewn church grounds toward the security office. It was time to address the situation more directly.

At the guardhouse, a new figure, robust and alert, with a thick mustache that balanced his squared face, stood waiting for him. Dante Ortiz, the new chief of security Dylan brought in, straightened up as Fr. Phil approached and extended a hand with a respectful nod. "Hi, Father. Heard about you saving Dylan's life when he first got here."

They shook hands. The priest's face broke into a smile. "I was there by God's grace. But what you did for Lily and Dylan a few months ago was a true act of bravery."

Ortiz dismissed the compliment with a humble shake of his head. "I was just doing my job." He exhaled and shifted his feet, his arms flexing as if straining against a frustrated resignation. "They wouldn't put me back in the field after that. I just can't ride the desk until sunset."

He gazed over Fr. Phil's shoulder, apparently lost in thought. "And then Dylan said he needed to upgrade the security here to prepare for the Ghost's imminent arrival. Can't turn down a cushy job like this." His chuckle, though light, carried a serious undertone.

Fr. Phil held up a hand. "You may change your mind after I tell you this. I'd like you to beef up security around the estate, especially around the restaurant."

"Understood. What's the specific concern there?"

He hesitated, glancing around as if the very air might carry his words beyond their confidential bubble. "The Irishman Gang was spotted here. They aren't a nice bunch."

Ortiz rubbed at his dark mustache as he processed this, his stance shifting to one of alert readiness with the precision of a former law enforcer. "Have they made threats to anyone?"

"No, not directly." Fr. Phil waved the question away. "For all I know, they could be passing through and stopped to grab a bite to eat. But given their history, uh, I want to be careful."

"What history?" Ortiz cocked his head. "If I'm not mistaken, this gang isn't active here. They're more known in the northeastern states."

"Quite right." Fr. Phil acknowledged with a nod. How much should he reveal to this man, a relative newcomer to their community? "Twenty years ago, they killed a couple in New Jersey. Their teenage son came home from a friend's house and witnessed it. He escaped, was relocated, given a new identity. He was supposed to return to the trial, but it never happened."

"Why not?" Ortiz lowered his hand, but he'd brushed one side of his mustache askew.

The priest shrugged. "Evidence mysteriously disappeared. Witnesses recanted. Prosecutors had accidents. All kinds of mishaps. That's just what I was told."

Ortiz looked at him sideways. "Why would the marshals send the boy here? The Marino criminal empire? My understanding is that they turned legit not long ago."

Ah, the man pieced together the implications quickly! One must be careful about what they revealed around him. Still, Fr. Phil leaned closer, lowering his voice. "Ah, you're mistaken. And I see you're not familiar with this part of the history. Ralph Marino turned himself in and cooperated with the Feds not long before this event. So, a little over twenty years ago. Because he was, uh, what you call a CI, I believe the underworld hadn't gotten wind of it yet. The US marshals, in their infinite wisdom, thought that nobody would dare mess with the Marinos. Where better to hide the kid than here?"

Ortiz's eyes widened. "And he's been here ever since?"

Fr. Phil nodded, a profound sense of duty pressing on him. "Yes, and that's why we can't take any risks—not with the safety of everyone here, and especially not with someone with a past as tangled as his."

Ortiz straightened up. "I understand, Father. I'll start by increasing patrols around the restaurant and reviewing our surveillance protocols. We'll keep a vigilant eye. Safety is our priority, after all."

CHAPTER 9

MARINO HOTEL

SIMON

The Marino Hotel, clad in stone and glass, stood proudly on the bustling city avenue. Tasteful lighting underscored its opulent façade. Lush landscaping framed the entrance, with meticulously manicured hedges, colorful flower beds, and gently bubbling fountains creating an oasis-like atmosphere. The crisp evening air was a welcome caress after the day's lingering warmth as Simon stepped out of his car, Olivia close at his side.

Lily and Dylan waited for them at the door. Apparently, the two hadn't bothered to leave after work.

"Where's the red carpet?" Simon feigned hurt.

While Dylan laughed, Lily sent him a scowl. "I'm sorry, Dad. You're not the honored guest this evening."

"Don't mind him, you two." Olivia waved them off.

"Okay, then, follow me." Lily led the group through the marble lobby and into a more secluded private banquet room set aside for the evening's event—an intimate dinner party hosted by Congressman Javier Jimenez. The clinking of glasses and the rumble of soft laughter punctuated a low buzz of conversation.

Cream linens draped elegant round tables, and each centerpiece, an artful arrangement of assorted roses and carnations, added bursts of color against the neutral palette.

"Hey, Simon!" Javier approached with a broad smile and an outstretched hand. The warmth in his greeting suggested his problem had since been resolved.

Introductions flew as familiar and new faces converged around him. Soon, a dark-haired woman sauntered over with an effortless charisma. Ah, yes, Liz, Javier's wife. She gave Simon a knowing smile as if acknowledging the unspoken bond of their shared experiences in political spheres. Then she beckoned over a college-aged young man with an easy smile and introduced him as Tyler, her son. The young man's handshake was firm, but his eyes and demeanor screamed something else.

Nina Rodriguez, the congressman's dynamic campaign manager, and Sam Tucker, his chief of staff, soon joined the growing group. Both were key figures in Javier's team, known for their strategic minds and relentless drive.

As conversations ebbed and flowed, Simon exchanged pleasantries with several acquaintances from his days as a senator. He noted Dylan's slight discomfort as Nina approached him first among the guests. Simon couldn't help but sympathize. Nina's reputation for tenacity in securing contributions was well-earned, and Dylan, the heir to the Marino empire, was a prime target.

Dinner unfolded with a pleasant cadence, and expertly prepared dishes wafted tempting aromas on their way to each table. Laughter and stories abounded, and glasses rose in toasts to old friendships and new beginnings.

As the meal neared its end, Nina approached Simon, her pitch polished and persuasive. The conversation was light, yet the intent clear—she was here to secure a substantial donation. Just as Simon prepared to respond, Javier waved her off. "Nina, leave the man alone. He's unemployed right now."

The room erupted in good-natured laughter, the tension

breaking like a thin sheet of ice. While the comment was technically true, Simon was far from idle. He had been consulting with the FBI task force, and the offer to run the Marino Foundation was nearly in his grasp, promising a new chapter tantalizingly within reach.

DYLAN

After bidding farewell to the gathering, Dylan led Lily and her parents toward the exclusive elevator servicing the penthouse atop the Marino Hotel. His grandmother's advice echoed in his mind, a convincing argument about keeping money within the family by occupying one of the hotel's most luxurious offerings instead of renting elsewhere. The elevator whisked them upward, its smooth ascent almost imperceptible.

"Just so everyone knows, they're just finishing an upgrade," he warned. "Might be a bit dusty, and some tools are still lying around. Workers are supposed to finish up in a few days."

The doors opened to a sprawling penthouse. The living room, dominated by wraparound windows, almost floated over a panoramic view of the city skyline, the lights twinkling like distant stars. The interior was elegantly appointed, with contemporary furniture to complement the sleek modern architecture.

"Wow, I like this." Lily stepped closer to the window, drawn to the view. Dylan moved to join her, their shoulders nearly touching as they looked out over the city.

"Kind of reminds you of Hong Kong, right? The scenery," he remarked, his voice low, almost reflective.

She nodded, her gaze still fixed on the view. "So, are you really taking this, then? It must be expensive."

His chest swelled. "I know. But I got a raise, and I get a reduced rate." His new position within the Marino empire came with perks that made even a penthouse seem within reach. "Have you decided what you're going to do with your condo in Hong Kong?"

She had inherited a condo from her uncle and had been toying with the idea of selling it. Now her face scrunched. "If I go back to visit, I'd like to have a place to stay."

"You can stay at the hotel. I'd arrange comp accommodation."

"That's nice of you. Anyway, Mom listed it on Airbnb and other sites. So, it's making some money." She gestured back to the view. "This is beautiful."

Simon, having quietly toured the space, joined them. "It's a smart move, Dylan. In a place like this, you're not just living— you're investing in your future." He gripped Dylan's shoulder. "You're now the public figure of Ms. Carol. You have an image to project."

OLIVIA

As the elevator descended from the penthouse's lofty heights, Olivia couldn't help feeling nostalgic. The scenic view reminded her of Hong Kong, and the city would forever be in her heart. However, her loyalty would always be to America since she accepted the offer from her CIA handler decades ago. It seemed she was the only one who hadn't voiced an opinion, so she said, "It's really nice. I like it."

"Thanks. I'm not moving in until the end of the month." Dylan tucked his hands into his suit pants' pockets.

The elevator dinged as it reached the ground floor, its doors sliding open with a quiet hiss. Simon stepped out first, fished out a wad of cash, and headed to the valet. A moment later, he returned.

Olivia stood beside him, Lily, and Dylan, the warm evening

breeze ruffling her hair as they waited for the car. But she waved them off. "Why don't you two go get your cars? No need to wait with us."

"Okay, then, see you at home." Lily started toward the garage with Dylan who also bid them farewell.

Years of training had ingrained in Olivia a heightened sense of awareness, making her attuned to her surroundings. As her gaze wandered, it landed on the side garden where two figures moved with agitated gestures.

"Is that Javier? And Tyler?" She narrowed her eyes as she tried to discern their identities through the twilight.

Simon, following her line of sight, squinted. "I think so. I wonder what's going on?"

Whatever it was, the tension between the two figures was palpable even from a distance. Javier's hands were animated, emphasizing his words, while Tyler's posture was rigid and defensive. Javier turned to leave, but Tyler's hand shot out and shoved him to the ground with a force that knocked the breath out of Olivia.

"Hey!" Simon reacted, racing toward his fallen friend. Olivia sprinted right behind him. Lily and Dylan must've heard the commotion because their footsteps pounded after them.

Simon reached Javier first, kneeling beside him and helping him to his feet. "Javier, you okay?"

Javier winced as he kneaded his shoulder. "Yeah, I'm fine."

Olivia's attention shifted to Tyler, who was about to slip away. Her instincts kicked in, and she grabbed his arm and twisted it behind his back into a hammerlock. "Not so fast, Tyler."

Tyler struggled against her firm grip. "Let me go!"

"It's okay. Let him go!"

At Javier's urgent request, Olivia hesitated and glanced back. Her grip, though still firm, lessened slightly. "You sure?"

"Yes, just let him go. It's... it's not what it looks like." Javier held up both hands, an earnest pleading gleaming in

his eyes.

When released, Tyler rubbed his arm and glared at her.

"This isn't over," he muttered before stalking off into the night.

Simon touched Javier's hand. "What happened, man?"

Javier sighed, his whole body deflating. "Just a disagreement. It's nothing, really."

Unconvinced, Olivia shifted her feet. What could she do beyond respect Javier's wishes?

CHAPTER 10

THE MITCHELL RESIDENCE

KYLE

A somber gray draped the day, the sky mourning in tandem with those gathered beneath it. Kyle stood amid friends and family, the air around him thick with the scent of freshly turned earth and muted grief. The funeral had been a somber affair, fitting for a man whose life ended as tumultuously as Doug Mitchell's had. Despite the revelations about Doug's secret life as a hit man for a Mexican cartel, a palpable sense of loss hung over the attendees.

After the service, the reception seemed a stark contrast to the morning's gravity in an effort to keep the atmosphere light, to celebrate Doug's life rather than dwell on the darkness of his demise. The task force members who had come to show their support now surrounded Kyle's mother, Sheila. Their presence added to the complexity of Doug's life—tangled in deeds that defied categorization as black or white.

Ron arrived late, shifting the dynamics of the gathering. Nods met his excuse, another memorial service. After all, life must continue its relentless march forward despite individual tragedies.

Dylan and Lily, too, mingled with the mourners, their interactions tinged with the unmistakable hue of new love. Kyle watched them from a distance, a twinge of something akin to loss but not quite as sharp passing through him. He had harbored feelings for Lily once, even imagined a future with her that now seemed as ephemeral as the sunlight dancing on the dust motes in the room.

Recently, Grace Benson alone offered true solace, her efforts to distract and comfort him not going unnoticed. Kyle appreciated her presence, a balm to the sting of witnessing Lily and Dylan together, and her vivacity and warmth provided a welcome counterpoint to the day's gloom and his heart's complexities—a heart not broken but bruised by the what-ifs and might-have-beens.

As the reception meandered on, he found himself in conversation with his mother, her resilient strength a constant source of awe. Then his phone vibrated. Excusing himself, he glanced at the screen—unknown number.

The voice on the other end belonged to Alex, Grace's brother, his words slicing through the reception's background noise. "Wait—hold on." Kyle shifted his grip on the phone. "Can you slow down?"

The only words that came through discernibly were "Someone took Grace."

His mother must've sensed something was wrong. Now she came up beside him, a frown creasing her saddened eyes. As soon as he hung up, she touched his arm. "What's the matter?"

"Grace got snatched." He patted her hand on his arm, eased it away, then hurried off in search of Ana, Grace's birth mother.

They had captured those responsible for threatening Grace's and Kyle's lives a week ago. Before then, she'd led a simple and quiet life—or so she'd said. So, why would someone abduct her now?

OLIVIA

Olivia stood in Sheila's house, the reception buzz surrounding her. Olivia hadn't attended many funeral services, mostly because she was often out of the country. She and Simon were here not because they knew the deceased but because they wished to support their young friend Kyle, who had just lost his stepfather. Although she understood there was no love lost between the two.

People gathered in small clusters. Others moved about slowly, offering condolences. Her gaze drifted, taking in the somber faces and subdued atmosphere.

"Weird. Kyle is rushing out of the door." Lily's voice cut through Olivia's thoughts.

Olivia glimpsed Kyle hurrying toward the exit with Ana and Ron close behind him. Why would he leave his widowed mother now? Her curiosity piqued, Olivia crossed her arms and tried to glimpse Sheila. "I wonder what happened."

"Maybe they got a case," Simon suggested.

"Bad guys don't take breaks." Dylan shrugged.

Did Lily shudder? Olivia frowned at her resilient daughter. Maybe she'd better shift the conversation to something lighter. "So, what are you guys doing after this?"

Dylan exchanged a glance with Lily. "We might catch a movie or—"

His phone's chime cut him off. At the same time, Lily glanced at her phone. "Oh no!"

Dylan muttered a curse as he read his text.

"Something wrong?" Olivia asked.

Before either could respond, Simon picked up his phone and frowned. "Nina. I contributed already. What does she want now?" He swiped to answer. "Hi, Nina... What? When? Yes, of course, I'll be right there."

"Oh my! Have they arrested her?" Lily asked.

Olivia frowned. "What's going on?"

Dylan scanned the surroundings while tucking his phone away. "The congressman was found dead."

"No," Simon was telling Lily. "But Nina is being held for questioning."

Javier was murdered? Nina was a person of interest? Just what had happened? Olivia frowned, then eyed her daughter and Dylan. Those two were like magnets for trouble. "Lily, Dylan, a murder investigation is not for amateurs. Can be dangerous. Stay out of it."

"It happened in the hotel. I'll get the incident report." Dylan jammed his hands into his pockets and rocked off his toes.

"And he was a Private Select member." Lily held up both hands. "Sorry, Mom, but unless I quit, I'm gonna be in the loop."

"Right, fine." Olivia rolled her eyes. "Just do your job. Stay in the hotel. Don't play detectives!"

"Yes, ma'am," Dylan intoned and Lily saluted.

CHAPTER 11

GRACE'S APARTMENT

GRACE

The sun filtering through the stained glass windows cast rainbow patterns along the quaint church hall where Grace Benson had spent her morning. The Bible study session had been a refreshing return to a routine she had missed dearly. With the melody of worship still echoing in her mind, she stepped outside into the crisp fresh air and breathed deeply, drawing in a sense of renewal and purpose. The recent turmoil, including the unexpected stint in an FBI safe house when she was targeted by an assassin, had left her yearning for the familiar comfort of her faith.

She had extended the invitation to Kyle, the FBI agent she met during her ordeal, hoping to share this part of her life with him. His polite refusal didn't dampen her spirits. It was just another step in their journey. "Work in progress," she mused to herself, a smile tugging at her mouth. In time, Kyle's heart would open to the spiritual guidance she found so vital—no doubt about it.

After sharing a light meal and engaging in conversations with her fellow attendees, Grace headed home.

During the mundane drive back, her thoughts adrift in anticipation for the dinner with Kyle, she answered her brother on the hands-free phone. His offer to upgrade her laptop with a new drive was just like him, always tinkering with gadgets and looking out for her in his tech-savvy way.

"Sure, that sounds great, Alex. I'll see you soon, then." The thought of a faster, more efficient laptop, a small but significant upgrade in her daily life, made her smile.

She parked her car, gathered her things, and strolled inside. Her apartment, dominated by her piano and scattered music sheets, welcomed her. She'd planned a quiet day of playing piano, organizing next week's lessons, and perhaps phoning her mother, who was always eager to hear about her endeavors. She'd barely kicked off her shoes and settled into the welcoming couch when a sharp knock at the door shattered the stillness—a knock far too soon to be Alex. With a curious frown, Grace leveraged the modern conveniences of her apartment and tapped into her doorbell camera through her phone. The screen flickered to life and revealed a deliveryman cradling a vibrant bouquet.

Her brow furrowed. How unusual. Flowers? For her? When was the last time someone had sent her flowers? It must be a mistake—a wrong apartment, perhaps. The deliveryman shifted from foot to foot, and a wild thought fluttered through her mind, igniting a flicker of hope. Kyle. Could he have orchestrated this surprise? He wasn't known for grand romantic gestures, but maybe, just maybe, he was trying to change.

Pushed by an emerging thrill at the thought of a secret admirer, Grace hurried to the door. Her heart skipped a beat as she unlocked it. The door swung open, and she gasped at the stunning bouquet. Roses and daisies danced together in a riot of colors, their fragrance wafting a sweet and intoxicating blend that drew her in.

"Miss Benson?" The deliveryman's voice was polite, yet it carried a hint of something else she couldn't quite place.

"Yes, that's me." So they were for her! She started to reach for them, despite the confused surprise stirring her up.

Before she could react, the man's demeanor changed. His hand shot out, gripping her with unexpected strength, and the cold, hard press of what could only be the barrel of a gun jammed against her back.

A chill surged through her veins, a stark, icy fear that rooted her to the spot. Her mind raced, the beautiful bouquet forgotten as she stared into the eyes of a man who had transformed from a mere delivery person into a clear and present danger.

CHAPTER 12

ON THE ROAD

ANA

The urgency in her actions was palpable as Ana barely acknowledged Ron's presence before gunning the engine, her mind a whirlwind as they sped through the streets. She only recently started a relationship with Grace, the daughter she gave up twenty-five years ago, and the fragile beginnings of that relationship were now under threat. The fear of losing her now churned into a sharp ache in her chest.

"Calm down." Ron's voice, steady and calm, cut through her reverie.

She took a deep breath. "I'm calm."

"You know, if this was a case, you'd be benched."

Her jaw clenched. She flexed it to force out words. "I'm just going to see what happened." Then she focused on the road, her hands gripping the steering wheel with white-knuckled intensity. They had scant information, and every passing second was another second Grace was in danger.

At the apartment complex, Kyle pulled up behind them, his expression grim. Alex was already there, waiting in his car, a bundle of nervous energy. As Ana and Ron approached, Alex got out with his laptop.

Once everybody surrounded him, he opened his laptop. "I'll show—let me back up. I was just dropping off her laptop. Got here about a half hour ago. I used the code to enter. She gave me the code, just in case. The door wasn't locked. These days since the threat, she's been security conscious." He inhaled deeply. "Her phone was still on the couch. And a flower bouquet was on the floor."

Now he woke his laptop up. "That's when I checked the door cam. I installed it and helped her set it up. I went to the cloud. And here's what I saw." He turned the laptop around to show them.

A deliveryman approached. The doorbell rang, and Grace opened the door. Seconds later, the flowers thrown haphazardly, Grace walked out with the man.

"I don't think she went willingly," Alex said.

Ana agreed. "No, she didn't."

"Back up a bit." Kyle pointed. "Okay, freeze. See that? It appears the guy's holding a gun to her back. That's why she went."

"I see a camera pointing to the entrance and exit." Ron gestured toward the device. "Let's check the footage."

They headed to the apartment complex's office where Ron showed his FBI credentials and asked to see the security footage. Soon, they were watching the delivery van coming in and going out.

"Would you please email the footage to me?" Ron gave the manager his email address.

Ana looked at the image over Ron's shoulder, memorizing every detail of the vehicle. The reality of the situation was setting in, and with it, a fierce determination. "We should canvas the area for any witnesses and put out a BOLO."

Ron met her gaze, his determination matching hers. "I agree."

"Let's split up," Kyle suggested. "I'll start knocking on doors around here. Maybe someone saw where they went."

Alex held up a hand. "I'll go with you."

Ron nodded. "Ana, let's look at the apartment."

"Oh, speaking of her apartment, Grace mentioned some weird things happening, but we thought it was connected to the contract hit a couple of weeks ago."

"Weird things?" Ana palmed curls away from her temples.

"Yeah, things were moved. Her piano settings were changed. Things like that."

She exchanged a glance with Ron. Was Grace's abduction well-planned in advance?

"Before you go knock on doors, would you come with us to check the apartment, Alex?" Ron asked. "You can tell if anything is out of the ordinary or misplaced."

"Of course."

As they proceeded to the apartment, Ana's thoughts went back to Grace. She sent up a silent prayer for her daughter's safety, hoping against hope they'd find her soon.

Before they stepped out of the elevator, Ron told Alex not to touch anything. He agreed. As they entered the apartment, nothing seemed to be amiss. The door itself showed no other signs of forced entry, which only deepened the mystery. Grace's phone now lay next to her purse on the kitchen counter—Alex must have moved her phone. Ana picked it up, turning to Alex. "Do you know the pin?"

He shook his head and flexed his hands into fists.

"Bag it," Ron, ever the voice of pragmatism, chimed in. "We'll take it back with us. Deanna can crack it."

They moved through the apartment with a practiced efficiency, spreading out to cover more ground. Ana took a moment to center herself, her mind racing through the possibilities as she began her own meticulous search. "Alex, let us know if anything looks out of place or if anything seems different to you," she instructed, her detective instincts fully engaged.

She approached the digital piano. The idea that someone had been inside, subtly altering Grace's environment, sent a shiver down her spine. She examined the piano, though it revealed nothing out of the ordinary. Not one to give up easily, she then turned her attention to the bench and opened it to a collection of music books.

As she lifted the books, something small and metal clinked to the floor. The sound, though faint, cut through the silence of the apartment like a whisper of a clue begging to be heard. She bent down, and her heart rate spiked as she saw the object.

She removed the ring from her finger and placed it beside the note on the nightstand. Papi and Prince weren't home. If she was going to make her escape, it had to be now. Her gaze swept the room, from the windows to the elaborate desk, over to the plush bed at the center, and finally to the bathroom and walk-in closet. She had no choice but to leave, and she would find a way to make it work.

"Ana!" The voice snapped her back to reality.

Ron's gaze shifted from her to the ring. "What do you have?"

She took a photo of the ring in situ, then placed it on the keyboard and tilted her head toward the door. He understood and followed her outside. "I need to tell you something."

KYLE

The apartment seemed frozen in time, a silent witness to its occupant's sudden disappearance. Despite the numerous times

Kyle chauffeured Grace home, he'd never crossed the threshold into her private world. Now he would search every nook and cranny.

Behind him, footsteps approached, and he didn't need to look to know it was Alex. "Anything?"

The word strung together a threadbare hope, fraying with each passing moment. How well Kyle could relate. Disappointment bowed on his shoulders. He straightened, his hands pausing in their meticulous examination of a drawer. "Nothing."

Alex's gaze drifted toward the front room, curiosity flickering in his eyes. "Seems they found something, though."

Prompted by Alex's observation, Kyle entered the front room in time to glimpse his dad and Ana stepping outside. "Where are they going?" he muttered, more to himself than expecting an answer.

"No clue." Alex's attention drifted to the digital piano. He leaned over, his focus caught by something. "Hey, look, I've never seen this before. Definitely not on her finger."

Kyle joined him, his gaze following to where Alex pointed. There, amid the ivory keys, lay a ring, solitary and significant. Kyle's detective instincts kicked in as he captured the ring's image with his phone. Then, after donning a pair of gloves with practiced ease, he picked up the ring. The crest emblazoned on it was intricate, a design meant to signify something or someone. "Looks like a Hogwarts crest."

Alex inclined closer. "But that's not it. It's a crest, all right, but not Hogwarts. She likes Harry Potter, but not enough to buy a ring like this."

They fell silent.

"Bag it and take it back." The voice, authoritative and familiar, broke the silence. Dad had returned, his presence commanding. Ana was conspicuously absent.

Kyle secured the ring in an evidence bag. "Yes, sir."

His dad's gaze swept the room, a silent assessment before he spoke again. "Kyle, go on canvassing. Alex, I need you to go to your folks' house. It's unlikely, but we can't rule out ransom demand. I'll send Hernandez over. He'll get your parents' phones set up so we can monitor."

"My parents! Dad is a pastor, and Mom works at the church. They don't have any money."

"I know it's highly unlikely, but we have to be prepared."

Kyle still didn't see Ana. "Where's Ana?"

"Chasing some leads."

CHAPTER 13

IN THE VAN

GRACE

The rhythmic pounding of Grace's heart seemed to keep time with the van's tires as they rolled ceaselessly along. Encased in a van masquerading as a flower delivery service, she shifted, the irony of her predicament not lost on her. As they'd approached the van, a gun at her back, the cheery logo on the panel seemed to mock her with its promise of beauty and life, a stark contrast to the fear gripping her.

Now, seated on the passenger side, she darted her gaze around for anything that might offer a clue to her whereabouts or her captor's intentions. "What do you want with me?" she asked. "Why am I here?"

The man behind the wheel, a silhouette of indifference, kept his gaze fixed on the road. "Quiet. You'll know soon enough."

But Grace wasn't ready to resign herself to silence. "Where are you taking me?" she pressed on, her voice gaining strength. "What's going to happen to me?"

"Look, just sit tight and keep quiet. It's better for you," he snapped, annoyance breaking his stoic façade. His brief flare of emotion spurred Grace on, a small victory in the oppressive atmosphere of fear.

Her mind raced through every crime show she'd ever watched, each scenario playing out in her head. She shouldn't have gotten in the van, but what choice did she have? *Help me, Lord!*

The van veered off the main road, the change in terrain noticeable even without looking outside. They were heading into more isolated territory, the likelihood of passing strangers dwindling with each mile. "Are we going to the coast?" Grace tried again, a strategy to keep the man engaged, perhaps to catch him off guard or glean useful information.

"No," came the curt reply, the man's patience clearly wearing thin. "And enough with the questions. It doesn't concern you."

Didn't concern her? Where he was taking her didn't concern *her*? Seriously?

Grace couldn't help herself. The silence was suffocating, each minute stretching into an eternity of dread. "If you're going to hurt me, just know, someone will be looking for me. They'll find you."

The man let out a derisive snort. "Bold words. We'll see about that."

The conversation, if it could be called that, fell silent as the van continued its journey. Grace took a deep breath to steady her nerves. She needed to remain vigilant, to remember every detail of the route, anything to help her or someone else piece together her whereabouts later.

Then the van swerved, and the sharp maneuver sent her heart into her mouth. Instinctively, her hands shot up to grip the overhead bar, bracing for an impact that never came. Then she glimpsed something in the side mirror, a fleeting image that sent adrenaline surging through her veins.

"What's happening?" she demanded, unable to hide her panic

as she peered through the mirrors, but she couldn't make sense of the reflection that had caught her eye.

"Just sit tight," the man ordered, his focus now divided between the road and whatever had prompted the sudden swerve.

With the tension in the van so palpable, the air so thick with unspoken fears and questions, she struggled to breathe. But she had to keep her wits about her and look for any opportunity, no matter how slim, to escape or find help.

She sucked in a gasp at the sight of another van coming faster and faster straight at them in the rearview and side mirrors.

CHAPTER 14

POLICE STATION

SIMON

Reanalyzing the events that led them here, Simon walked into the bustling police station with Olivia in tow. The fluorescent lights overhead cast a harsh glare, illuminating controlled chaos. Officers and detectives moved with purpose, their conversations a low hum of urgency.

"Senator." Detective Rick Spaulding, the stocky detective with graying hair and a stern face, raised a hand to flag Simon down.

Simon nodded in acknowledgment and quickened his pace. "Detective," he greeted as he approached. "This is Olivia Tso." They had agreed not to broadcast their relationship yet.

Detective Jessica Monnin, Spaulding's tall partner standing nearby, frowned. "You know she can't go in there, counselor."

He opened his mouth to argue, but Olivia stepped forward and produced her FBI credentials with a smooth, practiced motion. "I'd like to get up to speed on the case." The badge gleamed under the harsh lights, bearing the name and title bestowed upon her by Deputy Director Haskin.

Monnin and Spaulding exchanged a glance, a silent conversation passing between them. Monnin started to protest, "It's our—"

But Spaulding cut her off, his expression shifting from skepticism to acceptance. "Of course, Special Agent Tso. After the questioning? You can watch over there." He indicated a hallway with a clear view into the interrogation room, a small window offering a glimpse of the ongoing interview.

Simon walked into the room first. "Hi, Nina." He flicked a glance toward the camera to make sure the light was not on before sitting down. "Okay, what's going on?"

"About an hour after the dinner party, Javier told Liz and me to leave town right away. I assume he told Sam, but he wasn't with us. Anyway, he wouldn't tell us why. Just said it was for our safety. The earliest flight was a red-eye. Liz was trying to warn Tyler and get Sam. I don't know if she got a hold of Tyler, but Sam wasn't answering. So we waited till this morning. But then this morning, I couldn't find Liz or Sam anywhere. Sam wasn't answering his phone. I knocked on their doors, but no answer. So, I decided to leave by myself after leaving Liz and Sam a voicemail. I was at the airport, just got through TSA, when a security guard and a cop took me." Everything poured out in one breath. "They told me Javier was dead. Is that true?"

"I'm afraid so." This was not what he expected. Why did Javier ask them to leave? Would it have anything to do with the man he saw the other evening? How did he know they were in danger? "Did he receive any threat?"

She shook her head. "Not that I know of."

But the way she talked about Liz and Sam... "Nina, is there anything you're not telling me? I don't think you have anything to worry about, but if you know something, even if it seems unrelated, it could be helpful."

Her eyes shifted, and her hands rubbed against each other. "Sam, uh, they're having an affair."

OLIVIA

Olivia stood in the hallway watching the interview. The detectives had gone in when Simon told them they were ready. It seemed Nina didn't know anything other than that Liz and Sam were having an affair.

The door swung open, and Detectives Monnin and Spaulding stepped out. Monnin was the first to speak. "She's free to go, counselor." The slump of her shoulders betrayed her weariness. Even her sandy-brown ponytail seemed limp. "Tell her not to leave town."

Simon nodded. "Understood."

Spaulding's broad hand gestured for them to follow him down the hall. They moved as a unit, the air thick with a shared urgency.

The detective led them to a dull conference room with mismatched chairs pushed up to a utilitarian wooden table. Olivia took a seat, her posture straight and attentive, as Spaulding began to brief her.

"Housekeeping found the congressman with a bullet to his head. It was just after one p.m. when the maid got around to cleaning the suite. The room wasn't due to check out, so it wasn't a rush. It took another fifteen minutes before the police were called. Hotel security responded first. Then the duty manager reported the murder."

Olivia flattened her palms on the cool tabletop, piecing together the timeline.

"First officers secured the scene. Then the ME office arrived and pronounced death when we got there," Spaulding continued. "Then the usual activities following a crime."

Olivia leaned forward, her eyes narrowing. "I assume you talked to the maid who found the body?"

Nodding quick enough to jostle her ponytail, Monnin consulted her notes. "Yes, she knocked three times, announced herself, and opened the door. Screamed and didn't touch anything."

Simon, who had been silent, spoke up. "Did the ME give you a time of death?"

Spaulding flipped through his own notes. "Between nine thirty p.m. and one thirty a.m."

"We haven't been able to locate Mrs. Jimenez or the chief of staff," Monnin added.

Olivia drummed her fingers. "What did the security footage show?"

"Nothing." Monnin rubbed the back of her neck, her tense posture betraying her frustration. "We checked the lobby cam, the elevators, even the garage—nothing."

"They can't have just vanished," Simon remarked.

"No, but we couldn't find them yet." Spaulding scooted back on his seat, his wide shoulders and thick chest taking up most of the backrest.

Olivia's fingers slowed their pace. Just her index finger moved now, one tap now for each bit of information she sorted. Liz and Sam were having an affair, but would they conspire to kill Javier? And according to Nina, Javier had told them to leave town for their safety. What prompted him to warn them? Wait. Spaulding said it was a gunshot.

"It was a gunshot wound. But nobody reported it?" Olivia asked.

Monnin checked her notes. "No one reported it."

"Strange that nobody heard anything. A silencer? And that would mean a pro." Olivia's index finger rose. "I take it you haven't found the murder weapon?"

"Correct." Spaulding dipped his head while Monnin arched her eyebrows toward her sandy-brown hairline. "Are you suggesting Mrs. Jimenez and Tucker were abducted? And not skipping town?"

"I don't know. It's too early to tell. But I think you need to find them quickly to have some answers."

CHAPTER 15

DIVE BAR

ANA

The dive bar, with its shadowy lighting and the distinct smell of sour whiskey mixed with tobacco, felt like stepping into a different era, a sharp contrast to the bright, bustling city streets outside. Ana's eyes adjusted to the low light as she made her way through the crowd, the murmur of hushed conversations and the occasional clink of glasses creating a familiar soundtrack. Her focus was singular: Chucky, sitting alone at the bar, lost in thought with a beer in hand.

As Ana approached, she took in the changes time had wrought on him. The beard was new, giving him a rugged appearance distinct from the clean-shaven military man she remembered. Yet, despite the years and the burdens they carried, an unmistakable sharpness remained in his gaze.

"Long time. How you been?" She kept her voice steady even with her tumultuous emotions.

Chucky looked up. One brow rose. "As I live and breathe, if it's not the one who got away." He set his glass down with a deliberate motion as if marking the moment. "Princess, what are you doing in a place like this?"

She gave a casual shrug, an attempt at nonchalance. "Just needed to talk to someone from the old days. Still working for Papi?" Jorge Perez was Papi to everyone in his circle.

Chucky's heavy sigh, laden with resignation, spoke volumes. "Not officially. He said, 'no need for bodyguards anymore.' I worry about him."

That was strange. Papi always had bodyguards. "Why?"

He downed the rest of his beer. "I think he's not well, but he won't say."

While she was curious about Papi, she'd come here for another purpose. "Do you know where Prince is?"

"He's around. Oh, wait, your Prince. He took off soon after you."

She frowned. Why would he have left Papi? "What? That can't be right. Where did he go? I thought he'd have taken over the business long ago."

He shrugged. "Went to Europe, somewhere. From what I heard, got an education. Then he vanished."

"Vanished?"

"Papi blew a gasket when he took off. Tracked him to Spain, enrolled in the university. But then—poof! He disappeared."

"If Papi was having him watched, he couldn't have disappeared."

"But that wasn't the case. The old man had someone keep an eye on him, but not, like, twenty-four seven. One day, the guy reported he lost him."

She shivered to think what had become of the man assigned to watch Prince. If he was gone, then someone had to have taken his place. "Who's Prince now?"

"Who else? Hugo."

The conversation paused as the bartender approached, sliding a refill toward Chucky in a wordless exchange, a dance of familiarity in the chaos of the bar.

"Does Hugo still run the art gallery?" she asked.

"Far as I know."

"Thanks, Chucky. I appreciate it. If you hear anything—"

"I'll let you know. But, Princess"—he picked up his drink, raising it as if to salute her—"be careful. This isn't just about finding someone. You're stirring up old ghosts."

"Chucky." She braced both hands on the bar, leaning closer, close enough to smell his soured breath and crisp cologne, and dropped her voice to a whisper. "I'm not here to cause trouble. But someone left my ring in a place where I would find it. It means he's back, doesn't it? Or at least, he was."

Chucky glanced away, focusing on a crack in the worn bar top before meeting her eyes again. "You know as well as I do that the past has a way of creeping up on us when we least expect it. But that ring..." He paused, perhaps weighing his words. The beer sloshed in his glass as he gesticulated with it while making his point. "It could mean a dozen different things."

"But you think it means he's back," she pressed.

"I didn't say that." He clinked the glass back down. "Look, you're playing with fire here."

Her heart thudded, but determination pounded the fear down. "I need to know, Chucky. I can't explain it, but it's important."

He studied her, then sighed, picked up his drink, and downed it in a gulp. "All right." He wiped a drop from his beard. "Just be careful, Princess. Some doors, once opened, can't be closed again."

CHAPTER 16

TASK FORCE OFFICE

RON

Anyone in law enforcement knew that the first forty-eight hours in an abduction case was critical. The revelations Ana brought forth still churned in Ron's mind. How had she slipped through their rigorous background checks? Ana's connection, however distant, to a known crime family should have been a red flag during the recruitment process. Yet, here they were, facing a situation none of them could have anticipated.

The thought of OPR going after Ana nagged him. Her relationship with the Perez family would come to light soon. One person might be able to help. Even though he left the senate a few months ago, Simon still had friends and influence in that world. He knew Ana was a great agent.

If Ana believed Grace's biological father was behind her abduction, such a lead couldn't be ignored but necessitated a delicate approach. Ana wanted to—claimed she *needed* to— face Grace's father on her own. Ron understood, but would her approach be the best way to bring Grace home? So, while she went to do her own search, he focused on this Moneyman angle. Perhaps he could kill two birds with one stone.

"Where's Ana?" Tanner interrupted Ron's contemplations.

"She's following some leads. What do we have? Let's start with Grace's abduction." Ron's gaze swept across the room to settle on Kyle, indicating it was his turn to report.

Kyle straightened, his report ready. "The canvassing didn't give us anything. Nobody heard or saw anything unusual. Most weren't home. Deanna can tell you if we have any luck on the street cams. BOLO is out on the vehicle." He nodded toward the forensic specialist.

Deanna tapped on her tablet, drawing the room's attention to the big screen. It flickered to life and displayed the ring. "I'll start with this. The crest is the Perez family crest."

Hernandez let out a low whistle. "You mean the Jorge Perez family? They're a big deal in Mexico. Or were. Haven't heard anything in the last few years, though."

Hernandez would know. For a brief stint before joining this task force, he served on a joint task force with the Federales in Mexico.

"Yes, that one." Deanna lowered her tablet, and her nod underscored the gravity of the connection.

"We don't know how the ring has anything to do with Grace's abduction. But we'll chase down the lead. What else can you tell us, Deanna?" Ron encouraged her.

"Not much on the ring. It's been wiped clean. Interesting that it's a size 5. Men tend to wear bigger sizes, so it appears this belongs to a woman."

Ron already knew it was Ana's, but it wasn't the time to reveal that.

Deanna refocused on her tablet. "Now onto the cameras. I was able to find that vehicle leaving the complex and followed it." She maneuvered through her tablet, sending a map and video footage to the big screen, and guided them through the vehicle's path until it vanished from view. "As you can see, I lost it right here. No more camera coverage."

The room fell silent. Although it frustrated them, the abrupt end to the vehicle's visual trail was an all-too-common hurdle. Ron's gaze lingered on the screen, the vehicle's last known location burning into his memory. They'd have to start there, the boundary between what they knew and the unknowns they needed to navigate.

Ron's directive shifted the meeting's focus toward another crucial aspect of their investigation—the enigmatic figure known as the Moneyman. The room's ambiance, already thick with unsolved mysteries and complex leads, seemed to thicken further. "Let's move on to the Moneyman. Hernandez, dig deep into the dark web. Find everything and anything you can about the Jorge Perez family and Diego Morales."

"On it, boss. I'll see if the Federales has any updated information too."

"Tanner, any news from Agent Davis?"

"No, boss."

"All right." Ron slapped his hands together. "Let's get to it."

"BOLO just got a hit." Kyle pocketed his phone.

"Go, you and Tanner," Ron ordered. Maybe this would lead to something good.

CHAPTER 17

MARINO HOTEL

DYLAN

As he predicted, Dylan received the incident report promptly. When the email pinged on his phone, he opened it and skimmed sparse details, a bare-bones account of the discovery of the body and the initial response. Lily stood beside him, reading over his arm.

"It didn't say anything about a gunshot," she remarked, her brow furrowing.

He nodded. "I noticed that same omission. They're loud. You'd think someone would have heard something."

"How's it that nobody saw the killer?" Lily palmed her stylishly layered hair away from her face, her jerky movement displaying frustration.

Dylan shared her concern. "Let's check the security footage."

She arched a brow. "I think the cops already reviewed them."

He met her gaze. "True, but we might catch something they missed. Sometimes fresh eyes help—let's not forget we're more familiar with this scene than they are."

Her headshake let her hair feather back into place. "We could talk to housekeeping. I rotated through that department. I know them. They'll tell me things they won't tell the cops. Most of them don't trust cops anyway."

So true. Hotel policy only hired legal residents, but many were from countries where police were not to be trusted. Still, Olivia's stern admonishment earlier resounded in his mind. "But your mom said to stay out of it."

Lily's eyes flashed. "She said to stay in the hotel and do our jobs. We're staying in the hotel. And we aren't exactly playing detectives. Just asking questions."

He rubbed his jaw. Would he dare invite Olivia's ire? But talking to some people couldn't be that dangerous. He shrugged. "Well, it happened in the hotel. That makes it my business. Okay, let's go."

Minutes later, they entered the staff lounge where the housekeeping staff gathered after their shifts. Bright fluorescent lights showcased worn, comfortable furniture, a place where the staff could relax and unwind.

Lily approached a matronly woman just getting off shift, her face lined with fatigue.

"Oh, it was horrible. All the blood..." The woman pressed a trembling hand to her chest. As she spoke, several other women gathered around, drawn by the chance to share and hear the latest gossip.

Lily patted the woman's arm. "I'm sorry you had to see that. Does anyone here know who worked last night?"

"I did." Another Hispanic woman raised her hand. "I didn't see or hear anything. But..."

"But what?" Lily pressed, leaning in slightly.

The woman frowned, bit her lip. "It's probably nothing. I just have never seen him before."

Dylan tried to see her name badge, but she hadn't changed into her uniform yet. "Excuse me. What's your name?"

She smoothed down her blouse, eyes wide with surprise, head shaking. "Señor, my shift hasn't started yet."

He smiled his reassurance. "Don't worry. I know. You're fine. I just want to know your name."

"Jacinta," she nearly whispered.

"Thank you, Jacinta. Who did you see?"

"A server, like room service, but I never saw him before."

"What did he look like?" Lily's eyes sparkled.

"Um..." Jacinta scrunched her forehead. "White, about your height." She gestured to Dylan. "Nothing special. Ah, a drawing on his neck."

Dylan frowned. A drawing? "You mean, a tattoo?"

"Ah, sí, sí." Jacinta snapped her fingers. "Tattoo, this be the word."

"What is it? The, um, drawing?" Lily scooted closer to the new speaker.

Jacinta touched the left side of her neckline, the thoughtful scrunch to her forehead deepening. "I couldn't see clearly. Just a black line here."

"Anything else you can remember?" Dylan almost held his breath.

Jacinta shook her head. "No, just that. I thought it was strange because I know all the servers."

Lily gave Jacinta a reassuring smile. "Thank you. You've been very helpful."

They started walking away. Dylan and Lily exchanged glances. "A tattooed server no one recognizes," Dylan mused. "That's a lead."

Lily nodded. "We need to find him. He might have seen something or know something."

"Let's check the staff records and see if anyone matches Jacinta's description. And we should review the security footage ourselves, just in case."

Meanwhile, a lot of chatter rose among the other women in

another corner. Dylan slowed his steps. His Spanish was limited to the basic touristy phrases.

"...dígame..." Lily was saying something in Spanish. Dylan thought she had just started learning the language.

"Wait, Jacinta. What are they saying?" Lily grabbed the night shift lady.

"Rosita said she cleaned 1215." Jacinta translated. "She found two broken phones in the room."

"One of those must be Sam's phone." Lily released her grip on Jacinta, spinning to Dylan. "And I'm betting the other is Liz's."

"You think they are having an affair?"

Lily tried to ask the question in Spanish, but it didn't look like she knew the words. He saw her struggling.

Then Jacinta's face lit up. "Man, woman, love, bed, yes, yes."

Apparently, she'd gotten through the language barrier. Lily winked at him. "She's cheating on the congressman."

Dylan grinned back. "We need to tell the detectives. And these ladies need to give their statements. First, we'd better find that room service guy. Maybe he's new and might have seen something."

CHAPTER 18

POLICE STATION

OLIVIA

After the briefing, Olivia asked to see the security footage. The stocky detective took her to the media room, telling her the hotel cooperated fully and gave them complete access. The air was cool and slightly musty, a faint hum of electronics vibrating in the space. Beside her, Simon, with his brow furrowed in concentration, watched intently. Spaulding told the officer to play the footage from the day of the murder. Olivia didn't see anything worthwhile there.

"Could we see the lobby camera footage from Wednesday evening?" she asked.

"Why?" Spaulding eyed her, his expression weary beneath his graying hair and sallow skin.

When Simon opened his mouth to explain, she intercepted. "You'll see."

Spaulding waited a beat, then told the officer to play the relevant footage. The camera angle provided great coverage, capturing a wide swath of the lobby with its polished marble floors and grand chandeliers. People moved about, some checking in, others heading toward the elevators or the hotel bar.

"See Javier?" Simon pointed out, almost touching the screen.

"Yes." Olivia narrowed her eyes as Javier entered the frame. As Simon had said, Simon approached Javier, and they began chatting. At first, nothing seemed out of the ordinary. Javier appeared relaxed, even smiling.

Then something changed. Javier's demeanor shifted subtly as he spotted someone off-screen. His posture stiffened, and he made an abrupt departure, almost as if fleeing.

"Play the last couple of minutes again, please." Olivia's heartbeat kicked up.

The footage rewound and played again. This time, Olivia paid closer attention to Javier's reaction. Simon leaned in, scrutinizing the screen.

"That's the guy." Simon pointed to a Hispanic man in a well-tailored suit and appearing to be in his forties. Seated in a chair, he scrolled through his phone, seemingly oblivious to the world around him.

"Freeze, please," Olivia requested.

The officer complied, freezing the frame. The Hispanic man didn't seem suspicious at first glance, but Olivia's instincts told her there was more to this scene. She scanned the background for anything out of place.

Then Spaulding swore, and Monnin muttered, "Is that...?"

But Olivia's attention was focused on somebody else. A lanky man in a baseball cap standing close to the Hispanic man. He kept his head down, the cap obscuring half his face. Unlike the Hispanic man, he never looked at the camera, his movements deliberate and controlled.

Olivia's pulse quickened. Something about the way he carried himself, a certain fluidity and awareness, set off alarms in her mind. This man was an operative. If not active, then former.

The footage showed the man in the cap heading toward the elevators. He glanced around before stepping inside.

Who are you?

CHAPTER 19

UNKNOWN LOCATION

GRACE

Grace's consciousness flickered at the edges of awareness, a slow burn from the darkness into the haze of semiconsciousness. Her eyelids, heavy and reluctant, fluttered open. Disoriented, she tried to piece together her last coherent thoughts, but clarity was a fragile, fleeting thing.

She lay still, breathing shallowly, not yet willing or able to stir from her position. Her eyes, the only part of her body now obeying her desperate will, scanned from side to side. The interior of a cargo van enveloped her—the space both confining and eerily silent except for the engine's soft hum. The smell of lingering smoke mixed with something metallic, blood perhaps.

As her eyes adjusted to the scant light filtering through the two tiny windows, memories trickled back, each vivid against the dull throbbing in her head. First, the harsh impact, the bone-jarring collision with the SUV. Then the crunch of metal, the shatter of glass, and the explosion of chaos.

She stifled a scream at the recollection of being yanked from the wreck by rough, insistent hands. Then came muffled pops—

gunshots, her mind helpfully supplied—and her own voice, high-pitched and terrified, screaming into the void. The man who had abducted her from the safety of her apartment was now nothing more than a lifeless silhouette slumped in the driver's seat.

Panic clawed at her throat, and her arm twinged where the sharp prick of a needle proceeded a creeping dizziness that enveloped her senses like a suffocating blanket. Before darkness claimed her, she had a fleeting vision of him—her captor—shoving her in the back of a cargo van with another man, and then making a desperate U-turn, driving back the way they had come.

"Package secured... copy that," a male voice had said.

Then she heard no more. Now she took stock of her body. Hands and feet bound, mouth gagged, head throbbing. Otherwise, she didn't think she suffered any injuries. She sat for a long time. Hours? Or was it just her imagination? Maybe it hadn't been that long. Anyway, through the tiny grimy windows, the silhouette of a grand estate began to take form, its outlines reminiscent of the opulent Biltmore Estate. She recalled a conversation, perhaps days or mere hours ago, when Kyle had mentioned an estate, his friend Dylan's ancestral home.

No, it couldn't be. They wouldn't have brought her to the estate, could they?

After a short drive, the van came to a halt. The men opened the back door and hauled her out. She squinted, trying to make sense of her surroundings, but all she could see were trees. Were they in the woods? A hill rose nearby.

One of the men, the one with the ponytail, went close to the wall. She couldn't see over his mass of body what he was doing. Then she almost gasped—the stone wall before her split open! The other man with spiked hair untied her feet, and they guided her down a staircase into what looked like a doomsday bunker. What was their plan?

CHAPTER 20

COUNTRY ROAD

KYLE

K yle followed GPS to a country road. They had passed a strip mall and some housing developments.

"There!" Tanner pointed ahead.

A couple of cruisers were parked along the curb. As soon as Kyle saw the ME van, his heart dropped. Minutes later, he parked behind the cruisers. He and Tanner hopped out. Holding their credentials out, they approached the deputies. One deputy pointed to a woman who looked to be in her early thirties, in a flowery blouse and plain pants, average build, long brown hair tied up in a ponytail. "Detective Cassidy is in charge."

They trooped over to the detective who was talking to someone, likely the ME.

Tanner, a couple of inches taller than Kyle, stretched to look over the people. "Not Grace. Male."

Kyle let out the breath he was holding.

Detective Cassidy turned to them. "You the Feds?"

Their credentials were in front of them. As the senior agent,

Tanner took charge. "Special Agents Nathan Tanner and Kyle Peters."

"Kylie Cassidy." The woman shook their hands. "What's your interest?"

While Tanner explained their intention, Kyle checked the van. The body was still in situ, a gunshot wound on the guy's head. Execution style. This was the guy on the video posing as a flower deliveryman. So, where was Grace? Did she escape?

Cassidy's voice carried his way. "Sorry, no camera around here. But it looks like the van got hit, the driver was executed, and someone took her."

"Or she escaped." Tanner rubbed at one of his thick brows, the senior agent always one Kyle wanted to emulate, kept his calm.

"Well, I didn't see anyone when I drove here," Cassidy said.

"We didn't see her either. Which way did you come from?"

"I saw you guys drive up. I came from the other way. So, your girl didn't escape. Someone took her."

Kyle crouched by some tire tracks. "Tanner, look at these."

Tanner took pictures while Cassidy waved them off. "Got those already. Will see if we can match it to a particular model. Feel free to look around and see what else you find. I got this homicide to solve, and you got a girl to find. Let's work together."

"Yeah, let's." Tanner examined the van. "Did you check the registration?"

"Yup, came back stolen. Not surprised."

"Tanner, I remember seeing a strip mall about a half mile back. They might have cameras."

"It's a long shot—"

"Actually, that's a good idea," Cassidy cut in. "Not many people come this way, believe me. If we see this van and another vehicle going this way soon after, there's a good chance that's the vehicle. Speaking of, there's another store down the other way. They'll have a camera. We'll see if we catch the same vehicle driving away."

"Sounds like a plan."

After the van, Kyle and Tanner asked to see the body. While they'd spoken, the ME had removed the body from the van, and it was now in the ME van. They got the preliminary information from the ME, but Tanner still wanted to have a look. Kyle could do without it, but he had to learn to get used to dead bodies.

"Look here." Tanner pointed to a tattoo. "Take a picture. It looks like the same crest."

Kyle did. "It does." That wasn't good news. So, the Perez family was involved? But what was the connection between Grace and the Perez family?

CHAPTER 21

MARINO HOTEL

LILY

Lily stepped into the bustling hotel kitchen, as the clatter of pots and pans overplayed the lively hum of conversation. The rich aroma of freshly cooked food mingled with the faint scent of the soup of the day. The stainless steel counters gleamed under the bright overhead lights, and the floors were impeccably clean despite the constant activity.

Familiar with this environment, having rotated through the department during her training, she led the way with a purposeful stride, her heels clicking on the tiled floor. Dylan's steps followed closely as they approached the supervisor, a burly man in his fifties with graying hair and a friendly demeanor.

"Hey, Lily, what brings you down here from your swanky management office? Want to grab some bites?" Tony's wide mouth split into an even wider grin, but the smile faded as his gaze landed on Dylan. "Oh, hello, Mr. Roche."

"Hi, Tony." Dylan gave a half wave. "We just want to know who worked last evening."

Tony's brow furrowed as he walked over to the console. His

fingers flew over the keyboard with practiced ease. "Let's see." He scanned the screen. "Carlos and Ray."

She stepped closer. "We're looking for a white guy about Dylan's—er, Mr. Roche's—height with a tattoo on his neckline. Would either of them qualify?"

Tony shook his head. "That would be a no. Carlos is Hispanic and Ray is Black. And off the top of my head, I don't recall anyone with a tattoo on the neckline. Most of the visible ones are on the arms."

Dylan nodded. "Thank you, Tony."

Tony shrugged, head cocked to one side, his gaze switching between them. "Is everything okay? You guys seem... on edge."

She managed a small smile to put the supervisor at ease. "Just following up on some things. Thanks for your help."

They turned to leave, the kitchen staff casting curious glances their way. As they walked back through the maze of stainless steel and culinary chaos, Dylan leaned in slightly. "So, where to next?"

She picked up her pace. "Let's check the security footage. If this guy was here, he must have been caught on camera."

"Good idea. Let's go."

Minutes later, they entered a security office aglow from computer screens, the hum of electronics and the occasional crackle of a radio interrupting the silence. Monitors lining the walls displayed live feed from around the hotel. The guard, a lean man in a black suit, watched them with mild curiosity.

"Come on. Look up for once," Dylan muttered.

Lily shared his irritation. She palmed her hair away from her face as she scanned the footage. They had found the guy in question, but he never looked at the cameras, almost consciously avoiding being recorded.

"Sir, we don't have a hundred percent coverage. There are blind spots. All the entrances and exits are covered. And elevators," the guard explained.

"What about the employee entrance? And the delivery?" Lily asked.

"Yes, we do." The guard fiddled with the controls, and the footage on one screen changed to a grainy image of the employee entrance.

"That's him, isn't it?" Dylan pointed to the screen, his eyes narrowing as he scrutinized the figure.

"I think so," Lily said, but the angle wasn't the best. A guy matching the general description got into a truck, but they couldn't see anything else in the night sky. The time stamp indicated 1:25 a.m.

Dylan exhaled, running a hand through his hair. "Let's tell the detectives what we've found so far. And then we need to hit the road if you want to get home at a decent hour."

CHAPTER 22

ITALIAN RESTAURANT

ANA

After talking to Chucky, the first person Ana wanted to see was Susie Gorman, her former agent. She had to use her federal resources to locate Susie. Thank goodness, the agent was still in the area. The call was short. Susie, although surprised, agreed to meet for a predinner drink.

Ana was nursing a virgin mojito at the bar when Susie arrived. She waved to get the agent's attention and stood when Susie got close.

"Oh my! I wouldn't believe it if you weren't standing here in front of me. Princess, how are you?" The agent studied her from head to toe before taking a seat. "You still look good, but sorry, you're too old for the runway."

Ana stifled a laugh. "This is not what I want to see you for. I'm trying to locate Prince. Do you know where he is?"

Susie laughed. "I take it you mean your Prince. Nope, not a clue. He's gone, like you."

Ana took a deep breath to mask her frustration with a calm she didn't feel.

"Look, Susie..." Ana traced the rim of her glass, her chest tightening. "I need to find Prince because he's... he's involved in something big, something that could affect a lot of people. I thought you might have kept in touch."

A bartender floated by to take Susie's drink order. Then the agent leaned back. "My dear Princess, or should I call you Ana now? I wasn't lying. The industry has moved on. New faces, new names. People like Prince, they disappear into their own worlds. But if you're looking for Papi, there might be a way."

Ana shifted on her stool. "How?"

Susie sighed. "You were always one of the good ones, Ana. You'd have to go through Hugo, the new Prince."

So, Hugo would take over Papi's business. "And where is Hugo?"

"He still owns that art gallery, Mirage Fine Arts. You know, I hear Papi is getting out—or wants to. I also hear Hugo doesn't have the desire to follow in his footsteps."

"Really?" Ana fingered her short curls back behind her ears. Could the Perez family go straight?

Susie shrugged. "Just what I heard."

As Ana stood to leave, Susie gripped Ana's sleeve, stilling her. "Ana, be careful, okay? This industry, the people you're looking for—it's not just glitz and glamour. There are shadows too."

Ana paused, offering a small smile over her shoulder. "I know, Susie. I've seen them before. But thanks for the warning."

Ron had told her he'd have Kyle as her contact and backup. She called him.

"We're just wrapping up." Kyle updated her.

She was silent for a moment before exhaling a heavy breath. "So, she was abducted from her apartment. And now, someone shot the guy and took her."

"About the size of it. It appears the Perez family is involved somehow. At least, the dead guy had a tattoo resembling the crest. We don't have anything on the new abductor yet."

Her brows furrowed deeper. If the Perez family took Grace from the apartment, who was this new player? Anyhow, her gut told her finding Papi and Prince was the key. "When you get back to the office, can you find out everything you can about Hugo Perez? And Jorge Perez."

"Of course. You think they've got something to do with this?"

"I don't know."

She ended the call and made another one. This time, she dialed Ron. The line crackled to life, and his voice greeted her.

After he answered, she shook her head, frowning. "Kyle just updated me on Grace. It doesn't make sense. By the driver's tattoo, we know the Perez family is involved somehow. But then who would hijack their operation?" Her mind was already playing out different reasonings. Internal power struggle. She heard that somewhere. So, could someone inside the family be pulling this stunt?

"It had to be an inside job. Someone who knew about the abduction in the first place."

She nodded. "I agree. I'll proceed to look into the Perez family. Someone in that family knows something."

"We're working all angles. We won't rest until we find her. You be careful on your end."

"I will." The second she hung up, her phone flashed another call. A private number. Her finger danced on the screen. After debating if she should take it, she finally swiped to answer.

"Princess." A BMW with blacked-out windows stopped in front of her.

"Get in the car," a voice from the past said in her ear.

CHAPTER 23

UNKNOWN BUNKER

GRACE

Grace stumbled as the two men pushed her into a shadowy room. The air was thick and musty, the concrete walls pressing in on her.

"I'm bringing the van in," Ponytail said and exited the room, leaving Grace with the man she had mentally dubbed Spike Hair. He grabbed her hands, yanked them forward to untie them. As his hand moved close to her mouth, he warned, "I'm taking this off, but if you scream, I'll put it back on." Without waiting for a response, he yanked the tape off her mouth.

"Argh, that hurt."

Ponytail returned, a piece of paper in one hand and his phone in the other. He flipped the phone around and showed her a series of pictures. Her heart pounded as she recognized her parents in candid shots from several days judging by the different outfits.

"We can get to them anytime we want. If you don't want them to get hurt, read this," Ponytail said, his voice cold and commanding.

Spike Hair shoved the paper in front of her face. Grace's gaze darted across the text, a bizarre message filled with cryptic demands and code-like phrases.

"Wait, you guys got the wrong person. The message makes no sense to me." Her whole body started shaking. But her parents' images burned into her mind. What if they were in danger?

Ponytail's expression hardened. "Want your folks to get hurt? Didn't think so. Now, read it!"

Grace swallowed hard, the situation pressing down on her. She took a deep breath and started reading aloud. Her voice trembled, but she pushed through to recite the strange message as Ponytail held his phone up, recording every word.

She finished reading, her voice echoing in the bare room. Ponytail stopped the recording and, without a word, turned and walked out, leaving her alone with Spike Hair.

"We won't hurt you as long as you cooperate." Spike Hair sounded surprisingly calm. He gestured to a door on the right. "Restroom is over there. There's food and drinks in the fridge in the kitchen. You're free to roam around, but I can tell you there's no escape. You'd just get lost, and then you'd starve to death."

Grace's chin jutted up. Her jaw and hands clenched as she watched him leave, the door clicking shut behind him. Silence enveloped the room, a silence drowning out her racing thoughts.

She rubbed her sore wrists, the raw skin reminding her of her harsh captors. Then she pushed to her feet and walked to the restroom. The small space was basic but clean, with a tiny sink and a toilet. She splashed water on her face to steady her nerves.

Returning to "her" room, she inspected the sparse furniture—a simple bed, table, and chair. She moved toward the kitchen area, her stomach growling. Opening the fridge, she found sandwiches, apples, and water bottles. She grabbed a sandwich and a bottle of water, then sat at the table to eat.

As she chewed, she scanned the room for anything to help

her understand her situation. The unmarked concrete walls offered no clues. Why had they taken her? What did the message mean? And most importantly, how could she escape? There had to be a way.

How long it had been since the men left, she didn't know, but it seemed like a long time. She snatched more water bottles, then explored. Just maybe she could find a way out of this bunker. Mindful of Spike Hair's words, she looked for a pen or a piece of paper. Nothing. So she resorted to the sandwich's paper wrapping. She went out, ripped a tiny piece off, and dropped it on the side of the walkway at every turn.

True to Spike Hair's words, the place was a labyrinth. What was this place? But who built it? The longer she explored, the more it reminded her of the catacombs. She had gone on a pilgrimage with her parents to Italy and visited the burial chambers. After about ten turns, she came across a stretch of walls with strange markings. Codes?

Oh, Lord, I need You now!

She sighed. Maybe there was no way out. No, there had to be a way. She couldn't lose hope.

Thump-thump-thump.

She froze.

Scraaatch...

What was that?

It sounded like someone was scratching something. Thump-thump-thump.

Now the footsteps were going away.

Her eyebrows knotted together. She didn't think it was the men, but who or what was it?

CHAPTER 24

TASK FORCE OFFICE

RON

The squad room hummed with the quiet tension that always accompanied a high-stakes case. Fluorescent lights flickered overhead, and Ron's team gathered once more before the looming screen dominating one wall.

Ron stood facing the screen, as always. "Updates?"

Tanner stepped up first. He cleared his throat before diving into the details. "Evidently, a new player is involved. A vehicle hit the van, shot the driver, and took Grace. We're checking footage from a store about a half mile away."

Kyle, who had been working closely with Tanner, continued without missing a beat. "The driver had a tattoo just like the crest." He clicked the remote in his hand. The screen flickered and then displayed a high-resolution photo of a distinct tattoo on the deceased driver's arm.

Ron's gaze hardened as he patted his breast pocket for his glasses. He didn't need them yet, but at least they were there. "So, it's safe to say the Perez family took Grace initially. Now, we need to find out who this new player is. A rival family?"

Deanna snatched the remote from Kyle and clicked it. The screen image switched to video footage. "The tattoo is the Perez family crest. I got footage from two stores, actually. Let me put them side by side." The screen split, showing two angles. "Here, the first vehicle is the van. Minutes later, this"—she pointed with a laser pen at a cargo van now on the screen—"drives by. Now, about fifteen minutes later, this cargo van drives past the stores again."

Tanner leaned forward with his arms crossed, his brow furrowed. "That's got to be it. Cassidy mentioned that stretch of road rarely had any traffic."

Ron needed more than assumption. "Can you get the plate?"

Deanna nodded, her fingers flying over her laptop keys. "I found it going on the highway but lost it afterward. Here's the plate number." She displayed the information on the screen.

Ron turned to Hernandez, who was already searching. "Registered to... never mind, stolen plate. The plate is supposed to be registered to a Toyota Camry. The cargo van is obviously not a Camry."

"By the way, you set up the Bensons' phones?" Ron asked Hernandez.

"Yeah, boss. An agent is sitting with them. So far, nothing."

It was a long shot, anyway. This didn't appear to be a ransom situation. Ron shifted his stance. "Tanner, follow up with that detective. Deanna, keep looking into Perez and Morales online. And Hernandez, check in with the agent monitoring the Bensons' phones and help Deanna. Kyle, hang back."

A chorus of "yeah, boss" sounded.

"Uh, boss, that was Cassidy." Tanner swiped his phone to send one composite drawing on-screen. "She worked her magic and got the locals to talk. Evidently, a gas station attendant remembered seeing this guy getting gas and taking off. Moments later, he heard a loud crash, went outside to look, and saw the same vehicle. Said he thought there was a passenger, but he wasn't sure. Anyway, this guy took Grace. And likely shot the fake flower deliverer."

Ron put on his annoying "granny glasses" to study the drawing. A man with spiked hair. Ordinary looking, could be anyone. No distinguishable mark. "Deanna, is there any way to compare this to any database?"

A headshake. "Very unreliable."

He stared at the drawing, trying to make it come to life. Something about the spiked hair stirred a distant memory. Could it be? "All right, go!"

The team dispersed. He gestured to Kyle to walk with him back to his office. "I want you to go check in with Eva. Keep it low-key, like you're visiting a friend. Ask her about the composite drawing. She knows who she needs to see. Go now."

"Yes, sir."

CHAPTER 25

THE PEREZ MANSION

ANA

The chauffeur deposited Ana at the mansion's front door. Although she had never been here, she had seen pictures of it. She stepped toward the door. It opened on cue, revealing an interior that seemed to swallow her whole with its opulence.

Standing in the doorway was Papi, a shadow of the man she remembered. Chucky's words—"he's not well"—rang in her mind. His once robust and intimidating presence was now diminished, his body frail and bearing the unmistakable signs of illness. He sighed upon seeing her, a simple acknowledgment loaded with unspoken words. "Welcome, Princess."

She nodded, reminding herself to proceed with caution. Her eyes scanned their surroundings as she obeyed Papi's gesture to proceed past the foyer to the living room.

He sank into a chair with a weariness that seemed to age him further right there. She took a seat across from him, her posture alert, ready for whatever revelation was about to come. A cup of espresso was on the coffee table with the usual condiments. He waved over the coffee set. "It's for you. I don't drink that anymore."

Then Papi's voice, though weakened, carried through the room as he called out, "Mario!" A man, whom she didn't know, hurried over. "Play that video," Papi instructed.

Mario pulled out his phone and tapped a few buttons. Soon, Grace's scared voice emerged from the speakers. "Papi, they want you to relinquish control of your business and transfer it to Prince. Please do what they say."

Ana stiffened and reached toward Mario's phone. "May I see that again?"

The man replayed it. Grace was forced to read the message. Could Hugo have orchestrated this? And how did the captors know to use Grace? Somehow, the captors discovered the relationship between Papi and Grace.

"You knew? How?" She looked him in the eye.

His lips curved in a smile. "When we were looking for clues as to where you went—mind you, you weren't an agent back then—you left something in the trash."

The pregnancy test! How could she have been so dumb? "Does Prince know?"

"No, Julio doesn't know. I thought it'd be for the best. But" —he shrugged—"he left anyway."

"And you haven't seen him since?"

A shake of his head. "We tracked him to Spain. He went to university there. But then, he vanished."

This jibed with what Chucky told her. But if Papi had known all this time, why hadn't he found her and brought her back? "I don't understand. You didn't send anyone after me."

He waved Mario away. "You're the mother of my grandchild, Princess. That makes you family. I've been keeping tabs on you and my grandchild. I knew you were applying to be a government agent. I made sure your connection to us was scrubbed."

She swallowed hard, unsure what to say. "I wasn't involved in your business. I didn't even know."

"Yes, and that's why you left once you found out. I know, I figured it out. But let's not worry about that now. We need to find Grace. By the way, that girl has talent. Just like Julio. I was at her Christmas program. She did a great job."

Grace's musical prowess certainly wasn't from her. All thanks to her father. But Ana needed to focus. "Hugo is the current Prince, correct? Could he have done this?"

Another shake of his head, this one firmer. "He doesn't want anything to do with the business. He's got his own gallery."

"But why would they demand that?"

"I don't know, but let's focus on finding her. If we find her, there's no need to worry about all this."

"Did you ask him?" She couldn't just let it go. If it was Hugo, they could get him into custody and make him talk.

"You can talk to him, but it's no use."

"All right, send me a copy." She wouldn't get more from him on that. She'd ask Deanna to search for the location where the video was taken. For the caffeine boost, she took the cup and drank a good portion of it. "So, you ordered Grace to be abducted from her apartment?"

"I wouldn't call it an abduction."

Seriously? She scoffed. "What would you call it? Use a ruse to get her to open the door, drug her, and take her."

He waved away her sarcasm. "If I were to invite her here, tell me the odds of her coming willingly."

"You should have given her the choice." Although this type of "invitation" probably wasn't uncommon in his world.

He shrugged. "Anyhow, let's focus on finding Grace."

Assuming Julio was alive and well, even if he had found out about Grace, he wouldn't have done this. He could have come back, and Papi would gladly give him everything. Hugo? "I don't understand the demand, then. If Hugo doesn't want it, why would someone make that demand?"

"I've thought about it. If the business somehow got into Hugo's hands, he'd get rid of it as soon as possible. He wouldn't want to sully his hands."

"So, could it be an enemy who thinks they could take it off Hugo easily?"

"Could be."

"Does Hugo know? About Grace?"

"Yes, he does now."

"Okay. Who knew about your plan to abduct Grace?"

CHAPTER 26

MIRROR ESTATE

KYLE

The day was gray and heavy, clouds looming over the horizon as Kyle settled into his driver's seat. The leather felt cool against his skin in keeping with the brewing storm. He had just turned the ignition when an incoming call buzzed his phone. The screen displayed Alex's name, and Kyle almost considered letting the call go to voicemail. Alex would be anxious, and while Kyle's heart went out to him, he had nothing hopeful to offer yet. Still, he tapped the screen and answered the call.

"Hey, any news?" Alex's voice crackled through the speakers.

Kyle shifted the car into gear, whirring out of the parking lot. "We have some leads, and I'm chasing one now."

"What can I do?" Something rustled on Alex's end of the line, perhaps Alex moving around, unable to keep still.

Kyle navigated a sharp turn, his mind racing as fast as his car. If he had a sister and she were abducted, he wouldn't have wanted to be sidelined either. Yet, Alex was a civilian. "Why don't you stay with your parents? I'm sure they're worried. They'll want you with them."

"They're fine. They've been in church praying the whole time. And so far, nobody has called for any ransom."

Kyle's grip tightened on the steering wheel. Ransom didn't seem the goal here. His thoughts then drifted to his father's strict instructions to maintain Eva's cover, adding further complexity to his current mission—a visit to the Mirror Estate under the guise of a friend, not an agent. Maybe he could let Alex tag along.

As these thoughts marinated, he couldn't help thinking that not long ago he'd have gone strictly by the books. Hanging with Lily and Dylan, famous for defying orders, probably rubbed off on him. He let out a chuckle.

"What's so funny?" Alex snapped.

"Okay. I'll come pick you up and show you the Mirror Estate."

"Yay! Wait, why are we going to some fancy estate? I thought you said you were working a lead."

"Rule number one—no questions. You don't have to come along."

"Okay, okay, no questions. I'll be waiting."

ALEX

As they entered the gate to the Mirror Estate, the sheer opulence struck Alex. The estate sprawled across acres of meticulously maintained gardens, and its impressive architecture could rival any historical landmark he'd seen in magazines. "Wow! I've seen pictures before, but this is amazing!" He craned his neck to take in every detail as they drove along the winding driveway.

Kyle, who must've grown accustomed to the grandeur,

parked in the guest parking area, then gathered his things. "This isn't as famous as the Biltmore, but it's still something."

Eager to capture the moment, Alex reached for his phone on the impulse to share this sight with his friends. "Is it okay if I take some pictures?" he asked, half out of the car already.

Kyle led the way to the front door. "Later. Not now. And do not post on social media. And I mean it. Dad would kill you if you did."

Raising his hands in a gesture of surrender, Alex nodded, then slipped his phone back into his pocket, his curiosity about the estate growing. "Okay, I promise."

As they approached the ornate front door, it swung open to reveal a man in a neatly tailored suit. "Hello, Kyle."

Kyle stepped inside. "Alex, this is Max." Then Kyle led Alex away from the doorway and deeper into the foyer.

Once out of Max's earshot, Alex whispered, "What did he say? Major-something?"

"Majordomo, a fancy word for head butler or estate manager."

Alex absorbed this new vocabulary. So this was how the other half lived. They probably threw lavish parties and hosted quiet, opulent dinners under sparkling chandeliers.

"Hey, Kyle," a woman called out warmly, interrupting their brief reverie.

Curious, Alex followed Kyle toward the sound and found himself before a strikingly beautiful woman with stylish short brown hair, dressed in a comfy top and jeans. Her features suggested mixed heritage, perhaps some Asian ancestry. She looked around her twenties, poised yet approachable.

Kyle smiled at her. "Howdy, Eva. This is Alex, Grace's brother."

Eva's expression softened, and she extended a hand toward Alex. "Nice to meet you, Alex. I hope we find Grace soon."

He shook her hand. "Do you work here?"

"I'm Ms. Carol's personal assistant."

Kyle bumped her arm and tilted his head, some unspoken communication passing between them.

"Yes, let's go to the library." Eva tapped on her phone. "Alex, Max will show you around and introduce you to Ms. Carol."

Well, talk about being summarily dismissed.

Max showed up and gestured to the hall. "Mr. Benson, allow me to take you on a tour of the estate."

"Of course. But please call me Alex."

"And Ms. Carol would like to meet you."

Meeting Carol Marino was like meeting a celebrity. What a great business connection.

"Excuse us." Kyle and Eva walked off. Just what was Kyle doing here anyway? Was some lead connected to this visit?

CHAPTER 27

LORRAINE'S KITCHEN

FR. PHIL

As the late afternoon sun dipped behind the horizon, casting long shadows over the bustling streets, Fr. Phil agreed to meet with Jeremy at Lorraine's Kitchen. Ortiz's call had been abrupt but insistent. They arrived at the familiar establishment known for its cozy ambiance and hearty meals.

Upon entering, Fr. Phil scanned the room with a practiced eye, his gaze settling on Ortiz already seated at a side table, deeply engrossed in a plate of the restaurant's famed spaghetti. The chief of security noticed them and half stood.

"Fr. Phil, Fr. Jeremy, over here." Ortiz waved them over as he wiped his hands on a napkin.

Introductions cut through the formalities as Ortiz invited them to sit. "Might as well eat here. Order something if you haven't eaten yet."

"Sure." Fr. Phil sat.

Jeremy followed suit.

Connor approached their table with a smile. His presence was a common sight. Even as a manager, he was always ready to lend a hand during busy times. He pulled out his notepad. "Evening, Father. What can I get for you tonight?"

"I'll need a minute," Jeremy said while Fr. Phil ordered his usual.

After Connor poured water glasses for them and promised to be back, Fr. Phil pivoted to Ortiz. "You said you had something important to report."

Ortiz, acknowledging the prompt, pointed his fork at Fr. Phil. "Since you told me about the Irishman Gang, I've been on the lookout for strange or unusual activities. The guard manning the entrance noticed an unfamiliar van passing through. That, in and of itself, isn't too alarming. But the van never came back around. It drove past the gate and never returned."

"I assume you meant coming from town." Fr. Phil rubbed his chin. "There's no way out. It would have to come back out."

"Exactly. I suppose it could have encountered car trouble. So, I went to check it out myself." Ortiz put his fork down and wiped his mouth with the napkin, the linen rasping against his thick mustache. "The vehicle is nowhere in sight."

The tantalizing entrée options no longer holding his interest, Jeremy lowered his menu. "It can't have vanished."

Ortiz gave the young priest a brief glance. "I don't know what to tell you. I didn't see anyone out there. It's the woods back there. I suppose it could be parked under a tree and covered with camouflage."

"Now that is sinister thinking." Jeremy folded the menu and set it aside.

"Hi, Father."

Both priests turned as Eva approached with Kyle. "Hi, Eva, Kyle, have you met Fr. Jeremy Holmes?"

They shook their heads followed by quick introductions. "Want to join us?"

"Oh no." Eva held up a hand. "I just need to ask Connor something."

Connor walked toward them with a basket of bread.

"I know you're busy now." Eva swung her phone around to face Connor. "But could you take a look at this? Do you recognize him?"

His eyes grew wide. "I can't say for sure, but it looks like Finn O'Neill. He runs with Freddy Doyle's gang."

Fr. Phil cringed. "Was he spotted here?"

"No." Kyle waved him off. "No, at least not that I know of. If that's him, he likely took Grace."

Fr. Phil frowned. "Grace. A friend of yours, right? She's been taken?"

"Yes. A witness saw him in a cargo van."

"A cargo van?" Ortiz edged his plate aside and braced his arms on the faux wood table. "What color? Any signage?"

"Beige and plain."

"Are you thinking it's the same van?" Fr. Phil asked.

"Why? What same van?" Kyle gripped the back of the empty chair beside the trio and leaned over the table.

Ortiz nodded Eva to the seat, then explained about the mystery van that seemed to have disappeared.

Eyebrows rising, Kyle asked, "Here? In the estate? What time?"

"Yeah." Ortiz took his phone out, fiddled with it, then offered it to Kyle. "Time stamp 5:04 p.m."

When Kyle took it and played the video, Eva stood to look. Then he returned the phone to Ortiz. "I'm almost positive it's the same van. I'm gonna need to report this."

CHAPTER 28

TASK FORCE OFFICE

RON

After a quick pizza dinner, the atmosphere in the squad room gave way to a blend of tired energy and relentless determination. Ron stepped up to update the team before sending them home. The big screen glowed in the drab space, casting long shadows across desks cluttered with papers and coffee cups.

"Update." His voice cut through the scattered conversations. As the team shuffled to gather around the screen, the door creaked open.

"Sorry, looks like I'm a bit late." Ana breezed in and swung her bag over the back of her desk chair.

He surveyed her, her poised shoulders and alert posture suggesting she was okay. She caught his look, nodded, and stepped forward confidently. "I'll go first."

After he waved her the go-ahead, she began. "The Perez family is definitely behind taking Grace from her apartment, but they're now being blackmailed."

Hernandez, leaning against his desk, held up a hand. "I'm a

bit lost. What's the relationship between Jorge Perez and Grace? Why would they use Grace as leverage?"

From the corner, Deanna, arms crossed, muttered almost too quietly, "Can't you put two and two together?"

After a beat, Ana said, "Grace is his biological granddaughter."

The room fell into a surprised silence, broken only when Hernandez elbowed Deanna. "Did you know?"

At the back, Tanner, who had been tossing a stress ball up and down, caught it midair and held it tightly. "Wait, you're not saying Hugo Perez is—"

"No, his brother, Julio Perez is."

Ron, observing the pieces falling into place for his team, clapped once to regain control of the room. "All right, guys. Now that Grace's parentage is settled, let's focus on getting her back and finding out who this new player is."

Questions flew across the room as the team tried to piece things together. "Who knew about the plan?" "Who knew about Grace?" "Who would want to make such a demand?" Ron pondered these questions too as Ana unraveled more details.

Ana clicked through her notes. "Jorge Perez is still in charge, I believe. He said Hugo didn't want anything to do with it. And Hugo knows about Grace. As for who knew about the plan— Mario, that's his assistant, and the driver who got killed. I don't know if Hugo knew about it."

Ron cleared his throat. "Okay, we can consider Hugo a person of interest. Maybe he wants the business after all."

Ana's nod shook one tendril of glossy brown hair over her temple. "I'll talk to him, hopefully tomorrow. See what he knows. But I can't see him killing a loyal underling. Oh, Deanna, did you check the video I sent you?"

"Yes." The fun-loving forensic expert swiped her tablet. "It'll take time to trace it. It was sent through at least a dozen proxies. The video itself doesn't reveal anything. The background is plain. It's possible it's a basement, though, seeing that there's no window."

Ron crossed his arms and braced on the edge of a desk. They'd just have to keep digging. "Do a deep dive on Hugo Perez, his financials, especially. We need to know everything."

"Yes, boss."

He was about to tell them to grab a couple hours of shut-eye when his phone rang. He fished it from his blazer pocket. Kyle.

"Yes, Kyle. You're on speakerphone."

"The van came here! Grace is probably here somewhere—"

"Here? As in Mirror Estate?" Ron slid to his feet. *This* he hadn't expected.

"Yes." Kyle reported what Ortiz said. "I asked him to forward the video to Deanna. Maybe you can confirm it's the same van."

Ana's face showed the first sign of hope since this afternoon. "Let's go and search the estate."

"Here's the weird part." Kyle spoke slower now, drawing out each syllable as if still contemplating the words. "It seems to have vanished."

"How can it vanish?" They all asked the same question in one way or another.

"I don't know. But Ortiz can't find it. Eva and I are going out there with him to take a closer look. He said the van could have been parked under a tree and covered with camouflage."

"All right, let us know."

"Yes, sir."

"If Grace is out there"—Ana grabbed her purse and slung the strap over one shoulder—"I need to be there."

"The best way is to find out where they're hiding her. The estate is a big place. If they can hide a van, they can hide Grace. So, keep working on the Perez family angle. You'll be the first to know when we have her location, I promise."

Her shoulders slumped and her lips tightened. But she

nodded and started scrolling her phone. "Guess what?" She held up the phone. "Hugo's gallery is hosting a show. I'll go talk to him now."

CHAPTER 29

MARINO HOTEL

LILY

After calling Detective Spaulding, Lily and Dylan grabbed their stuff and headed to the garage. The day had already been a whirlwind, but what they had stumbled upon last felt different—urgent. As they waited for the elevator, the cool, sterile air of the building seemed to buzz with tension.

Lily caught movement out of the corner of her eye—someone emerging from the staircase leading to the penthouse. Was that a shadow of something along his neckline? Her pulse quickened. It wasn't just anyone.

She tapped Dylan's arm. "Hey, that's him."

"Who?" Dylan followed her gaze, his eyes narrowing as he spotted the man in worker overalls heading to the stairs. He sucked in a gasp. "Let's go!"

They hurried after the man, their footsteps echoing in the corridor. They reached the staircase and service elevator just as the elevator doors were closing.

"Shucks!" Lily exclaimed. They were too late.

Dylan pulled out his phone. "I'll alert security."

"He came out of the penthouse staircase." Her breath still came in quick bursts.

He finished his call and tucked away his phone. "But how? Nobody should have access."

"What about the workers? You said they were supposed to finish up in a few days."

"Yes, but only the supervisor has the access code." He forked his fingers through his short wavy hair, then jerked a thumb toward the doorway. "Come on. Let's have a look."

They strode to the guest elevator bank. But Lily gripped his arm, stopping him from punching the button to summon a car. "Maybe we should take the staircase leading up to the penthouse? After all, that's where the man came from."

"Good plan." He stepped aside and let her lead. When they entered it, the stairway was quiet, almost eerily so. Still, she couldn't shake the feeling of being watched. But they saw nothing unusual as they ascended.

He unlocked the penthouse door. The click of the lock echoed in the silence. He pushed the door open slowly, peering into the dimly lit room. "We'll just have a look at—"

The door swung open, revealing the scene in horrific clarity. Dylan gasped and moved to block her sight, but it was too late. Her eyes widened at the tableau.

The first body, bound to a chair with coarse ropes, was slumped forward, its head lolling unnaturally to the side. The face was bruised and bloodied, evidence of the torture endured before death. The skin was pallid, the lifeless eyes staring at the floor.

Beside it, another body lay sprawled on the couch. However, this one looked serene, like she was sleeping.

Lily had to close her eyes. Two murders!

CHAPTER 30

MIRAGE FINE ARTS

ANA

From the outside, Mirage Fine Arts presented itself as nothing more than a humble storefront nestled among a row of similarly unassuming buildings on a busy street. The façade, worn by the years yet charming in its simplicity, bore no hint of the elegance tucked behind the aged exterior. The only clue to the treasures within was a modest sign, swaying in the breeze, announcing a show featuring the works of artist Cathy Foley.

Julio mentioned Hugo's gallery countless times, but Ana never stepped foot inside until today. Her steps slowed as she approached. Her gaze caught on the sign before she pushed open the heavy wooden door into a luxurious interior displaying tasteful decorations while soft, ambient lighting highlighted exquisite pieces of art. The subtle scent of varnish and expensive perfume wove an almost palpable spell of sophistication through the expansive space.

"Welcome!" The voice cut through the tranquil gallery,

pulling Ana's attention to the speaker. An ordinary-looking man, clad in a tailored suit that hung on his lanky frame, greeted her. His glasses caught the light as he moved, and a name tag pinned to his lapel declared him as Shane. Early forties, Ana guessed, taking in his earnest expression and neatly combed hair.

"Nice place," she responded.

"Feel free to browse." Shane waved to the walls. "Her work is absolutely stunning..." He began to drone on about the unique style and revolutionary techniques of the artist currently featured, delving into details that soared far above Ana's head. She nodded as she pretended to absorb the information.

With a vague gesture of appreciation, she excused herself from his enthusiastic art lecture and wandered deeper into the gallery. Her eyes skimmed over the artworks, appreciating their beauty, her thoughts elsewhere. She was here for Hugo.

Soon, she spotted him at the gallery's far end, engaged in an animated conversation with an elegantly dressed couple, likely potential buyers. His hands elaborated his speech with expressive gestures, his voice a smooth pitch of persuasive enthusiasm. Taking a deep breath, she stepped into his line of sight.

The effect was immediate. His words trailed off as his eyes met hers, and for a split second, his mouth slid open. "Uh, sorry, would you excuse me?" He stammered to the couple, who looked mildly baffled but consented before he made his way to her.

"Princess, is it really you?" he exclaimed, his composure slipping into astonishment.

"In the flesh." She gave in to a small smile.

Hugo responded with air kisses that whisked past each cheek, displaying the flamboyance she remembered so well. He looked around to find someone, then beckoned Shane over. "Please take care of Mr. and Mrs. O'Leary." Then he gripped both of Ana's hands and squeezed. "Come, let's talk."

As she followed Hugo to his office, she noticed Shane's keen eye on her every step. Her instinct told her Shane was more than an employee.

"Sit." Hugo tilted his head toward the chair facing his desk. "What would you like?" He grabbed a bottle of sparkling water from the mini fridge. "Sorry, I don't stock booze anymore. Just got my ten-year chip."

She sat. "I didn't know. Congratulations! And water would be fine."

"No reason you should know. Flat or sparkling?"

"Flat, if you have it."

He handed her a bottle and sat behind his desk. "So, I heard you talked to Papi. When he told me about you, I thought he was blowing smoke. But look at you, you're really here."

"What else did he say?"

"Well..." He let out a low whistle. "Everything, I guess."

"Did you know about Grace?"

He uncapped his water. "I found out when he changed his will. You see, I needed to investigate if he was being swindled by some con artist."

"Right, you can't be too careful these days. But how did you find out? Did you hire a PI?"

"You can say I did some snooping. I saw the DNA results he got from the attorney."

"Did you know about his abduction plan?"

"Not specifics, but I knew they were planning something." He finished his water. "Look, I know you're some government agent now. Let's cut to the chase. I have nothing to do with what happened to Grace. I run a legit business here."

"I'm curious. After Julio ran away, I thought you'd be the one to inherit the business."

He unfolded his handkerchief and dabbed at the water by his mouth. "Yes, indeed. But guess what? You left. Then Julio followed you. Or so we thought. Anyway, Papi always knew I had no interest in the business. I guess he didn't want to drive me away too. So, he kind of accepted it. Besides, once he turns himself in—"

"What did you say?!"

CHAPTER 31

MARINO HOTEL

OLIVIA

As soon as Olivia heard about the dead bodies, she and Simon rushed over to the hotel. The detectives had already arrived and were securing the scene.

"Thank goodness the killer wasn't here when you came up!" Olivia exclaimed as she approached Lily. "You're not supposed to chase after the killer."

"We didn't!" Lily protested. "We didn't go out. Dylan alerted security. We stayed in the hotel. And how were we supposed to know this? Nobody was supposed to be up here."

"All right, you two, let's just be grateful you're both okay," Simon interjected, always ready to defuse the situation. He opened his arms wide. "Let's have a hug."

He enveloped Lily and Olivia in a warm embrace, providing comfort amid the chaos. They were in the kitchen, away from the grim scene in the living room.

Olivia glanced around, noticing Spaulding with Dylan, likely taking his statement. She smoothed back her daughter's glossy hair. "Did you give your statement?"

"No. I guess I'm doing it now." Lily blinked, looking past Olivia.

Monnin approached and shook her ponytail back over one shoulder, the gesture impatient and likely habitual. "Excuse me. I need to ask her some questions."

Olivia and Simon stepped back. Olivia motioned for Simon to sit in one of the dining room chairs while she ventured over to the crime scene. The living room was a stark contrast to the pristine kitchen. While a death investigator with the name tag Polanski meticulously noted details on his phone, Olivia's focus was drawn to the bodies: Sam slumped in a chair and Liz sprawled on the couch. The scene was grim, made more so by the objects on the coffee table—a gun, a syringe, and a flash drive.

"May I see these?" Olivia asked.

Polanski glanced up, frowning. "You a detective?"

When Olivia flashed her FBI credentials and introduced herself as a special agent, Polanski gestured to the spread as if beckoning her to partake of a buffet. "Help yourself."

Olivia picked up the flash drive with gloved hands, inserted it in an SD card reader, plugged it into her phone, and was about to review the content when Spaulding's stern voice floated over. "It's my crime scene."

"*Our* crime scene," Olivia clarified. "These murders are obviously connected to Javier's."

"You're thinking they were killed by the same perp?"

"I'm leaning toward Sam and Liz conspiring to kill Javier. Someone else killed them."

"What made you say that?"

"The broken phones in Sam's room. Lily and Dylan spotting the fake room service dude. The syringe. The gun. And the flash drive. Let's have a look."

Simon sidled up to watch. She pressed Play and saw Liz inject Javier while hugging him. Javier struggled before falling on the floor. Then Sam used a pillow to muffle the sound when he shot him. All the while, they were saying this would look like a hit. How naïve! Olivia almost tsked. Autopsy and forensics would prove all that they did.

"Dylan, check your text!" Lily, apparently finished with her statement, rushed over.

From the corner of her eye, Olivia caught Dylan fiddle with his phone.

"Oh no," Dylan said. "I need to go help."

"Me too. Tell Mom we're going to the estate." That was Lily. She must be talking to Simon.

"Oh, wow. There's a spy cam in the room. He must have retrieved it before Crime Scene showed up." Spaulding rubbed at his temples, making the wiry, graying hairs there stand up. "Who do you think killed them? And why?"

Olivia shrugged. "Guess that's why they pay us the big bucks to find the answers."

Spaulding scoffed. "You, maybe. Definitely not us. Over-worked and underpaid is what we are." He beckoned Monnin over. "Will you follow up with security about the suspect? The fake room service guy?"

Monnin's nod jostled her sandy-brown ponytail. "And what are you doing?"

"I'll get Crime Scene Unit to check Tucker's room and here. Then I'll need to make the notification to the son." He flicked his gaze at Olivia. "By the way, we found the kid in a drunk tank at Sector E earlier. I had him brought to our sector."

Poor kid! Tyler was already suffering from addiction. Now he'd lost his support system. "We'll need to authenticate the video." If she asked Deanna, she'd have to brief Ron. Unless she could tie any of these murders to the Perez family, she couldn't take them to the task force.

"We can do that." Spaulding clamped a hand on Monnin's shoulder. "Cliff notes version, Tucker and Liz killed the congressman. Someone recorded it. Presumably, the same someone killed these two."

Monnin frowned. "This is getting complicated."

Recalling the scuffle between Tyler and Javier, Olivia asked, "Do you know why Tyler was arguing with Javier?"

"Planning to ask that when I make the notification." Spaulding pointed at her. "You want to tag along?"

CHAPTER 32

MIRROR ESTATE

KYLE

Kyle and Eva climbed into Ortiz's rugged off-road vehicle, the sun casting long shadows across the sprawling estate. While Kyle took in the dense forest bordering the property, Ortiz, a sturdy man with a calm demeanor, settled into the driver's seat and turned the key, bringing the engine to life with a low rumble.

"As you know, I'm new here," Ortiz said. "But I drove around the whole estate the first day, just to get the lay of the land." He maneuvered the vehicle onto a narrow unpaved road that snaked through the trees.

"I've never been out this way." Eva scanned the thick underbrush flanking the road.

"Neither have I," Kyle admitted. He'd spent most of his time at the main house and Lorraine's Kitchen, although he had seen the guesthouse, the chapel, and the closed orphanage from a distance.

"We're on the other side of the buildings," Ortiz explained as they traveled deeper into the wooded area. The trees loomed tall and ancient, their branches forming a canopy overhead. "As you see, it's a wooded area. There's no way out. So, I have no idea where that van would have gone."

"It must be hidden, right?" Kyle ventured.

"I suppose." Ortiz shrugged.

"There are a lot of secret tunnels and hideaways, I heard," Eva said. "Do you think it could have been in one of these spots?"

"I don't know. I'm new. Don't know anything about secret tunnels," Ortiz replied. "But if that was the case, these guys must know the area well."

They continued in silence. The only sounds were the engine churning, the gravel crunching under the tires, and the wildlife occasionally rustling in the underbrush. The road twisted and turned, and the forest seemed to grow denser, the trees pressing in from both sides.

Soon, Ortiz slowed the vehicle to a stop. "Let's check out the area." He opened the door and stepped out. "I'll show you the tracks."

Kyle and Eva followed, the cool, earthy scent of the forest enveloping them as they stepped onto the uneven ground. Ortiz led them to a patch of disturbed earth a short distance from the road. The tracks were faint but discernible, leading deeper into the woods.

"Here." Ortiz pointed, kneeling to get a closer look. "These tracks are fresh. Could be from the van."

Kyle studied the tracks. "Do they lead anywhere specific?"

Ortiz pushed to his feet. "They stopped by a hill. And then nada. But speaking of tunnels, we need to ask Sean. If you believe Max, the kid has been crawling in the tunnels since he was in diapers. He might know something."

CHAPTER 33

TASK FORCE OFFICE

RON

Ron sat at his cluttered desk, scanning the Perez family file for what must have been the hundredth time. Papers and digital screens surrounded him in the cramped office, casting a faint blue light over the room as he searched for any hint that could lead to Grace's whereabouts. The air churning through the climate-controlled ventilation smelled stale, only relieved by the faint draft and hum of distant city life creeping in through the open window.

The sharp ring of his phone interrupted his concentration. With a grunt, he grabbed it, eyed Ana's name on the screen, and swiped to answer, already holding the phone to his ear.

"Yes, Ana?"

"Any news?" Her voice crackled through.

"No. Kyle said they'd ask Sean to help. The kid knows the tunnels well. Maybe he knows something. If I hear anything, I'll let you know. What do you have?"

"Jorge Perez plans to turn himself in."

Ron jerked upright in his seat, leaning closer to the phone.

"Turning himself in?" he repeated, as if saying it out loud would make more sense of it.

"Yes, and I don't think Hugo is involved, but I got a bad vibe from his employee, Shane Collins."

Ron kneaded his temples, trying to piece together too many scattered fragments of information. He glanced over at a photo of Hugo Perez pinned on his wall, staring back with a confident gaze. "Wait." Ron pressed cold fingers to his now-closed eyes. "Word on the street is Hugo's in charge."

"I don't know," Ana admitted. "If Hugo is lying, he's very good at it. Did Hernandez find anything useful on him? And I'd like Hernandez to check Collins out."

Ron scribbled a note on a pad, feeling the situation unraveling further into chaos. He clenched his jaw. "I'll tell him. But why would people think Hugo is in charge?"

During the brief pause on the line, Ron could imagine Ana working through what they were dealing with. "Maybe someone is doing business in his name?" she suggested. "It's interesting—when I asked the old man if he was in charge, he changed the subject."

"Okay, but it doesn't get us any closer to who is blackmailing Perez and where Grace is."

Tanner skidded to a stop in his doorway. "Boss, we found something."

"I'm going out to the squad room." Ron told Ana. "I'll put you on speaker."

Once they were gathered around the screen, Tanner nodded to Deanna who swiped her tablet to send a mug shot to the screen before Tanner spoke. "Based on what Kyle reported, this is the guy driving the van. Finn O'Neill."

Ron pulled his granny glasses from his breast pocket and fit them in place as Finn O'Neill's image, spiked hair and lanky, posted above several aliases. But wait, O'Neill's gang affiliation was listed as Irishman? Was the gang here for Connor or Grace? Was Grace's abduction more complicated than Ron thought?

He cleared his throat. "They aren't active around here."

Hernandez typed something on his keyboard and projected a screenshot next to the mugshot. "Well, they've been, er, rebranding themselves as hired guns. I found this, uh, ad, on the dark web."

Ron squinted to read the words.

"You don't need to read it. It's in codes," Deanna said. "Anyway, someone answered the ad. It took some doing, but we traced it back to an IP address registered to Mirage Fine Arts."

"Hmm, but we can't pinpoint the person who used the computer, correct?" This came over the phone from Ana.

"Correct," Deanna confirmed.

"So, someone with access to the gallery network ordered the abduction. Ana, we need to narrow it down to who else knew about the plan," Ron said. "Tanner, give her a hand."

"Yes, boss."

"Hernandez?" Ana's voice crackled through the speakerphone. "Can you dig into Shane Collins? I got a bad vibe."

Hernandez responded, "Will do."

"Let's get to work!" Ron ordered.

CHAPTER 34

TUNNELS

GRACE

Grace couldn't tell how long it had been since she'd returned from her initial exploratory escape from the room where she'd been held. Upon her return, she had gulped down a bottle of water, her throat parched and her body drained from the tension. Yet, her captors remained absent, their unsettling silence feeding her resolve to find a way out. She equipped herself with two more bottles and a pack of sandwiches, then ventured back into her prison's labyrinthine passageways.

This time, she was slightly more prepared, stuffing her pockets with rolls of toilet paper she'd found in a utility closet. As she retraced her steps, she dropped small pieces of the paper behind her, marking her path like modern-day breadcrumbs. At the first fork in the corridor, she hesitated only momentarily before choosing the unexplored path, leaving a trail of her makeshift markers—which would also lead her captors right to her should they follow, a risk she deemed worth it.

As she wandered through the endless twists and turns, her spirits began to wane. The light from the bulb hanging on a string along the wall grew dimmer with each step, casting long shadows that seemed to dance mockingly around her. Doubt crept in, suffocating her initial burst of hope. What if there was no way out?

Images of her family flashed before her eyes—her parents, likely taking their worry out in prayer—and her brothers, especially Alex, who had always been her protector. Kyle drifted into her thoughts, stirring a pang. *If only I had my phone, Kyle would find me. Lord, please help!*

"Hey, who are you?"

Lost in her thoughts, she jolted back at the sudden voice. The words echoed eerily down the corridor.

She pivoted, scanning the area but not seeing anyone. "Who are you? Where are you?"

"Look to your left." The voice sounded like a young boy.

She did, and indeed, a young boy's face peered at her through a hole in the wall. It was hard to tell his age from only a portion of his face, but based on her dealings with her students, she guessed he was either a fourth or fifth grader. The light emanating from his side seemed to be brighter, or perhaps he was holding a flashlight? So many questions she wanted to ask, but the most pressing was, "Do you know a way out of here?"

"Sure, why? Can't you just go back the way you came?"

A logical question.

"I wish. I was abducted. How do I get over to you?" She looked all around her, remembering the turns she had made. Would one of the turns she missed take her to the boy?

"I don't know. I haven't walked all the way through. Unlike the other ones, this one is like a maze. I mark on the walls, so I don't get lost."

Was that what she heard earlier? While she figured out a way to get to the boy, she asked, "Do you have a phone with you?" Nowadays, a lot of her fourth and fifth graders had cell phones.

Why they would need one? She had no idea. "Can you call a friend of mine? He'll come find me."

"Yes, but it doesn't work here. No signal. You said you were abducted. You mean like kidnapped?"

"Yes, please, maybe you can go back and call Kyle. No, wait. I don't have my phone. Um, Google FBI Kyle Peters, Orlando. Something should come up. You know how to Google, right?"

"Pleeeaase. I'm not five. But I told you. No signal. And it's a long way back. Did you say you're a friend of Kyle's?"

"You know Kyle?" She didn't know who was more surprised.

"Yeah, he comes by sometimes. A bit uptight, not like Dylan and Tommy. They're cool. Still, you're his friend. I'll get help and get you out of here."

The sweetest words she'd heard since she was taken! "Thank you!" Who was this kid? Kyle often mentioned Dylan. Wasn't he the millionaire or billionaire? He said Kyle came by sometimes. "Where are we?"

"Mirror Estate."

CHAPTER 35

LORRAINE'S KITCHEN

KYLE

Kyle, Eva, and Ortiz returned to Lorraine's Kitchen, seeking Sean. The dinner rush was over, and the once bustling dining area was now quiet. The priests who had been dining earlier had left, leaving a serene ambiance in the air. Connor, Lorraine's husband and Sean's father, spotted them from across the room and motioned them into the kitchen.

As soon as Kyle saw Alex, he cringed inside. He'd forgotten about him. "Hey, Alex, you met Ms. Carol?"

"Yeah, Max gave me a tour. Ms. Carol is nice. Any news on Grace?" Alex's gaze kept going to Eva.

Eva ducked her head, perhaps uncomfortable under the stranger's too attentive gaze. "We don't know anything for sure yet, but she could be here somewhere."

"That's fantastic!" Alex, previously braced against the counter, lurched to his feet. "What are you waiting for? Let's go get her."

"Hold up." Kyle held onto Alex's shoulder. "Relax, we're working on that."

"Sorry to interrupt." Connor stepped forward. "But have you found anything? Are they here?"

"Not really," Ortiz said.

Lorraine wrung her hands. "Nobody has seen Sean. He ate with us earlier, but then he's gone again."

"That boy?" Ortiz's crooked his mustache to one side. "I bet he's exploring the tunnels."

"Yeah, I'm usually not concerned. The estate is a safe place." The worry lines etching Lorraine's face belied her words. "But when Connor told me about the Irishman Gang showing up, I just got worried."

Kyle shared a glance with Eva, understanding Lorraine's underlying fear. Ortiz said Sean was very familiar with the tunnels and secret areas in the estate. They surely could use his help to find Grace. In fact, that's why they were here. "Would you feel better if we go look for him? Probably in the tunnels, like Ortiz suggested."

"Would you?" Lorraine's stiff shoulders edged down from near her ears. "I can't leave yet. A couple of tables outside still have guests."

Connor took off his apron. "I'll go with you. Kate can take over."

"Go." Lorraine's mother, who had been helping out, swapped her kitchen apron for a fancier one, ready to step in. "I'm sure he's down in the tunnels exploring like he always does."

"Hang on. Let me swing by the guardhouse to get Cedric and Ronnie. They'll track him. Be back in a few." Ortiz started to walk out, then spun. "Connor, bring a piece of Sean's clothing for them."

"They're his Australian shepherds," Eva explained. "They're retired from search and rescue. Really cute. I think he's training them to be guard dogs too."

Soon, Ortiz returned with two adorable Aussies. He pulled

the blue leash up. "Meet Cedric." Then he raised his other arm with the pink leash. "Meet Ronnie."

"We can get acquainted later. Let's look for Sean now." Connor headed to the back stairs.

CHAPTER 36

POLICE STATION

OLIVIA

A little while later, Olivia walked into the police station, or the sector as they were called in Orlando, with Simon by her side. She inhaled air thick with the scent of stale coffee and the faint hint of disinfectant. The hum of conversations and the occasional ringing phone created a backdrop of organized chaos. Simon wanted to offer help to Tyler once Spaulding and Olivia finished with the kid.

As an intelligence operative, Olivia had never done a death notification. The task weighed on her while they wended through the maze of desks and officers. Tyler, still in the drunk tank, had sobered up. As she entered, he rubbed bloodshot eyes, and his posture slumped. She let Spaulding take the lead, his years of experience making him the natural choice for this task.

The stern-faced Spaulding cleared his throat, stepped closer to the cell, and gentled his tone. "Tyler Jenkins?"

Tyler looked up and winced. He stumbled to his feet, approached the bars, and gripped them tightly. "Yeah." His voice rasped. He cleared his throat. "That's me."

"Tyler, I'm Detective Spaulding, and this is Special Agent Tso." Spaulding unlocked the door and let the kid out. He took them to a small conference room, then gestured Tyler to one of the chairs. "Sit."

When Tyler complied, Olivia sat next to Spaulding, leaving Simon outside observing.

"We need to talk to you about your mother," the detective began. "We're very sorry, but she was found dead earlier today."

Tyler's face fell, air rushed from his lungs, and he gawked, frozen in place like a deer caught in headlights. "Mom? What happened to her? Who did this? *Why*?"

Spaulding raised a hand to calm the kid's frantic questioning. "It's early in the investigation. We don't know much yet."

Olivia leaned forward, her heart aching for the young man. "Mr. Roth, Lily, and I are very sorry for your loss. I know this is a bad time, but we have a few questions to ask you."

Tyler took a deep breath, his chest rising and falling as he tried to compose himself. He blinked a few times and raised his hand to wipe his eyes. "Okay," he whispered.

"Last evening, we saw you arguing with your stepfather. What was that about?" Olivia focused on his body language.

Tyler's face twisted. "It was stupid. He accused me of using again. I told him I wasn't. I don't think he believed me. He said he wouldn't bail me out again. Anyway, I got sick of defending myself and wanted to leave. He was in the way, so I shoved him away. Didn't mean to push him so hard."

Olivia watched him closely for any signs of deceit. She saw none. His pain and frustration seemed genuine. A glance over at Spaulding confirmed he believed Tyler too. The detective nodded subtly, their shared assessment.

"Thank you, Tyler." Spaulding stood, then dropped a hand on the kid's shoulder and squeezed it. "We're doing everything we can to find out who did this."

As they started for the door, Tyler called, "I remember something. I didn't think anything of it."

She turned back. "What is it?"

"Javi said something weird. He said his past was finally catching up with him."

CHAPTER 37

TUNNELS

SEAN

Sean panted as he made his way through the dimly lit passage, retracing his steps from where he had seen the woman. After reassuring her he'd get help, he followed the markings he left on the stone walls to navigate the labyrinthine hallways.

Then a voice echoed from somewhere nearby, halting him in his tracks.

"I don't know. Something about him looks familiar," one deep voice said.

"You're imagining things," another raspier voice responded.

"What are we supposed to do with the girl?" Deep Voice asked.

"Keep her until we get further instructions," Raspy replied.

After a brief silence, Deep Voice spoke again. "I think I know who that is. I wonder if he's the kid they stashed away after the O'Keefe job."

"That was, what, twenty years ago?"

"About that."

"Then stop worrying about it. There's never gonna be a trial anyway. Concentrate on finding the map."

A string of curses echoed before Deep Voice said, "If they built it, they should have a map."

"Don't you know where we are? This is the Mirror Estate. It belongs to the Marinos. Their ancestors built it. So, why would an outsider have the map?"

"They found the bunker and this!"

"I don't know. Let's go back to the bunker."

Sean held his breath as he pressed his ear closer. With a faint mechanical whirr, the wall started to open, revealing a secret room beyond. The sight made his eyes grow wide and heart pump loudly. He bolted down the corridor, his footsteps echoing wildly.

Grace

After the boy promised he'd return soon, Grace stood at the site waiting, praying she'd be found. The dismal flickering from a bulb hanging on a string along the wall was the only thing cutting through the oppressive darkness. She sucked in short gasps of breath, drawing in air too damp and cool, and hugged her arms around herself to keep from shivering. She didn't dare lean against the walls, not with them covered in a thin layer of grime and moss, giving off a faint musty smell. She held her breath as she listened for his return.

Grace crouched in the dampness, gave in, and pressed her back against the cold stone wall. The musty air felt thick in her lungs as she tried to quiet her rapid breathing. Then the faint scuffle of approaching footsteps echoed through the passage and her heart pounded. She tensed, waiting.

"Oh, it's you."

She recognized the voice before the boy's small frame emerged from around the corner. Relief washed over her, tempered by the urgency in his expression. She scrambled to her feet. "You're back. Did you get help?"

The boy shook his head, panting as the stomp of his feet slapped against the rough-hewn tunnel. "I must have made a wrong turn. Where's the bunker? They said they were coming to check on you."

Grace pointed to the path she'd come from. "It's that way. So, you didn't get help?"

He shook his head more emphatically this time. "Not yet. I overheard them talking. Then the door opened, and I had to run."

Grace sank back against the wall, disappointment draining her. "I was hoping—"

The boy's hand shot out and grabbed hers with surprising strength. "Did you hear me? They're coming. We gotta go."

You can't lose hope! She pushed herself away from the wall. "If they're coming from the way you came from, we should go the other way."

She motioned toward the right tunnel, and they took off together, sprinting headlong into a narrower tunnel. The walls seemingly closed in around them as they ran. She'd been this way earlier, but would it lead them to safety now?

Almost as soon as they started, the thud of footsteps behind them grew louder. Voices bounced off the walls, distorted and menacing.

"I see her. That way!" one voice shouted.

"A kid is with her," another voice added, closer than the first.

"Hey," she called out, but no, she couldn't keep calling him hey. "What's your name? I'm Grace."

"Sean."

Grace and Sean picked up speed to put more distance between them and their pursuers. The shouts and footsteps grew louder, echoing ominously in the narrow tunnel.

Then Sean tripped and fell, skidding on the damp ground. Grace dropped to her knees and helped him up, her heart hammering her rib cage. As she struggled to pull him to his feet, a door to their left creaked sideways.

"This is the door with the strange codes," Sean said, his eyes widening.

He hopped up and pulled her into the room. The door automatically closed behind them! Faint lights came on. Were they motion-sensor lights? She looked for a handle but found none.

Sean clutched at her hand. "I must have accidentally triggered something to unlock this door."

Grace leaned against the wall, her breathing ragged and her knees wobbly. "Well, then, let's hope they don't find the trigger."

Outside, the sounds of their pursuers grew fainter, but they weren't safe yet. To get her bearings, she surveyed a room filled with old crates and forgotten supplies, much like the storage rooms they'd seen before. But coated in dust and strung with cobwebs, this one had an eerie sense of abandonment.

Sean, however, was fixated on the door. "Only problem is how do we get out?"

CHAPTER 38

TASK FORCE OFFICE

RON

Ron glanced at his watch, scowling at the late hour. The long day was drawing to a close, and the fatigue was starting to wear on him. But he'd check in one last time before sending the team home to resume their efforts in the morning. The buzz of his phone interrupted his thoughts, and he read Kyle's text, his jaw clenching. Sean seemed to be missing, and while Kyle suggested the boy might be exploring the tunnels, Ron's gut churned.

With a determined stride, he made his way to the squad room where the hum of conversation and the clatter of keyboards belied the team's waning energy. Shane Collins's photo was displayed prominently on the screen, accompanied by his vital statistics. The suspect's face steeled Ron's resolve.

Gathering their attention, Ron nodded to Tanner who stood up and motioned everyone to get up. "Listen up, everyone. Kyle just informed me that Sean Murray seems to be missing. He thinks Sean might be exploring the tunnels, so they're going to search for him. In case you never met the ten-year-old boy, he's Ms. Carol's butler's grandson."

A murmur rippled through the team. Hernandez, who had been studying the screen, looked up, then gestured toward the information displayed. "This is what Deanna and I have found so far."

Deanna, standing next to him, added, "The guy has no social

media profile. Nothing. And we can't find anything prior to 2020. It's like he didn't exist until then."

Ron furrowed his brow. Perhaps because of Olivia, he couldn't help thinking this guy might have been an operative of one kind or another. Either that or he was running from the law.

Hernandez went on. "We've checked all the usual databases and come up empty. It's like he went to great lengths to erase his past."

"Or someone did it for him," Deanna suggested.

"Maybe you can get his fingerprints." Scratching his forehead, Tanner glanced at Ana. He'd rubbed one of his thick brows the wrong way, leaving wiry hairs distractingly askew.

Ana shrugged. "I can try."

Tanner grabbed the remote, and several names now came up on the screen. "Here's the list of all the employees and anyone who has access to the gallery network. As you can see, there are only six people."

"But..." Deanna raised a finger. "If someone were to piggyback on that network, you wouldn't see it."

"We've checked all of them. The only one in question is Shane Collins. He does most of Hugo's grunt work."

"Is there any connection between this Collins fellow and Grace or the Irishman?" Ron stifled a yawn.

"Not that we can find." Tanner bounced his stress ball up and down. "Maybe Deanna can probe deeper."

"Yes, Deanna, see what you can find out." Ron rubbed his eyes. "It's late. Go home, get some shut-eye, and come back tomorrow fresh."

"Any more updates from Kyle?" Ana asked.

It had been a while since the last update. Ron took his phone out and called. It went straight to voicemail. "If he was underground, he might not get signals."

"Didn't he say Grace might be there?"

True, Grace could be there, but they didn't know that for

sure. A two-prong approach would still be better. But Ana would want to join in the search. "Okay, call the estate, let Max know you're coming. He should be able to tell you where to go."

Ana stood up. "Thanks. I'll call on the way."

He nodded. "The rest of you, we still need to find out the one behind this blackmail scheme. He or she could give us the exact location, in case Grace isn't at the estate. And we don't want Jorge Perez to change his mind about turning himself in."

CHAPTER 39

TUNNELS

DYLAN

Dylan drove with a determined focus, the engine humming as the estate came into view. Lily sat beside him, her face taut and hands clenched in her lap. They had to find Sean, and quickly.

He stopped in front of Lorraine's Kitchen where the group had planned to gather before heading into the tunnels. As they stepped out, another car pulled up behind them and Ana got out, hustling to catch up.

"Wait up!" she called out.

Dylan and Lily paused and let Ana close the distance. "What are you doing here? Do you have news on Grace?" Dylan asked, then held his breath, pushing down the rising hope.

Ana shook her head. "Not really, but Kyle said she might be here. Your security chief said the van drove here, but they couldn't find it."

Lily frowned, her brow knitting. "How can it disappear?"

"I don't know." Ana's shrug only briefly loosened the poise

her shoulders always carried. "Anyway, Kyle isn't answering his phone. I'd like to know what the status is."

"Let's hurry!" Dylan led them toward the tunnel entrance. "We asked them to wait for us. Let's hope they did."

As they approached, Ortiz stood there with the dogs, Cedric and Ronnie. He waved them over. After quick introductions, he handed Dylan a blue leash. "Take Cedric with you."

Cedric, a well-trained search dog, stood at attention, his nose already twitching. Ortiz had trained the dogs with Dylan as a backup, and a surge of gratitude warmed Dylan over the man's foresight.

Ronnie got excited, her tail wagging as she strained toward Ana and Lily. Ortiz kept a firm hold on her leash, but her enthusiasm was clear. Cedric, in contrast, merely looked up at the newcomers with a calm curiosity.

Ortiz's radio crackled to life, a voice coming through with a hint of static. "He left marks on the wall. We are following them."

Ortiz responded into the radio. "Okay, we're coming now." He turned to the group. "Connor didn't want to wait, so they started about five minutes ago. Let's go."

Then he bent down, held out a pair of shorts for the dogs to sniff, and commanded, "Search."

Cedric and Ronnie picked up the scent. Their bodies tensing, they strained against their leashes. Dylan, Ortiz, Lily, and Ana followed, matching the dogs' pace down the dark, narrow tunnel.

The air hung thick and musty, seeming undisturbed for eons, and only their footsteps and the occasional bark or whine dared intrude in the heavy stillness. The faint light from their flashlights cast eerie shadows that danced with their movements, illuminating the rough tunnel walls.

Dylan kept a firm grip on Cedric's leash, trusting the dog's instincts to navigate the twists and turns. He could hear the others breathing heavily behind him, the urgency of their mission driving them forward.

Then Cedric stopped moving, sniffing at a spot on the wall. Dylan crouched down and shone his flashlight on the mark. It was a faint smear, almost invisible in the dim light, but it was enough.

"They went this way." He straightened up and urged Cedric forward again.

The group moved quickly, their pace increasing as they followed the dogs deeper into the maze. The walls seemed to close in around them, the darkness pressing down like a weight. But they pushed on, driven by the hope of finding Sean and Grace.

Ortiz's radio crackled again, the voice now clearer. "We found another mark. Keep coming straight."

"Roger that," Ortiz replied, and Dylan's flashlight, glancing off him, caught the determined set of his jaw. "We're getting closer. Stay sharp."

They continued on, the dogs leading them with unerring precision. Dylan's heart pounded, his mind racing over what they might find. Every sound seemed amplified in the confined space, the echoes of their footsteps blending with the distant noise of dripping water.

Finally, they rounded a corner, and a faint light glimmered ahead. With a surge of hope and renewed energy, Dylan urged Cedric forward. While drawing near, they could make out figures moving in the light.

"Kyle!" Dylan called out, his voice echoing down the tunnel.

Kyle turned, waving him closer. "Dylan, over here! We found something."

CHAPTER 40
THE ROTH RESIDENCE

OLIVIA

After she spoke with Tyler, the weight of the day pressed down on Olivia. They could do nothing more until the autopsy was completed, possibly the next morning. Spaulding and Monnin were off following other leads, leaving Olivia with a nagging feeling she couldn't shake. The shadowy figure next to Hugo Perez haunted her thoughts.

Simon drove her home, their silent contemplation a companion for the ride. Once home, Olivia went to her desk. She snagged a screen grab of the man next to Hugo, but his face was too obscure for facial recognition software. However, she could still approximate his height and other physical attributes.

Sitting behind her computer, she leveraged the various networks she had access to and combed through databases, forums, and any possible lead. The process was tedious, but she was relentless.

"Liv, Ron is trying to get a hold of you." Simon's voice broke through her concentration. He stood at the edge of the alcove where her desk was situated, holding out his phone.

She mouthed a thank you and took the phone. "Sorry, Ron, I forgot to turn the sound back on. What's up?"

"That's okay," Ron replied. "Do you know a Shane Collins?"

Olivia racked her brain, searching her memory. "Don't think so. Why?"

"Ana got a bad vibe. Let me back up a bit. Not sure if you heard through the grapevine, Grace has been taken—"

"When?" Simon asked at the same time she said, "Earlier this afternoon. That's why you all left?"

"Yes, long story short. It's connected to the Perez family. This Collins character works at Mirage Fine Arts, owned by Hugo Perez. And the deep dive didn't yield anything prior to five years ago. It's like he didn't exist before then."

Olivia stiffened at the implications. "Well, you know how it is. Unless I worked with him, I wouldn't necessarily know who he is. That's to protect us. Compartmentalize everything. But if you have a photo, I might be able to look into it."

A beat later, her phone buzzed with a new message. "Just sent it. Thanks. If he happened to be a foe, would you know?"

Olivia opened the message and swiped to the photo of his driver's license. The man in the image looked ordinary. Suit and tie, nothing special about him. She might have seen him before. "Um, it says he's five eleven."

"Yeah, so?"

"Nothing, I'm just thinking out loud. I'll get back to you. Oh, and if you need any help finding Grace, just holler." She ended the call and gave the phone back to Simon, who was looking out the tiny window. Something in the back of her mind floated to the forefront. "Hey, what did Spaulding say when we were viewing the footage?"

He turned around, eyebrows knitted. "Hmm, he said the man who got Javier's attention was Perez. Hugo Perez, I think."

One lightbulb went on. She had requested all the hotel footage via Dylan. Now she retrieved them from her emails and viewed them. The mystery man was standing by Hugo Perez. And Shane Collins worked in the gallery Hugo Perez owned. She studied the footage from the hotel where this mystery man posed as room service staff. Yes, there was this mark on his neck. She put them side by side and examined them.

"You're thinking they could be the same guy?" Simon asked.

"What do you think?"

"Hard to say. Their build is similar, but we can't see if Collins has that mark on his neck. And there's not enough of a face to really see the features."

"I know, but we have video of them walking... hang on." She searched the internet for any significant public event held in the gallery. There were several, and she hit the jackpot when she found one with a newsclip. "That's Collins, isn't it?" She pointed to a figure walking behind the reporter.

He leaned in to look. "I think so."

"I'm sending these to Deanna. She can do a gait analysis."

He put his hands on her shoulders. "You know it's not your job to solve the crime. You're a consultant and really just a conduit between the Ghost and the task force."

"I know, but Javier was your friend." She leaned into his grip, his miracle fingers working out the tension kinks in her neck. Concentrate. What was she saying? "It looks like there is a Perez connection. And this Collins, if he proves to be an operative of some sort, I'd like to know."

"Do you think he is?"

The stiffness came back. "If these prove to be the same guy, Shane Collins, I do believe so. He knows how to avoid cameras. He knows to wear a cap to make facial rec difficult. The way he carries himself. And of course, he doesn't seem to have a past beyond a few years."

"Of course, you're right." He bent to give her a kiss and went back downstairs.

Assuming Collins was an operative, who was he working

for? Hugo? Assuming the Perez family was involved somehow, what was the connection between Grace's abduction and Javier's murder?

CHAPTER 41

TUNNELS

GRACE

Grace shivered. How long had it been since Sean had pulled her into this room? Initially, relief claimed her when their pursuers were locked out, but as time stretched on, anxiety crept in. How would they get out of here? How would anyone find them?

"I saw them go in—"

She heard it and leaned against the wall to listen.

"There must be a way in," a second voice said.

She turned to Sean. "We have to think of something. They'll find a way in."

The boy, full of boundless energy and curiosity, had barely been still since they entered. After raising the question of their escape, he set off to explore the small, dingy space. Grace sighed and decided to join him. It wasn't as if she had anything better to do.

The room they found themselves in—some sort of forgotten storage facility—wasn't furnished, but just housed a few old, dusty crates and a metal shelf lined with disorganized stacks of paper. The concrete walls were bare except for a single door. Every now and then, they walked around to reactivate the light.

"Grace, do you know what this language is?" Sean held up a piece of paper with strange symbols scrawled across it.

She took one glance and shook her head. "I don't know." Then she leaned in, taking a closer look. "It's not written in any alphabet I recognize. It doesn't look like any Asian languages I've seen, and it's definitely not Arabic. Russian, maybe? No, not that either."

The symbols looked vaguely familiar, but she couldn't place them. Then it struck her. "These symbols—they're the same as the ones on the door." She pointed to the intricate markings carved into the metal.

Sean was about to toss the piece of paper back onto the shelf when Grace grabbed it. She'd hold onto it just in case. They continued their search but found nothing useful.

"This is odd." She pointed to an old doll on the shelf. "I didn't see any other toys. Why would someone keep a doll here?" Sean shrugged. "I don't have dolls, but I have action figures and stuffed toys. Mom always tells me to sort them out so she can donate the old ones."

Grace reached for the doll. It was sitting on a map. She picked up the doll and eased the map from underneath it. "Look at this—"

A mechanized sound startled her. Had their pursuers figured out how to open the door? The breath caught in her throat, and both of them pivoted toward the entrance. But the sound wasn't coming from there.

Sean bounced off his toes, the first to react. "Look, another door opened! I must have touched the right place. Let's go before it closes." He started to run toward it.

"How do we know where it goes?" Grace hung back, hesitant to follow.

But Sean snagged the map. "We got the map here. Let's go."

With no time to argue, she followed him toward the newly revealed door. But would it lead them to safety or trap them even further?

KYLE

Kyle followed Connor along the dimly lit corridor with Eva and Alex close behind. The air, so thick with the musty smell of damp concrete and dust, made every breath feel heavy.

"Look over here," Alex called out, pointing to a series of scratches on the grimy surface. They were subtle, almost invisible in the poor lighting, but there nonetheless.

Connor led the way as they followed the marks, the group's footsteps echoing through the narrow passage. Somehow, the echo rebounding off the wall gave the impression those walls were closing in around them, adding to the claustrophobic atmosphere. After a few minutes, the marks stopped.

"What happened?" Connor's question emerged almost in a growl. He fisted a hand around his flashlight, swinging the light wildly along the walls. "Why is there no more mark?"

Kyle touched the slimy wall. "Maybe he just kept going this way and didn't think it was necessary to mark it?"

"Let's keep going this way and see," Eva suggested in her soothing voice.

"All right, let's do it." Connor marched forward with renewed determination.

Kyle followed, scanning the walls for any sign of the markings while Alex stuck close to Eva, the two of them chatting.

They continued down the corridor but found no more notations—and no Sean. Kyle's hope began to wane. What if they were going in the wrong direction?

"I think you stepped on something," Alex said.

Kyle looked down, not seeing anything. But no, Alex was talking to Eva. She bent and pulled something off the bottom of her shoe. Alex's eyes widened.

"She's here. Grace is here!" Alex held up a sticker. "She went to a Bible study this morning. I think it's a new session."

Kyle stepped closer to see what prompted Alex's comment. Eva held a hi-my-name-is sticker, with the name *Grace* written on it in familiar handwriting. "A new session. I guess it makes sense that they had these name tags on."

"It's her handwriting," Alex confirmed.

Kyle could have said that too. He'd know Grace's neat looping script anywhere. His heart surged. Somehow, Grace was here. Could she and Sean be together? Or maybe Sean had found her?

"Connor, look at this." Kyle brought him the sticker.

Connor squared his slumped shoulders. "That's great news. They have to be nearby."

Eva smiled. "Let's keep going. If Grace left this behind, she must be trying to lead us to her."

They pressed on with renewed vigor, every step now echoing a purpose. The corridor twisted and turned, but they kept moving, spurred on by hope. The dull light seemed less oppressive now, each shadow less threatening.

As they curved around another corner, they came across a small door, slightly ajar. Kyle's heart pounded when he pushed it open, gun in hand, revealing a room cluttered with old furniture and boxes.

"Grace? Sean?" Connor called out, his voice echoing off the walls.

Barks rang out. Then Dylan and Ortiz, each holding a leash, followed the bounding dogs. Lily and Ana trailed them. That was a surprise! Kyle waved them over. "I think we found something."

Ana reached for the sticker. "She's got to be here somewhere. Do you think the dogs can sniff this?"

"I doubt it," Ortiz said. "It's been here mingled with all the scents around. They'll get confused. Alex, do you have anything of Grace's?"

Alex patted his clothes. "I don't think so."

"What if Sean and Grace are together?" Lily suggested. "The dogs are tracking Sean."

"Good point," Dylan and Ortiz agreed together. Then Ortiz added, "Let Cedric and Ronnie do their job."

The Aussies continued to track the scent. And they followed. So far, they hadn't seen Sean or Grace. At one fork, the dogs seemed lost.

"I think they lost the scent." Ortiz guided Ronnie toward the left fork. "Let's split up. I'll take Ronnie, Kyle, Eva, and Alex. Dylan and Cedric go with the rest of you."

Kyle went after the group while Dylan and Cedric took the other fork with Lily and Ana. This was so frustrating. Shouldn't Grace be nearby? When did she lose the sticker?

Minutes later, they rounded a corner and ran into Cedric.

"Huh, it's like we walked in a circle," Dylan said, just as surprised as Kyle was.

"Did you find anything?" Ana asked.

"Nothing," Ortiz replied.

"The sticker is here." Alex's fist balled up. "Grace has to be—"

"Shush." Ana's brows furrowed, and she cocked her head to one side.

Kyle listened intently. A voice echoed through the tunnels. "You stay here in case they come out."

The acoustics made it difficult to gauge the distance, but it didn't seem close.

Connor must have heard the man too. Before anyone could

react, he charged forward. "It's you! Where is my son? Don't you harm my son!"

A curse was followed by, "Who... oh, you! I knew I'd seen you before. Older now, but I can see your dad in you. So, that boy is your son." Someone hooted and laughed. "Just my lucky day!"

Ana leapt out, gun raised, and yelled, "Federal agent! Drop your weapon! Now!"

Kyle's training kicked in. He moved to back up Ana, but Ortiz grabbed his arm. "Cover me!" Ortiz handed Alex the leash and rounded the corner with his gun raised. Kyle positioned himself at the corner, aiming at the two men, ensuring Ortiz could get Connor back safely.

Connor stumbled back, visibly agitated.

"Stay back to protect the others," Ortiz instructed him before stepping forward again.

Tension crackled.

"No shooting! Ricochet risk!" Ana warned, keeping her gun aimed but steady.

The situation grew more intense. Voices rose, dogs barked, and anticipation nearly thrummed. Dylan and Lily were poised to engage, while Eva, looking serious, shielded Alex with her gun at the ready. Kyle hadn't known she was armed.

The two men began to retreat under the pressure. "Stay calm," Ana commanded, her focus never leaving the targets. One of the men stumbled, injured but not from a bullet.

"Ortiz, render aid," Ana ordered, keeping her gun trained on the other man. She moved cautiously, minimizing the risk of a ricochet as she pursued the second suspect.

ANA

Ana sprinted down the tunnel, her footsteps echoing off the damp stone walls. The suspect had a head start and knew the labyrinthine layout. Each turn felt more confusing than the last—no wonder Sean had marked the walls.

"Stop! Federal agent!" she hollered, her voice reverberating through the tunnels. The suspect only quickened his pace, disappearing around another bend.

By the time Ana reached the next intersection, she'd lost him. She punched the wall, the sting in her knuckles grounding her anger. Breathing heavily, she retraced her steps. "I lost him in this maze."

Back at the rendezvous point, Ortiz held a suspect with spiked hair. "He'll live," Ortiz said. "I think he injured his knee when he fell. Probably hit the ground at the wrong angle."

"Cuff him, Kyle!" Ana scanned the group. Good, everyone was safe. She zeroed in on Spike Hair. "Where are Grace and Sean?"

"I don't know."

Ana and Ortiz continued to press him, but he remained tight-lipped until he finally nodded toward something. "They disappeared in there."

"Where is there?" Ana jammed her hands on her hips, looming over where he sat on the tunnel floor.

"Back there." He jerked his cuffed hands down the tunnel. "They went into that room with the strange code."

Ana turned to the group. "Anyone notice a door with a strange code?"

Alex raised his hand.

"Yes?" Ana advanced on him but couldn't pull the information out of him fast enough to still her racing heart.

"I think I know where it is." He spoke too slowly, perhaps thinking it through as shared his thoughts. "Back where we found that sticker, I noticed some markings on the wall."

"Ana, we got to call this in," Kyle interjected. "Anyone have service?"

Everyone checked their phones, shaking their heads.

"Well, you'll need to escort him out and call it in," Ana told Kyle.

Kyle jutted up his chin. "I'd like to stay and help look for Grace."

"No, you need to call it in and report the situation to Ron."

Eva held up a hand. "I can escort him out and call it in."

"No, he's the only active agent here."

"Yes, ma'am." Kyle's shoulders slumped.

Alex caught her attention again. "I need to look for Grace."

But Ana stared him down. "As soon as we have news, we'll radio it in." She waved them all off. "You all need to head back."

"I'm staying," Connor protested. "I can't go back when Sean is in here."

Ana clenched her jaw. She could empathize. After all, she was here because Grace was her daughter by birth. "Connor, I promise you we'll find him."

Ortiz touched his arm. "You don't want us distracted. If you stay, we'll have to split our attention watching you and the bad guys."

Connor slunk back a step, wavering. "But..."

"I promise we'll get him back," Ana reiterated. "You need to be with your wife and stay safe."

Finally, the man sighed. "All right."

"Let's move," Ana commanded. "We'll go with you all. Alex, you'll point out where you saw the codes, okay?"

Alex saluted. "Yes, ma'am."

We're coming, Grace!

DYLAN

Dylan trudged back with the group, his thoughts racing. The air in the tunnels was cool and musty, their footsteps echoing his thudding heartbeat.

"Here it is!" Alex called out, pointing to a section of the wall illuminated by the dim flashlight beams. "See these?"

Dylan leaned in by where Alex indicated and gasped. The symbols closely resembled those on the map he and Tommy found in the time capsule. The intricate designs seemed to pulse with hidden meaning, their cryptic nature drawing him in.

"Are you thinking what I'm thinking?" Lily elbowed him, her eyes wide.

"I think so, but now is not the time." He'd have to return later. They continued, with Dylan and the dogs in front and Kyle bringing up the rear.

Then a cry rang out. "Argh!"

Dylan spun around to see the prisoner on the ground. Eva had bent to help him up, but the moment her grip loosened, he twisted violently and yanked his arm free. With surprising agility, he kicked out at Eva and sprang to his feet, bolting down the tunnel.

Without thinking, Dylan let go of the leashes. "Go get him!"

Cedric and Ronnie took off after the prisoner. Dylan ran after them, the others close behind. Their scrambled footsteps slapped the stone flooring, and their flashlight beams bounced off the walls, casting eerie shadows.

Moments later, barking and growling resounded through the tunnels. "Argh! Get off me!" the prisoner screamed. By the time Dylan reached them, Cedric and Ronnie had the prisoner pinned to the ground, their teeth bared and growls low.

Eva trotted over to the Aussies and petted them. "Good boy and good girl!" she praised, her voice steady despite the adrenaline surely coursing as strongly through her veins as it was through Dylan's.

Lily bent to grab the leashes. Dylan and Alex each held onto the prisoner, ensuring he couldn't escape again. The man's face now twisted with pain or fear, a stark contrast to his earlier defiance.

Connor stepped forward, his expression fierce and unyielding. He leaned in close to the prisoner, his voice a low growl. "Try this again, and they won't just tackle you."

CHAPTER 42

TASK FORCE OFFICE

RON

Sunday morning, Ron sat at his desk in the task force office. The clutter of papers and files spread before him mirrored his chaotic thoughts. In the last twenty-four hours, he'd learned a jumble of pieces to a jigsaw puzzle. Now he just needed to put the pieces together. But there was no *just* about it. Where did it all fit?

Late last night, Kyle had reported in. They had secured a suspect in the abduction of Grace and perhaps Sean. As of the last call, they hadn't found them yet. From what Kyle said, they couldn't have gone far. It would be a matter of getting to them.

And then Agent Davis called to let him know the deal was going down today. One reason why he called his team in on a Sunday.

"Morning, boss." Tanner appeared in the doorway. Had his senior agent even gone home? With his eyes red-rimmed and his clothes the same as yesterday, it didn't look like it.

"Morning, Tanner. What's the status?" Ron leaned back in

his chair, hands locked in his lap, projecting a calm that belied his churning gut.

Tanner scowled. "The suspect still won't say who hired him. And he invoked."

Ron pressed his locked hands against his twisted gut. Didn't help. He'd need an Alka-Seltzer. "All right. Let's get the team together." He stood and grabbed his coffee mug as he walked out of his office. The strong aroma of the freshly brewed coffee offered a momentary comfort.

In the squad room, Tanner, Hernandez, and Deanna were gathered around the large screen. Kyle had escorted the suspect back to the task force and planned to head to the estate as soon as the briefing was over. Last Ron heard, Ana was still deep in the tunnels.

"Okay, folks." Ron clapped once. "Let's do a quick update before Agent Davis shows up."

Hernandez clicked the remote, and a photo of the suspect, Finn O'Neill, appeared along with his vitals. He was affiliated with the Irishman Gang.

"He's not the one to deal with whoever hired him. Deanna and I can't find any call or text pertaining to that," Hernandez explained.

Ron swirled the coffee in his mug, the tension mounting. "What about his background? Any connections that might give us a lead?"

"We haven't found anything yet, but we're still digging," Hernandez responded.

Tapping his fingers against the black porcelain, Ron scowled at the dregs remaining. "Okay, let's go at it from another angle. Hugo Perez. The gallery. Update."

Tanner stopped squeezing his stress ball. "I've checked the list. Nobody stood out except for Shane Collins. Perez may have Collins do his dirty work—"

"Or he could be working for somebody else." Ron slugged

the last sip, then clunked the mug to the closest desk, Hernandez's. "Ana will need to follow up with Hugo. I've asked Olivia to look into Collins. Hopefully, I'll hear back soon." They needed more information on the Perez family. "Hernandez, you still have contacts with the Federales?"

"Yeah, I do."

"We need to know who the Perez family's business associates are. Who would Jorge Perez hurt the most if he does turn himself in?"

"On it, boss."

"I'd like to head back to the estate." Kyle inched toward the door, obviously eager to get back to the search for Grace.

Ron waved his son off. "Go."

Tanner held his phone, mouthed "Agent Davis," and stepped away. He must be escorting her in. Yep, sure enough, Tanner came back in with Agent Davis.

She wasted no time. "We have a situation. The intel we received confirms the deal is about to go down. We need to act —fast."

Ron straightened, his attention fully on Davis. "What's the plan?"

Agent Davis fiddled with the remote without success. Tanner came to her rescue. A map showed up on the screen. She used the laser pointer to pinpoint a marked location. "The deal is happening here, at a print shop on the east side. Our undercover agent, code-named Hawk, is already inside. They're planning to exchange a significant amount this afternoon, at sixteen hundred hours. Hawk has been embedded with the operation for months, and we can't afford to blow his cover."

Ron nodded. Four p.m. Not a lot of prep time. "You want us to provide backup? Or would you like a joint operation?"

"This would be a joint operation as planned. We'll set up a perimeter and cover all possible exits. Meet us there at fourteen hundred hours to prepare. Hawk will signal us when the deal is confirmed."

"We'll be ready," Ron said. "Tanner, make the necessary preparations."

Davis checked her watch and started for the door. "See you later."

When Ron was about to dismiss, his phone rang. Spaulding. His finger danced between the answer and the decline buttons. In the end, he swiped to answer. "Peters."

CHAPTER 43

TUNNELS

GRACE

Consciousness slowly crept back to Grace. Her left arm had fallen asleep from lack of circulation. She opened her eyes and shifted her position, a dull ache spreading through her limbs. Wait! Where was she? Panic surged through her, and her heart rate jolted. Right—the kidnapping, the tunnels, the little boy. She drew a slow breath and willed her heart to settle.

"Hey, I think I know where we are." A familiar voice broke the silence. She rotated her body to her side where Sean hunched over, staring at the old map. The boy didn't look tired at all, his eyes wide and bright.

"Did you sleep?" Still groggy, she rasped the words.

"A little, but this is too exciting. Look here." He showed her the map, his fingers tracing the faded lines. "I'm sure we started here, the room. Then we walked straight through to here. And I think this is the chapel. I mean, we ran and walked for quite a long time." He tipped his gaze skyward, the dim light of their flashlight casting shadows on his face. "We probably passed under the restaurant, and now we're close to the chapel, if not further. I never knew there was a tunnel underneath the restaurant."

"How can you be so sure?" She studied the map. With only symbols she didn't understand, they could be anywhere. But she didn't know the Mirror Estate. Sean did.

"Well, I'm not sure, but I believe I'm right. See this, it says north is that way." He pointed to the four-point marker on the map. "Dad told me the back of the main house faced north. And this symbol here is the emblem of St. Ann. That's the name of the orphanage."

She followed what he was saying. St. Ann was at the far corner. "But why wouldn't there be an exit, so to speak, to the restaurant?"

He shook his head. "I don't know. But I know the restaurant inside out. There's no hidden door—I'd have found it."

She thought back to the previous night. "Is it just me? I feel like we were running downhill, then level for a while."

He cocked his head to the side, considering. "Yeah, see, I'm right. We were going deeper underground and passed the restaurant. And now we're at the chapel. If we keep going, we'll hit the orphanage. The chapel should be the best way to get out."

Grace recalled the previous night vividly. They thought they would find a way out, but it wasn't meant to be. They had gone back and forth, but there was no way out. They couldn't go back to the room. No matter what they did, the door wouldn't open. It took a while to find this alcove, and she insisted they needed some shut-eye before they collapsed.

"And look at this." He turned the paper over to reveal some drawings. "What do you think this is? It looks like another map, but I can't figure this one out. It has the same strange words."

She took it. Indeed, the few notations on the map, if it was a map, looked the same as the markings on the door and on the paper she carried. "And it looks like it cuts off here." She felt the jagged edge.

Sean grabbed the map back. "I want to go home. Let's get out of here first. Then we can figure this out."

"Smart boy!" She stood up. "Let's go."

Sean got up too. "We haven't gone down this way. Let's check it out. Maybe there is a door to the chapel."

Grace stood up, shaking off the remnants of sleep. "All right. Be careful." *Lord, please lead us to safety!*

ANA

Ana didn't sleep. Without caffeine, her head threatened to explode. Ortiz, on the other hand, managed to nod off, leaving her both frustrated by and envious of his ability to sleep under such circumstances. But, of course, it wasn't his child out there being hunted by bad guys in an underground labyrinth. She shifted. This tension was almost unbearable, each second ticking by like an eternity. The excitement when Ortiz triggered the mechanism to open the door had lifted her spirits. She dashed in, hoping to see Grace and Sean. Instead, they entered an empty storage room—and the door closed, trapping them inside.

They searched for some mechanism to open the door but hadn't found it. Desperation creeping in, they investigated the room more thoroughly and uncovered signs that Grace or someone had been there recently.

"Someone searched this place," Ortiz had commented, running his fingers over disturbed dust and disheveled items.

Ana nodded but found nothing of immediate value or significance. With nothing to go on, she pounded on the walls just to check if they were all solid.

"Oh, hey, open sesame!" Ortiz exclaimed when the left wall opened up. "You think that's where they went?"

She didn't care where it led. "I don't know, but let's find out."

They stepped inside, and the wall closed behind them with an ominous thud. The new passage was short, leading to what seemed like another dead end. The small space felt even more claustrophobic.

"This is just great! We're stuck here." She'd yelled, her voice echoing in the confined space. How had Ortiz remained so calm? He'd simply said, "I'm sure we'll find a way out." That was hours ago.

Now she went to the end of the tunnel and examined every inch of the place, determined to find an escape. The cold stone grated under her fingers, the rough texture providing little comfort. Then she saw it.

"Ortiz, wake up!" she hollered. "Look!"

"What?" Already, he was beside her, groggy but alert.

She pointed up.

High on the wall, nearly obscured by shadows, was a hatch. Barely noticeable, it blended seamlessly with the stone. "There, do you see it?"

His eyes widened. "How did we miss that?"

"Doesn't matter. Give me a boost."

He knelt on one knee, creating a step with his hands. When Ana placed her feet in his palms, he lifted her up. Thank goodness it was a low ceiling. She grasped the handle and pushed the lid open. A clank reverberated when the lid hit the ground.

"Good eye! Get out and get help!" Ortiz said.

"I'll find something to pull you up." She hauled herself up and over and—into the middle of the woods. She wouldn't find anything of use here. So, she lay down on the grass and reached down. "I'll pull you up."

Ortiz eyed the opening. He was more stocky than tall, but he could still reach the opening if he jumped. And jump he did, but he almost missed. She scrambled back as he hoisted himself up.

Reality finally hit her. She sat down on the grass hard. *Lord, I know I don't pray enough and don't go to church often, but Grace does. Don't punish her. Help me find her, please!*

CHAPTER 44

MORGUE

RON

After Spaulding's call, Ron headed to the morgue. A US congressman's murder would fall under the FBI's jurisdiction. Oftentimes, the Bureau would investigate jointly with local law enforcement. But why did Spaulding think Ron would be interested in this murder? Agents from the local FBI office would likely handle it. But Spaulding called him. The thought gnawed at him as he navigated the city's traffic.

He had just parked when Olivia called.

"Sorry, I was at church and didn't call earlier. Still working on Collins. But I want to alert you to a US congressman's murder. Javier Jimenez from Texas. Spaulding may be contacting—"

"He already did. I'm walking into the morgue. Do you know why I'm here?"

"I'll let him brief you." Olivia ended the call.

He shook his head. Typical Olivia!

The morgue's chill seeped into his bones as he stepped through the heavy door, a stark contrast to the warmth he left outside. Stern-faced Spaulding stood waiting, waving him in. Beside him, Dr. O'Bannon, the medical examiner, appeared as a silhouette against the harsh fluorescence. Not long ago, Ron had met the ME, a friendly bald, slim man. Ron scanned the room and didn't see Monnin. "Where's your partner?"

"Chasing other leads."

Ron shifted his gaze toward the covered body. "Is this Congressman Javier Jimenez?"

"Yes." Spaulding nodded to O'Bannon. "Show him."

O'Bannon turned toward a nearby screen, clicking through to display an image that drew Ron's attention. "The victim had a tattoo removed. Thanks to IR photography, uh, that is infrared photography, you can see its faint outline."

Ron leaned in, his eyes narrowing as he tried to make out what it said. And then it dawned on him—the outline matched the Perez family crest outline. But could it be? "Can you send this to me?"

"Yes, of course," the ME said.

"So, you agree it might be the Perez family crest, huh?" Spaulding asked.

"I don't want to draw any conclusion yet. Hopefully, Deanna can work her magic and make this clearer. But do you know of any connection between this congressman and the Perez family?"

"Well, the only other interesting tidbit is that Hugo Perez showed up in the hotel where the congressman was staying a few nights ago. According to the senator, the victim freaked when he saw him and bolted."

"I need—"

Spaulding held up a thick hand. His stubby fingernails looked like he must've bitten them in his spare time—*if* the guy ever had any spare time, unlike Ron. "The footage. Yes, I'll get it to you. Your agent filled you in?"

Eyebrows arched, Ron asked, "My agent?" Who would that be?

"Olivia Tso. Is she not your agent?"

So, Olivia was hiding her CIA affiliation and used the FBI credentials Vera had given her. "Yeah, sort of. She's consulting with the task force."

"Excuse me, gentlemen. I do have other posts I need to attend to. Any more questions?" O'Bannon signaled his assistant to take care of the body.

"TOD?" Ron asked.

"Time of death would be between nine p.m. Friday and two a.m. Saturday."

"Cause of death?"

"Gunshot—" Spaulding started to say.

But the ME interjected. "Waiting for tox to confirm potassium chloride, but it's cardiac arrest. Gunshot wound would be a contributing factor."

"No kidding!" The detective noted it down. "Who would shoot someone after poisoning him?"

Ron shrugged. "Stranger things have happened. Who knows? Maybe there were two killers."

"Just know the two events happened very close in time. If there were two killers involved, they would have to be in on this together. Of course, that is only my opinion," O'Bannon said. "Oh, another interesting thing of note. The congressman had had plastic surgery. Details will be in the report."

"Now you know why celebrities never age!" Spaulding said.

CHAPTER 45

MIRAGE FINE ARTS

OLIVIA

Olivia sat in the passenger seat, waiting, while Simon chatted with another parishioner. Mass had ended, and the parking lot was beginning to empty. She had just updated Ron about the congressman's murder and the situation with Shane Collins. Her gut told her Collins was an operative, but she didn't find anything last night. She had also put in a call to Jay, her boss, who knew all the who's who in the espionage world. But she hadn't heard back yet. Given that Jay had recently been appointed deputy director and now worked out of Langley, she didn't blame him for not responding pronto.

As soon as Simon got in, she said, "Hey, you up for some undercover gig?"

He raised an eyebrow. "What do you have in mind?"

"Oh, just a little shopping." She flashed a mischievous smile. "Mirage Fine Arts is open at eleven a.m. today. I'm thinking we can go check it out."

A frown crinkled Simon's forehead. "How is that undercover?"

"It may just be in and out if Collins isn't there. But if he is, we'll chat him up so I can get a read on him and get his finger-prints. Just follow my lead."

Simon chuckled. "Since you'll be with me, sure. I know how lethal you can be, so I feel very safe."

While he pulled out of the lot, she scrolled on her phone. "Did you know Lily asked Sheila to help with our wedding?"

"Of course, why not? She's a wedding planner. And Lily is busy at work, especially now that she's always hanging out with Dylan."

Before long, they were at Mirage Fine Arts. The gallery was known for its exquisite collection, a place where the city's elite often visited. Simon parked a few blocks away at her urging to approach with caution.

As they entered the gallery, the cool air-conditioned interior offered a reprieve from the warmth outside. Paintings of various styles and eras, each one more captivating than the last, enriched the airy space. Olivia scanned the room, her gaze landing on Shane Collins deep in conversation with a woman by an abstract painting.

"There he is," Olivia whispered to Simon. "Let's get closer."

They meandered through the gallery, pretending to admire the artwork. She eavesdropped on snippets of his conversation about the art market, his voice smooth and confident.

"Excuse me." She stepped forward with a polite smile. "I couldn't help but overhear. Your insights on this painting are fascinating."

Collins turned to her, his eyes flickering with interest. "Well, thank you. Art is a passion of mine."

"I'm Olivia. This is Simon."

When she extended her hand, Collins shook it, his grip firm. "Shane Collins. A pleasure."

As they chatted, she observed his mannerisms, his expressions, to gauge his reactions for any signs of deception. Simon played along, engaging in the conversation, adding his observations about the artwork.

"Do you have a sell sheet or—"

"Of course." Collins opened a drawer, took out a pamphlet, and handed it to her. "Here's all the information on the artwork on display."

She smiled, careful not to touch where he handled it. "Thank you, Mr. Collins. You've been very helpful."

Collins nodded. "Anytime. Enjoy the rest of your visit."

CHAPTER 46
CHAPEL, MIRROR ESTATE

FR. PHIL

F r. Phil exhaled his relief as Jeremy approached, having taken on the responsibility of the earlier Mass. This Sunday, with Jeremy handling one service, Fr. Phil could afford more time to focus on other matters. After the usual chitchat with parishioners, Fr. Phil changed out of his vestments and donned a black shirt and pants and clerical collar. His routine would typically lead him to the new Adoration Chapel to pray, but today he had other concerns.

He was worried about Sean and Connor. He had seen the family at the early Mass, but they left before he could ask for updates. Now, when he tried calling the restaurant phone line, Lorraine answered. She said they had no news yet, but Agent Ruiz and Ortiz were still down in the tunnels. "Father, please pray..." Her voice started cracking.

"Of course. I'll be there in a minute. We'll pray together." He hung up and walked out of the sacristy.

"Have you heard from Connor?" Jeremy stopped him, the deepening circles under his eyes heavy with concern.

"I'm heading there now. I just talked to Lorraine. No news yet."

"I'll go with you."

Taking the tunnel was easier, so they headed down to the basement. The bluish lighting and cool air contrasted with the warmth of the church above. As they descended, Jeremy glanced at Fr. Phil, a question in his eyes.

"Is this what you warned me about? That I should remember what I learned in the corps. Being aware of my surroundings, etc.?"

Fr. Phil nodded. Ron had approved Jeremy after a strenuous vetting process, during which Ron checked with military intelligence before giving the new priest the green light. "This is not an everyday occurrence. I'm more concerned about the near future when Marge—known as the Ghost— comes to live in the closed orphanage. Dylan made sure it was secured, but..." He shook his head, his thoughts trailing off. "I just don't—"

Jeremy hushed him. "Listen!" he whispered.

Fr. Phil strained his ears. Tap, tap, tap. He frowned, looking around to determine the source. Jeremy, with his younger ears and likely better hearing, walked toward the alcove where Marge had almost killed Dylan had Fr. Phil not intervened. Fr. Phil followed the younger priest, his curiosity and concern growing.

Jeremy pointed to the far wall.

Tap, tap, tap. The sound was getting louder.

"It's coming from behind that wall." Jeremy narrowed his eyes. With a frown creasing his forehead, he cocked his head to listen. "It's Morse code for SOS. Listen, three short taps, three long taps, and three short taps again."

Who would be doing this? The only people missing would be Sean and Grace. According to Lorraine, Connor went back into the tunnels by himself.

Jeremy pounded on the wall and hollered, "Anybody there?"

A faint voice called, "This is Grace Benson. I'm here with Sean Murray."

Fr. Phil crossed himself. So did Jeremy. *Thank You, Lord! Now help us get them out.*

CHAPTER 47

TUNNELS

GRACE

Grace and Sean had been banging on the door for what felt like an eternity. The dim light from the single bulb in the corridor cast long shadows on the walls, making the place feel even more oppressive. The door in front of them was different from the surrounding stone walls—it was metal or steel, solid and unyielding. They had tried everything: pushing, pulling, even sliding it sideways in hopes it might open like some hidden passage in a mystery novel. But nothing worked.

Desperation was setting in. Their hands were sore from pounding, their voices hoarse from shouting. Grace glanced at Sean. Her young companion, despite his age, was handling the situation with remarkable composure.

If Sean is right and this is the chapel, then someone should be going to church today. Lord, let someone hear us!

"Hey, let's try SOS," Sean suggested.

Grace's mouth dropped open. She closed it and swallowed hard. "You know what that means?"

Sean rolled his eyes. "I'm ten, not five. Dad told me what it meant when we were watching a movie once. The guys made a big SOS on the beach so the searching planes could see them. And Dad also said three, three, and three. Short, long, and short. Let's do it."

Grace couldn't help but smile, despite their dire situation. This ten-year-old was something else. She nodded, and they both started tapping on the door in the pattern for SOS: three short taps, three long taps, three short taps.

They repeated the pattern over and over, hoping against hope someone on the other side would hear them. Time seemed to stretch endlessly. Just as she was about to lose hope, she heard a faint sound.

"Listen!" she whispered, holding her breath.

The sound grew louder, more distinct. It was a voice, muffled by the thick door, but definitely a voice. Someone was asking if anyone was there.

She yelled as loud as she could that they were there.

"It doesn't sound like Fr. Phil. I wonder if he's the new priest," Sean murmured, his face lighting up.

Then, from the other end of the passageway, someone cried out, "There you are!" Maniacal laughter then sent chills down Grace's spine.

"I'll have myself a twofer. You and your old man," the voice continued.

Grace turned toward the voice. One of their captors had found them! He stood at the fork in the corridor, grinning like a maniac, his eyes glinting with malicious intent.

"Sean, get behind me." She kept her voice steady despite the chill gripping her heart.

The man stepped closer, his laughter echoing in the confined space. "You really thought you could escape, didn't you?"

Grace stiffened her spine. She needed to protect Sean, to find a way out of this nightmare. She took a deep breath, steeling herself for whatever was to come. "We're not going to let you take us."

The man stopped, his grin widening. "Oh, but you see, you don't have a choice."

Now would be a good time for a miracle, Lord!

CHAPTER 48

ABOVE THE TUNNELS

ANA

After her little self-pity party and heartfelt prayer, Ana dusted herself off and stood up, her resolve hardening. She needed to find Grace. The morning sun filtered through the tree canopy, dappling golden light on the forest floor, and the fresh scent of pine and earth grounded her.

"You all right?" Ortiz touched her arm.

"Yeah." She surveyed the endless expanse of trees. "Do you know where we are?"

Ortiz scanned their surroundings, his brow furrowed. "I have a vague idea of where we are in relation to the restaurant and the main house. The sun is going up this way, so if we walk in this direction, we should hit the restaurant at some point."

Ana's heart sank at the thought of returning to the restaurant empty-handed. "What's beyond the restaurant in the same direction?"

"That would be the chapel and if you go farther, the orphanage."

Her gaze fell on the hole they climbed out of. Ortiz must

have covered it up again without her noticing. "This looks like an escape hatch. What would you bet this isn't the only one?"

His mustache quirked to one side. "I like the way you think. Let's have a look."

They began walking, the forest thick with underbrush that crackled under their feet. Nature sounds enlivened the air—birds chirping, leaves rustling, squirrels scrambling.

Urgency propelled her forward. They had to find Grace—and quickly.

As they moved, Ortiz kept glancing around, his senses probably as much on high alert as hers were. "You know," he said, "these escape hatches must've been designed for emergencies. If there are more, they might lead us straight to where Grace is."

Ana nodded. "We need to find another one. It could be our best shot at finding her."

After walking for some time, they stumbled upon a small clearing. In the center, partially hidden by a large rock, was another hatch. This one looked older, the metal rusted and the edges worn.

Ortiz knelt and traced the edge with one finger. "This one's seen better days, but it might still work." He tugged on the handle and, with some effort, creaked the hatch open, revealing a narrow, dark tunnel.

Ana peered into the darkness, her heart pounding. "Do you think it leads to the orphanage?"

"Only one way to find out." Ortiz hunkered closer, peering into it. "Stay close."

CHAPTER 49

CHAPEL, MIRROR ESTATE

KYLE

After the morning briefing at the task force office, Kyle hurried back to the estate. His thoughts were a jumble of anxiety and determination. Ana still hadn't reported in, and he was sure Grace was there. Urgency gnawed at him. As he turned into the estate's driveway, his phone buzzed with a new text message.

DAD

Head to the chapel. Priests need help.

Kyle frowned at the message. Why would he need to go to the chapel? Despite his initial hesitation, the message's authoritative tone made it clear this was not a mere request. He steered his car toward the chapel.

Minutes later, he walked into the chapel, the cool air and dim light providing a stark contrast to his earlier rush. An older lady approached him.

"Are you Agent Peters?" she asked.

"Yes, ma'am."

"Father wants you to head down to the basement by the alcove. They're down there. A few other men are helping them too."

Kyle's curiosity deepened into concern. What was going on? He followed her directions and descended into the basement. The dimly lit corridor felt almost eerie as he approached the alcove.

When he got there, the two priests—Fr. Phil and the new priest, Fr. Jeremy—were engaged in a serious discussion. Fr. Phil spotted him and called out.

"Ah, Kyle, come over here."

"Grace and Sean are behind this wall," Fr. Jeremy explained. "It's not drywall. It could be part of the foundation. But then, it sounded like they were pounding on a door, wanting it open."

Worry creased Fr. Phil's narrow mouth, jutted out his hard jaw, and dimmed his blue eyes. "But they aren't tapping anymore. Neither are they answering questions. I fear what's going on behind the wall."

A chill ran down Kyle's spine. The silence from the other side of the wall was ominous. He took a deep breath to keep his composure. "Okay. First, let's confirm that they are still there and safe."

Fr. Jeremy rummaged around in the basement and closets. "We can use this." He held up a PVC pipe, probably left over from previous repairs or construction.

"Let's try." Kyle put one end of the pipe against the wall and the other to his ear. He didn't hear anything at first. Then he heard some voices. "You listen. Tell me what you hear." He handed it back to Fr. Jeremy for independent confirmation.

The priest listened. "They're still there."

Fr. Phil exhaled in a rush as if he'd held his breath far too long.

"But I hear another voice. Loud."

"That's what I heard too."

Fr. Phil began searching for something on the wall. "Looking for something?" Fr. Jeremy asked.

"Just a hunch. There might be a hidden switch. If it's a door on the other side, it can't be a wall over here."

"The wall is a cover-up." Fr. Jeremy let out a low whistle. "Clever."

As Fr. Phil searched, Kyle's heart thudded against all the possibilities. The estate was old and filled with hidden passages and secrets. The old priest might just be right.

The wall slid open!

CHAPTER 50

MIRROR ESTATE

DYLAN

In the crisp morning air, Dylan made his way through the estate's sprawling gardens. After Mass, a calmness settled over him, though concern for Sean and Grace quickly replaced it.

Last night, he and Lily had talked late into the night about what they saw in the tunnels and what it could mean. After an intense conversation, filled with theories and fears, Lily ended up staying over. Alex, too, had stayed. He didn't want to leave until his sister was found. Max had prepared two guest rooms for them.

Early this morning, Dylan spotted Eva and Alex in the gardens. They seemed deep in conversation, but by the time he went to Mass with his grandmother, Lily, and Eva, Alex was nowhere in sight. Later, he found Alex playing with the dogs in the guardhouse.

"Want to take them out for a walk?" Dylan asked. "Lily is coming."

Alex glanced up, then shook his head. "Nah, but thanks. You

guys go. I'm going to the restaurant to check for some updates. I may help search again."

"We'll be heading that way once we take care of them."

A few minutes later, Dylan and Lily each held a leash. Ronnie was full of energy as always, wanting to chase after anything and everything, while Cedric was more mellow, content with a slower pace.

"Let's check out the woods," Dylan suggested.

The woods were dense and silent, save for the rustling of leaves and the occasional birdcall. They walked for a long time, the tension from last night's conversation lingering between them. Eventually, they found themselves near the area where Ortiz had said the tire tracks disappeared.

"Hey, what are you doing?" Lily hollered at Ronnie, who was pulling hard at the leash. Lily had to run to keep up.

Dylan jogged after them, the leaves crunching under his feet. "Now you too!" he said when Cedric showed sudden interest in the same direction.

The dogs seemed fascinated with a particular bush and kept digging.

"Look!" Lily cried out.

Dylan looked up from the dogs and gasped. The hill was opening up. Momentarily still, he gawked, unable to believe his eyes.

"They must have triggered something. It's the van," Lily whispered, but the last word emerged in an excited low-pitched squeal.

Dylan pulled the dogs back and searched the area. "Oh, here it is." He toed a button on the ground cleverly disguised in the foliage. The dogs' digging must've tripped the mechanism.

Lily pointed down to what looked like a carcass of a squirrel or some other small animal. She wrinkled her nose. "I think they were after this."

The hill opened to reveal the "vanishing" van.

CHAPTER 51

RESTAURANT

OLIVIA

After her visit to Mirage Fine Arts, Olivia lifted the prints from the information sheet using a crude but effective method. She preserved the original sheet just in case it was needed later. Once she had a clear image, she emailed it to Jay who could have it identified much faster than she could. By the time she finished, they were back at home, but not for long.

A short while later, Jay texted a name and contact information. He said the guy would be able to give her more information on Collins. Now she found herself at a coffee shop, waiting for Jay's friend, Hank.

"Olivia?" a server asked.

Olivia looked up. "Yes?"

The girl handed her a piece of paper. "Some guy at the drive-thru window said to give this to you."

Olivia took the note and thanked the girl. It directed her to the soccer field a block away. She walked there. As she approached the field, she noticed an ordinary-looking middle-aged man wearing a New York Yankees baseball cap. Several kids were playing soccer, their laughter and shouts creating a lively background. A few parents sat on a bench, watching and chatting. Olivia approached the man and sat next to him.

"I wasn't followed."

"I know." He held out a bag of popcorn. "Want some?" They rarely used names.

She declined with a shake of her head. "I was told—"

"You're dealing with a dangerous fellow. Back when I knew him, his name was Charles Moore. He was MI6." The man shook the popcorn bag, the rustle of fluffy kernels rattling her. "The love of his life was disavowed when an operation went awry. He never got over it. Last I heard, he was working for Rafael Montoya."

The name rang a bell, but she couldn't place it. "Who is this Montoya?"

"He runs a team of, uh, what you might call 'fixers for hire.' My guess is he's here on a job."

"Would he be freelancing?"

"Could be, but I think not. One, it's against Montoya's policy. Two, he's being generously compensated by Montoya's clients."

"So, assuming he's still on Montoya's payroll, we'd need to find out what his job is."

"Good luck with that! I can tell you one thing. Since he's still around, the job is not finished yet. Otherwise, he'd be long gone."

What was his job, though? Assuming he was the one who killed Liz and Sam, why? Whoever hired him couldn't have known Javier would be killed. So, what was he really up to? And who hired him?

CHAPTER 52

TUNNELS

DYLAN

Dylan stood over the freshly discovered van, his pulse racing as he tried to call Kyle, Ortiz, and Agent Peters. The ominous silence from their phones only heightened his anxiety. Frustrated, he dialed Max, who was waiting anxiously at the restaurant for any news.

"Max, I've found something." Dylan scanned the deserted area. "I've tried calling Kyle, Ortiz, and Peters, but none of them are picking up."

Max's voice came through the line. "Once I hear from Ortiz, I'll let him know. You and Lily need to come here. Do not go in by yourself. An extremely dangerous man's down there. Ms. Carol wouldn't want you getting hurt."

Dylan nodded, though Max couldn't see it. "Yeah, don't worry. We'll be back soon." He ended the call and turned to a beaming Lily, who bounced closer. He reached for her hand. "We need to head back."

But Lily drew her hand away, her eyes alight. "Nobody's here, and we're not in the tunnels. Let's just look around."

Dylan sighed. It would be futile to argue, would it? "Fine, but we won't go far."

The van suggested there might be another way into the tunnels nearby. Cedric and Ronnie were having a great time sniffing, digging, and playing in the underbrush.

"Come look!" Lily called out from deeper in the woods.

"Come on. Let's go," Dylan said to the dogs, pulling their leashes as he jogged to her.

Lily was standing by something like an outdoor electrical outlet. She pointed. "Check this out."

Dylan lifted the lid, but instead of outlets, it housed a keypad.

"I wonder what it's for?" Lily echoed his thoughts.

He studied the keypad, leaning in to inspect smudges on a few numbers. "Hey, look at the numbers zero, three, seven, nine. Don't they look dirty?"

Lily squinted at the keypad, nodding. "Yes, I can even see the prints. So, that must be the code."

"Four numbers. If my math is correct, there should be twenty-four possible combinations if no repeat is allowed. Otherwise, it'd be, hmm, two hundred and fifty-six." But would they get locked out for too many failed attempts?

Lily started punching in the numbers while Dylan kept count. "Four down, twenty to go."

A mechanized whirring reverberated. Lily beamed and squeezed his arm. "Seven is the lucky number!"

Much like the garage, the hill appeared to open up, revealing a set of steps leading down. Dylan held his breath as he peered into the darkness.

CHAPTER 53

TASK FORCE OFFICE

RON

Ron checked his watch, the minute hand ticking closer to one o'clock. The squad room, with its standard-issue furniture and cluttered desks, hummed with the low buzz of activity. After a quick lunch, he returned to the weight of responsibility pressing on his shoulders. It was time to bring the team up to speed.

"All right, everyone," he called out. "Gather around the screen. We've got updates."

The team filtered in, taking their usual places. Tanner leaned against a desk, one hand squeezing his stress ball. Olivia, usually absent from these meetings, stood off to the side. The others formed a semicircle, attention fixed on Ron.

"Got a call from Kyle," Ron began. "Grace and Sean were fine, as of an hour ago. Unfortunately, something happened, and they lost contact with them. He, the priests, and other expert volunteers are trying to find a way to them. Apparently, Grace and Sean made contact on the other side of a foundation wall. He'll update us."

Tanner frowned, drawing the rugged lines on his face into deeper creases. "Any news from Ana?"

Ron shook his head. "No updates. It's worrisome. She would at least text if she could. Maybe her phone is dead. Or she's in the tunnels with no cell service."

Olivia downed half a bottle of water, then wiped her mouth. "Ana is capable. I'm sure she's fine. If it's okay, I'd like to share some details about Shane Collins."

When Ron waved her on, giving her the floor, Olivia took a deep breath. "Shane Collins, former MI6 agent, now works as a gun for hire. Latest intel indicates he works for Rafael Montoya. Collins is meticulous, skilled in surveillance and close-quarters combat. He's not someone who takes random assignments. His jobs are always planned and executed with precision."

Ron blinked several times, jaw clenched, and ran his hand through his hair. "What's his job? It can't be killing the wife and chief of staff. Who hired him?"

"That, we don't know yet. He works at that gallery—"

"Yes," Tanner interjected. "We have a list of the people who have access to the network. Everyone checked out, but him."

"Do you know how long he's worked there?" she asked.

"No, I don't think so."

"We need to find out when he was hired. That'd give us a timeline of when he got the job."

Good thinking. Ron inclined his head. "Deanna, what have you found out about that video of the congressman's murder?" He told Spaulding he needed his team to authenticate it even though the police tech already did.

"It's authentic. Not manipulated."

"So, why did he leave it there?"

"To justify his killings?" Tanner dropped the ball.

"But he was also spying on the congressman." Olivia stretched to scoop it up. "He was there a few evenings prior to the killing. So, why monitor the congressman? It would appear Javier was his mark."

"Oh, by the way"—Deanna raised her hand—"the tattoo is the Perez family crest. I'm ninety-five percent positive."

"What tattoo?" Olivia, about to toss the ball back to Tanner, stilled, frowning at Deanna.

"Autopsy shows him having a tattoo removed." Tanner snagged the ball back. "Deanna just confirmed it was the Perez family crest. We need to find out how he was connected to the Perez family."

"Question." Hernandez stopped typing. "His mark got killed by someone else, would he still get paid?"

Ron and Olivia both said no, and Ron continued. "We're missing something. It doesn't make sense that he would kill the people who killed the congressman, assuming that was his mark. Usually, they would just pack up and go. Maybe try to negotiate for a partial payout."

"Unless his job isn't to kill Javier but is related to him somehow. And that's why he hasn't left yet." Olivia frowned, and a faraway look glazed her intelligent eyes. "Could it be that he needed something from the congressman? And that's why he had a spy cam in his room, but then he got killed. Maybe this made Collins's job harder. What's he looking for? Perez family crest... tattoo removed... What'd he say? Family..."

Ron was thinking what others were wondering. Olivia was thinking out loud. And suddenly, she uttered, "Deanna, can you find out everything you can about Javier Jimenez? Dig deep."

CHAPTER 54

TUNNELS

GRACE

Grace's heart pounded in her chest, her breath catching as the desperate shouts echoed through the damp, musty tunnel. A moment ago, relief nearly overwhelmed her as voices came from the other side of the wall, rescue imminent. But now, the nightmare was far from over.

They charged through yet another dimly lit tunnel, more shadows flickering and dancing across the rough, damp stone walls. Cold and clammy air, rich with the scent of earth and decay, tainted each heavy breath. She clutched Sean, blood rushing in her ears. The maniac's twisted laughter echoed through the tunnel, sending chills down her spine and tightening the grip of terror around her heart.

"What do you mean? Twofer?" Grace called out, trying to keep her voice steady despite the fear gnawing at her insides. She strained her ears to decipher any clues hidden in his words.

The maniac laughed again, and the sound, both cruel and chilling, reverberated off the stone walls. "I've got his daddy," he taunted, his eyes gleaming with malice, reflecting the dim light like a predator's.

"No! Daddy!" Sean yelled and charged forward.

Grace grabbed him. "No, Sean, he might be lying."

Sean hesitated, his small body trembling. Tears pooled in his now-wide eyes and threatened to spill over. The maniac smirked, clearly enjoying their torment. "You don't believe me? Wait here!"

"What's your dad's name?" She whispered.

"Connor."

The maniac stepped back into the shadows and reached to his left, yanking something. A figure stumbled out into the dim light, and Grace's thudding heart sank.

"Daddy!" Sean yelled again, almost wrenching free from her grip.

Connor wobbled. Barely keeping him on his feet, his body slumped forward, each breath seeming to take immense effort. Blood oozed from his mouth and nose, bruises mottled his face and arms, and his left eye was nearly swollen shut.

"Don't you dare hurt him!" Sean shouted.

"I'm sorry, Sean." Connor's words rose, barely above a whisper, each one seeming to come at a struggle.

The maniac pointed a gun at the man, malevolent glee darkening his expression. "You two, come over here!" He waved the gun, the barrel glinting in the dim light.

She couldn't lose hope. No matter what, she would get out of this. Even if, with the present situation, she couldn't see a way out. *Lord, please, we need a miracle!*

CHAPTER 55

MIRAGE FINE ARTS

OLIVIA

Olivia paced in front of the gallery. The crisp air tickled her skin as she replayed her plan in her head. She pulled out her phone and dialed Spaulding's number. After she explained what she wanted, the detective agreed to meet her at the gallery. As she waited, she called Simon to confirm what Javier said about the family business.

Moments later, Spaulding arrived, the taller Monnin at his side. Both approached her.

"Hello, Agent." The stocky, stern-faced detective eyed her with curiosity.

She nodded her greeting. "Detectives."

They entered the gallery, stepping into soft lighting and the murmurs of patrons admiring the art. Olivia scanned the room and spotted Collins engrossed in conversation with a couple by a large abstract piece. She slipped around a series of paintings to avoid his line of sight.

Reaching the staff-only door, she glanced back to ensure Spaulding and Monnin were following. They had badged their way in seamlessly. Inside, they found Hugo Perez's office. He looked up from his desk as they entered, his expression shifting from surprise to cautious politeness.

"Detectives, Hugo Perez." He stood to shake their hands. "How can I help you? Please sit. Anything to drink?"

They declined. Then Spaulding took the lead. "Mr. Perez, we're investigating the death of Congressman Javier Jimenez."

Perez's face paled, his eyes widening. "The congressman is dead? When? How?"

His genuine surprise mirrored Olivia's reaction when she heard the news. She observed him closely, noting the way he clutched the edge of his desk.

"Yes, he was found dead yesterday." Spaulding then questioned where Hugo was at the time and asked other general questions. Then he said, "We understand you had a conversation with his campaign manager, Nina Rodriguez."

Perez blinked. "Yes, I'm planning to open a gallery in Texas. Nina approached me for a contribution. And we talked a bit about business in Texas in general."

"When was this?"

"Oh, Wednesday or Thursday evening. Shane was there with me. But he didn't stay long."

Olivia saw her opening. "Shane?"

"Pardon me. Shane Collins, my assistant here."

"How long has he worked for you?"

A frown creased his brow. "A few months. How is that relevant?"

She ignored him. "Did you hire him from an ad? Or staffing agency?"

"I don't see what he's got to do with this. But no, he came highly recommended."

"By whom?"

"My mother."

CHAPTER 56

TUNNELS

ANA

Ana grabbed her phone, the bright screen glaring as she prepared to call in her status. She and Ortiz had found an opening to the tunnels beneath the estate, a critical lead in their search for Grace and Sean. Just as she was about to dial, the phone's screen flickered and went black.

"What's the matter?" Ortiz asked as she stuffed the phone back into her pocket.

"Phone's dead," she grumbled. "I don't know about you, but I'm going in."

Without waiting for a response, she moved toward the opening. Ortiz followed, his flashlight casting long, eerie shadows against the tunnel walls. They descended the rusty ladder, and she almost held her breath waiting to see what they might find below.

"I wonder why this one has a ladder and the other one didn't," she mused aloud to distract herself from the claustrophobic feeling of the narrow tunnel.

"I guess this one is deeper." His response echoed in the confined space.

Finally, they reached the bottom. Her feet thudded onto the cold, damp ground. She shivered, not just from the chill but also from the oppressive darkness surrounding them. His flashlight cut through the blackness, revealing rough stone walls that seemed to close in on them.

He pointed to the right, his voice a whisper in the silence. "If I remember correctly, the orphanage is that way."

Ana looked the other way, her brow furrowing. "Should we check the opposite way? Or do you think Grace and Sean would be over by the orphanage?"

Ortiz paused, probably considering. "If we head straight the other way, we should hit the chapel or under the chapel."

"Should we split up?"

"No, we need to watch each other's six."

Ana's nod jostled her curly bob, annoying wisps tickling her cheek before she palmed them away. "Let's check out the orphanage and double back."

"Let's."

It didn't take long at all. The tunnel ended in a series of steps, then a wall. There was no way out. "That's weird. How is it that there's no way into the orphanage?" Ana asked.

Ortiz pounded on the wall and listened to the sound. He tapped the middle again. "Here, it's hollow. Somehow, this must open to the orphanage."

To her, this was a dead end. "We'll check this later. Let's go back the other way."

They doubled back, and she stopped, put a finger on her lips, and whispered, "You hear that?"

He cocked his head. "Voices."

They crept forward, and the noise came from around the corner.

CHAPTER 57

BUNKER

DYLAN

Dylan crept through the dimly lit tunnel. Even though a dangerous man was lurking somewhere in these underground passages, his thoughts kept drifting to his aunt. Did she know about these tunnels? Had she been planning an escape route all along? Maybe her obsession with living on the estate wasn't just about the treasure.

"Hey, do you think we could get from here to the wall with the strange symbols?" Dylan asked, his voice rebounding in the confined space.

Lily shrugged. "You're asking me? I don't know." She scanned the walls as if trying to see through them. "But I would like to check it out. We may have to go back to the restaurant entrance. But then again, we can always explore this way. We found the van. And now, this entrance."

"Yeah, but we're supposed to stay out of it." Still, the thrill of discovery vibrated through him.

"Right, we are supposed to." Her eyes glinted mischievously. "But we have the dogs. Yeah, Cedric, let's go."

Ronnie, not needing any encouragement, was already tugging on Lily's arm, eager to continue the adventure. Cedric and Ronnie led the way down the stairs, their footsteps padding along the quiet tunnel. If anything sinister lurked in the shadows, surely the dogs would sense it and bark a warning.

As they descended, the atmosphere shifted. This part of the tunnels looked more modernized than the sections they previously explored. The rough stone walls gave way to smoother, more uniform concrete. Electrical conduits ran along the ceiling, and the occasional fluorescent light flickered overhead, casting an eerie glow.

"Is this a bunker?" Lily asked.

Wow. Shelves stocked with canned goods and bottled water lined the walls, and a low whistle escaped him. "I've only heard of places like this. Look, must be enough food and water to last for months."

He frowned at a metal file cabinet in the corner, then walked over, and opened a drawer. Empty. He pulled out another, same. What a bust!

"Look," Lily called. "I think this is a phone number. Not a local number."

He pivoted. She'd retrieved a folded sticky note from the trash can. She took a picture of the note.

"Send it to Agent Peters," Dylan suggested. "I bet he'll want to know. I don't see anything else here."

"Me neither. I wonder why I don't see a security system here. They hid the van and the keypad to come in. You'd think they are security conscious. So, where is it?"

What she said made sense.

"Maybe it's in another room?"

"Or maybe it's hidden like everything else," she countered and started searching.

He joined her in the middle of the room and surveyed The layout. A bed on one side. A fridge and cases of water and canned food against another wall. A desk and a filing cabinet on the wall facing them. But... "Do you think it's strange that the desk and the cabinet are so far apart?"

Lily left his side and went to the wall. "It is." She felt the wall. Nothing happened. "Now, why wouldn't they hang the picture in the middle of this wall?" She stretched to reach the picture above the cabinet. He stepped up and grabbed the picture.

"Voilà!" she exclaimed as the wall slid open to reveal an office with monitors and computers. "I bet my mom would love to see this, but I don't want to call her. She's gonna be mad that we're doing something *dangerous* again."

"Let's call Alex. I think he's in IT, and he's close by."

CHAPTER 58

CHAPEL, MIRROR ESTATE

KYLE

Kyle's heart thudded against his ribs as he navigated the dimly lit corridor, the sound of his own breathing loud in his ears. The ancient wooden door groaned open, revealing the dust-covered room beyond.

"Whoa! You did it, Fr. Phil," he exclaimed. The intricate lock that had barred their way was now a twisted mess of metal on the floor.

Fr. Jeremy stuck his head in the door. "I don't see them," he whispered.

Kyle stepped in front of him. "Stay behind me," he commanded. His hand steady, his senses on high alert, he drew his weapon. He moved cautiously, every creak of the floorboards beneath his feet amplifying the tension in the air.

The corridor was empty. His gaze darted from corner to corner, searching for any sign of movement. Where were they? They had just been here, hadn't they?

A faint rustling caught his attention. He spun toward the

noise, his finger tightening on the trigger. "Freeze!" he shouted, his voice echoing off the walls.

A shadow leaped out from around the corner. "Federal agent!" he hollered, his training taking over.

"Kyle?!"

The voice was familiar. As the figure stepped into the light, Kyle's eyes widened. Ana stood there, her gun lowered, relief slackening the tightness gripping her shoulders. Ortiz sidled up beside her, his expression equally surprised.

Kyle let out a breath he hadn't realized he was holding and lowered his weapon. "Ana! Ortiz! How'd you get here?" He scanned the room for any sign of the others. "Did you see Grace?"

Ortiz rasped a finger over his bristly mustache, his brow furrowed. "We heard voices and thought they were here. But it's clear they're not here anymore."

Kyle's gut clenched as a wave of frustration sluiced over him. "Where could they have gone?" He walked to the center of the room, turning in a slow circle as he tried to piece together their next move.

Ana stepped forward, her gaze following the path they had taken here. "We didn't see them going that way, but they could have turned somewhere without us passing them."

"So, how did you get here?" Kyle holstered his weapon. "You went in that room last night."

Ana updated him on how they followed a dead-end path but climbed up to the surface and found another hatch close to the orphanage. "What about you? How did you come from there? And where is there? We thought it would be the chapel."

"It is. Fr. Phil heard Grace and Sean. I did hear some voices. But it looks like a wall on the other side. Fortunately, Fr. Phil somehow opened the door."

"So, that means they couldn't have gone far." Ortiz kept

tapping at his lip, the sound grating. "But why would they leave if they knew you were coming to their rescue?"

"I don't know." Kyle huffed out his frustration. "And these tunnels are like a maze. We need a map."

"I hear you," Ortiz empathized. "Old estate tend to have secret hideaways and tunnels. I wonder if Max knew anything about these. He's been here forever and his father too, I think."

"Let's go ask him. Where would he be?" Ana slid her gun into her shoulder holster.

"Kyle." Fr. Jeremy touched his arm. "Max just called Fr. Phil. Dylan found something. They're all meeting in the bunker to regroup. He texted a map."

CHAPTER 59

THE ROTH RESIDENCE

OLIVIA

Olivia stepped out of the gallery, the late afternoon sun casting long shadows across the pavement. She glanced back at the building, its sleek modern lines in stark contrast to the grim events that unfolded within. Hugo Perez was genuinely surprised by the news. His body language all conveyed truth. He didn't know anything. But her instinct about Collins was right.

She joined Monnin and Spaulding. They had been at this for hours, piecing together fragments of a puzzle that grew more complex with each revelation.

Monnin, her brow furrowed in thought, broke the silence. "Why were you so interested in the Collins fellow?"

"Just a hunch." Olivia crossed her arms as she leaned against the gallery's stone façade. "He's former MI6 and matches the description Lily and Dylan got from the housekeeping staff."

Monnin raised an eyebrow toward her hairline. "Former MI6, huh? That's quite the leap."

Olivia shrugged, her gaze steady. "It's more than just a leap.

He fits the profile. Plus, his particular set of skills would be useful in this kind of operation."

Spaulding smoothed back the graying hair his frustrated fingers had mussed. "But did you positively identify him? You saw a tattoo?"

"No," she admitted. "That can be done later. Right now, I'm more interested in finding out who's behind all this. You saw the bodies. Sam was tortured. Whoever was spying on Javier and killed Sam and Liz is after something. I'd like to know what."

The detectives exchanged glances, their expressions thoughtful. Olivia could imagine them weighing her theory against the facts they had gathered.

"I believe once we know that, we'll know who ordered the hit," she continued. Whether they believed her or not, she didn't care. They compared notes for a little longer, then parted ways.

Back home, she sat at her desk with monitors in front of her and jotted down everything she knew about Javier's death and Sam's and Liz's subsequent murders.

"You just can't let go." Simon walked by.

"No, I'm intrigued. Besides, he was your friend." She'd been presented with a puzzle she needed to solve.

He sat down. "Do you need a sounding board?"

"Yeah, that'll be good." She had a whiteboard up on her screen. "Let's start with Javier. He was killed by Sam and Liz. But someone was spying on him. He had a Perez family crest tattoo removed. What did he say about his family?"

"First, he said he lied about growing up in a foster home. Said he couldn't get involved in his family business. His mom agreed not to tell people about his lie. That he might follow my footsteps to resign."

"Okay, something about the family. Could the business be illegal?" She put a question mark next to Javier's family business. "And he mentioned his mother, not his father?"

He frowned and tapped a finger to his lips. "Yes, I'm sure he said his mother. What are you thinking?"

"Nothing yet." She put another question mark next to Javier's mother. "Now, Sam and Liz. They were having an affair. The recording is real. So, they killed Javier, basically for money. Sam was tortured." She closed her eyes, visualizing the scene again. "Not enough blood." She opened her eyes. "We need to find out if he was tortured before or after his death."

"Why would anyone mutilate a corpse?"

"To stage the scene. But if he was tortured before his death, then someone wanted information from him. He was Javier's chief of staff. What would he know that Liz wouldn't know?"

"Well, anything to do with House business. Javier was a congressman. There are a lot of things he shouldn't be telling Liz, but Sam, being his chief of staff, might have access to."

"So, I would say whoever killed them wanted something about Javier. Killing them seems to be a revenge for Javier."

"But why?" Simon rubbed his eyes. "Only someone who loved Javier or cared about him very much would do that. So, who? Not Liz. He didn't have any siblings that I know of. And no kids."

"His mother, maybe?" She circled the words *his mother* on the screen. "He mentioned his mother."

He frowned. "For argument's sake, how would she have known about the murder? It wasn't even public. Unless you're saying she's the one spying on him."

She shrugged. "I don't know. Let's talk about Collins. He's a former MI6, now working for Rafael Montoya as a hired gun—assuming he's here on a job, and since he's still here, he's not finished yet. Hugo Perez said he only started working for him a few months ago and he came highly recommended by Perez's mother."

"Really? Who's his mother?"

"A rather famous artist, Cristina Navarro."

"Sounds legit. Doesn't sound like a lead."

"No, but it's an interesting tidbit. Remember Javier removed a tattoo of the Perez family crest. He was somehow connected to the Perez family. I've asked Deanna to do a deep dive on him. Maybe we'll find something there."

"So, what are you gonna do?"

She had been thinking about it. Collins was the one she was interested in. While Hugo might be the one behind it—she didn't think so—she didn't get the killer vibe from him and doubted Hugo had the stomach to do what the killer had done to Sam. "I'll watch Collins."

CHAPTER 60

BUNKER

DYLAN

Dylan leaned back in a chair, admiring the state-of-the-art technology in this secret computer room. He thought he had located all the tunnels, but there must still be a lot of hidden secrets beneath the estate. And his aunt, the Ghost, probably knew about this bunker and all the tunnels.

In the dim room, the computer equipment radiated a soft glow, and their hum filled the silence. The supplies stocking the shelves along the walls seemed untouched for years, yet the computers and other high-tech devices indicated recent activity.

Max, Eva, and Alex had arrived moments ago. "We come bearing gifts." Alex put two large Lorraine's Kitchen to-go bags on the table. "Lorraine made lunch for everyone. We ate already. So, they're all yours. Kyle, Ana, and Ortiz should be here soon. And maybe the priests too." He let out a low whistle at the sight of the monitors in the secret room. "Oh my! I gotta check this out."

Dylan hadn't realized he was hungry until he smelled the sandwiches and subs. "Lily, want one?"

Already digging into the bags, she picked out a tuna sandwich. He grabbed a turkey sub. They sat at the only table to eat.

"So, what have you guys found?" Eva asked.

In between eating, Dylan updated her on how they discovered the van and the entrance.

"We found a phone number on a sticker. It's still in the trash. But I took a picture." Lily showed Eva the photo.

Eva called the number, held a finger up to silence them, and pressed the phone to her ear, her expression unreadable. After a brief moment, she hung up. "A man answered. He didn't say his name. Instead, he asked, 'What's so urgent?'"

Dylan exchanged a tense glance with Lily. Who was that?

Max, who had been pacing the room, huffed and flopped on a nearby chair.

"Max, we'll find Sean." Dylan patted the older gentleman's knee and tried to inject some optimism into the tense atmosphere. "And Connor."

Max sighed again, deeper this time. "I didn't think this bunker was still in operation. They obviously upgraded it."

Dylan, Lily, and Eva looked at each other.

"You know about this bunker?" Dylan asked.

Max ran a hand through his hair. "They built it when they constructed the estate. As you know, your ancestors were involved in illegal activities, and they needed a bunker for emergencies. But it hasn't been touched in years, not since your grandfather turned himself in. Or so I thought. Someone must have found it and upgraded it. There was no computer, nothing fancy like this. And there was no secret entrance."

If his grandfather knew about it, then his aunt would know about it. "I knew it!" Dylan exclaimed. "She's got something to do with this."

"Who are you talking about?" Max frowned.

"Who else? The Ghost. All this upgrade doesn't come cheap. She's got to be the one financing this." But he didn't admit he knew his aunt wanted the rumored treasures somewhere in the grounds. And that was why she finagled a deal to live here. He shook his head. Every bad thing came back to his aunt.

"But, Dylan"—Lily touched his arm—"what's the connection between her and Grace? There's no reason she would want to abduct her."

"I don't know, but this place—I bet anything she had something to do with the upgrade. Who else would have known about this?"

"Wait. I thought the guy in custody was in the Irishman Gang," Eva said. "I haven't read anything about your aunt colluding with the Irishman Gang."

"There's always a first." He just couldn't let go of the idea.

Alex, who had been examining the computers, spoke up. "This is some serious tech. Whoever upgraded this place knew what they were doing."

Eva went over to where Alex was sitting. "What have you found?"

Apparently in his element, Alex tapped the keyboard, typing rapidly. Dylan had only seen Olivia code that fast. Alex's gaze shifted from one monitor to the next. "If I'm not mistaken, this is a surveillance program in the tunnels. Dylan, you need to upgrade the estate security system. It's been hacked. This one has access to it."

"What?!" Dylan muttered a curse.

"No worries. I kicked it out. So, you're good for now."

"Wait. It's a surveillance program?" Wadding up a napkin, Lily rushed over. "Can you find Grace and Sean?"

"That's what I'm trying to do. The labels are screwy, so I have to go through each one."

"There!" Eva cried.

They all looked where she pointed.

Max gasped. "Oh no, Connor!"

Dylan sucked in a deep breath. Connor looked like he'd gone ten rounds with Mike Tyson. But Grace and Sean appeared unharmed, at least physically.

Alex did something to stop the camera feed from changing to another camera. "Anyone recognize that room?"

CHAPTER 61

MIRAGE FINE ARTS

OLIVIA

Olivia sat in her car, the hum of the engine providing a steady background noise as she waited. The city lights cast a faint glow through her windshield, and the rearview mirror reflected her furrowed brow. Javier had the Perez family crest tattooed on his arm, a mark of significance. He had mentioned his mother but had avoided talking about his father. What was the connection? The Perez family was notorious, and only family members or those deeply trusted in their inner circle bore that tattoo. Was Javier part of that circle?

She discarded half-formed theories when Collins exited the art gallery. Time to focus. She got out of her car, keeping a safe distance as she tailed him through the bustling streets.

Collins was good. He pivoted down a narrow alley, entered a convenience store, and vanished. She hesitated only a moment before following him inside. Inside the cramped and cluttered store, the shelves packed tightly together made it easy for someone to disappear. She scanned the aisles, but Collins wasn't in sight. There—the back door was slightly ajar.

She slipped through it into the lot of a run-down shopping center. The place was almost deserted, with many empty store spaces unoccupied. The hair on the back of her neck prickled, and her instincts screamed at her to be on guard.

Before she could react, a presence hovered behind her. Her training kicked in. She spun around, grabbed the arm reaching for her, and used her attacker's momentum to flip him over her shoulder. But her assailant was skilled. He turned the flip into a somersault and came up on his feet, his hands open wide.

With quick reflexes, she pulled out her own gun, pointing it at him. "Federal agent!" she yelled.

The man didn't flinch, and his posture remained relaxed. "Relax, we're on the same side, Jade—or is it Olivia?" He waved his empty hands. "No weapon."

Olivia's heart pounded. How did he know her aliases? She didn't recall ever working with him on any joint operation. She kept her gun at the ready but lowered it slightly. "Explain," she demanded, her gaze never leaving his.

Collins lowered his arms. "I'm undercover, reporting directly to Seymore Gladstone. Operation Iron Shield. Code name Falcon." His British accent was more pronounced now. "You shouldn't have come in with your senator fiancé. He's too well-known. Although I would say it was plausible seeing that you two were getting married. A painting would be a nice addition to a new home. But then your agent called and hung up."

She frowned. What was he talking about? Who called him? But that wasn't the priority here. "If MI6 had an operative here, we'd have to be notified." When she asked Jay about Collins, he never said anything about that. Instead, he sent her to Hank. "Stop lying. I know you're Charles Moore. Former MI6. Now working for Rafael Montoya as a hired gun."

He smirked. "That's to show you how good my legend is."

Her pounding heart slowed, her breath now came in steady, but her thoughts wouldn't still. True, when she was undercover as Jade, everybody believed Olivia was dead. Only a handful of people were aware of her assignment. But that still didn't mean Collins was telling the truth. "If you were undercover, you wouldn't have tortured Sam Tucker and killed Liz Jimenez. I know it was you. I can even see your scar on the neckline." The scar could easily be mistaken for a tattoo. How had he survived a knife wound so close to the jugular?

"You're assuming I killed them. And you don't know everything about him. He wasn't just shagging the wife—" He stopped, cocked his head to listen.

Olivia heard it too. Someone was coming. She glanced toward the noise. Just a worker taking a smoke break.

"Will catch you later."

She turned back, and Collins was gone. The man was good.

The first thing she did back at her car was call Jay. After explaining everything, Jay put her on hold. Moments later, he came back on the line. "I spoke to Gladstone himself. Falcon is real."

"What's this Operation Iron Shield? Why didn't they liaise with us?"

"An operation to foil a plot to assassinate their PM. Since a US congressman and his staff were involved somehow, he couldn't risk it."

Surely, Simon's friend wouldn't have been involved in such a plot. "But Javier?"

"We don't know how he was involved, if at all. But they had evidence of his chief of staff's involvement. Falcon will brief you in due time." Click.

CHAPTER 62

TUNNELS

GRACE

Time had blurred into an endless loop since Grace had been ushered along with Sean and Connor into this dingy room. Their maniacal captor paced, a gun held in a causal grip. His erratic ranting indicated he and Connor had some sort of history —a dark, vengeful past that now ensnared her and Sean too.

She sat on the ground, her back pressed against rough, unfinished drywall, Sean and Connor beside her. Their captor yammered on a phone, and the musty unpainted walls scarcely contained all the tension surrounding them. A tiny red dot in the corner of the room caught her attention, flickering faintly. Could it be a camera? She prayed it was. If there was any chance Kyle or his colleagues could see them, it would be through that lens.

Her heart raced. How could she send a message to whoever might be watching? *Think, Grace, think!* She needed to communicate without their captor noticing. Then it hit her— ASL. She had taken one semester of American Sign Language in college, though she never had the chance to practice it much. *Lord, please help me remember.*

Connor, who had been slumped against the wall, seemed to find a reserve of strength. He straightened up, glaring at their captor. "They have nothing to do with the past." His voice came through steadily despite the fear in his eyes. "Let them go."

The man laughed, and the chilling sound echoed off the walls. "I have to keep the girl. That's the job. Now, your son, I won't make the same mistake this time. Nobody would be a witness."

Sean's gaze flicked between her and the red dot. He saw it too. The boy's face hardened, and his hands fisted. "Then get on with it."

Grace's heart skipped a beat. Why was Sean taunting the man? Then it clicked. He was creating a distraction. She scanned the room. The door had a number and letter stenciled on it. Yes! She would sign the number and letter. *Please, Lord, let someone see this.*

She glanced at the captor, now focused on Sean. Without lifting her hand, she signed. Her movements were hesitant, rusty from lack of practice. She held up four fingers and kept her thumb tucked against the palm, then transitioned to a fist with her thumb on the side facing outward, praying it made sense.

The man didn't seem to notice her, his attention still on Sean. Grace continued to sign, repeating the number and the letter, watching the red dot, willing it to relay her desperate message.

Sean continued to provoke their captor. "You talk too much. Just do it if you have the guts."

Their captor's face contorted. He stepped closer to Sean, his grip tightening on the gun. Grace's heart hammered her chest. Had Sean gone too far? She lurched to her feet. "He's just a kid. Leave him alone!"

The man, clearly unhinged, pointed the gun at Connor, then Sean, then her, as if figuring out who to shoot first.

CHAPTER 63

POLICE STATION

OLIVIA

After her tense encounter with Collins, Olivia strode to her car, the cool evening air doing little to soothe her rattled nerves. She needed answers, and she needed them now. Sliding into the driver's seat, she unlocked her phone, connected to the hands-free speaker, and dialed Simon's number. He picked up on the second ring.

"Hey, how well did you know Sam Tucker?" She started the car and glanced around to ensure she wasn't followed.

"Not well, why?" Simon's voice crackled through the speaker.

"Did he have access to classified information?"

Simon hesitated. "That would depend on his clearance. He would have had access to certain classified info, but not top-secret stuff. And I don't think Javier was in the intel committee." There was another pause. "So, how did it go? You were going to watch that Collins fellow."

Her grip tightened on the steering wheel as she pulled out of the parking lot. "Not my best moments, but it's okay. Gotta go.

Love you." Before Simon could respond, she hung up and dialed Spaulding.

"Olivia, I'm in the sector," Spaulding's stern voice answered.

"Meet me at the station in ten." Again, she didn't wait for a reply.

Minutes later, she walked through the station's fluorescent-lit halls. Spaulding and Monnin waited for her near the entrance. Spaulding, ever the professional, gave her a brief nod. Monnin, on the other hand, towered over Olivia with a smirk that hinted at skepticism.

"Sorry, best we can do." Spaulding led her to a cramped interrogation room. The single light overhead cast a harsh glare against the bare walls and stark table.

Olivia didn't care about the room's size. She needed information. "Did you look into the victims?"

Monnin's smirk widened. What was up with her?

"No, we were just made detectives." Monnin paused, probably enjoying Olivia's brief irritation. "Of course we did."

When Olivia remained silent, waiting, Spaulding took the hint, opened a file, and scanned the contents before reading aloud. "Nothing suspicious until we got to his job. The congressman's office keeps stonewalling us."

She could find out more about that later. "Did you check his calls, texts, emails?"

"His personal phone and emails, yes." Spaulding flipped through the pages.

"Squeaky clean." Hands laced in her lap, Monnin leaned back in her chair. She tossed her ponytail back over one shoulder. "But he had a burner too."

A burner? Olivia cocked an ear. "Did you manage to get any information from it?"

Spaulding shook his graying head. "We found the phone, but it was wiped clean. No call logs, no messages, nothing."

That didn't sound good. So maybe Collins was right. "Did the ME do the posts yet?"

Monnin checked her phone. "He sent over a prelim report."

Spaulding was reading the physical report. Old school. His eyebrows rose. "Oh, not what I expected."

"What?" Olivia slipped her hands into her pockets to keep from reaching for either his report or Monnin's phone.

"Tucker died of insulin overdose. Jimenez died of asphyxiation."

"The beatings and the wounds are postmortem." The way Monnin's mouth twisted, as if holding back her gag reflex, she looked like she had just been made detective and this was her first ME report. "Why would someone do that?"

So, Olivia's first instinct was correct. Someone staged the scene. Assuming Collins was telling the truth, he did it. He needed to maintain his cover as a ruthless assassin. She ran several scenarios in her head. "Did the ME say anything about how the insulin got in his system?"

"An injection site on his arm." Spaulding skimmed the paper. "We need to—"

"I'm checking." Monnin scrolled her phone. "Here it is. There is a syringe. I'll have it printed."

"How was Liz suffocated? Any ideas?" Olivia asked.

"There's fibers consistent with the pillow on the couch." Spaulding scanned the text. "So, what are you thinking? You don't think Hugo Perez is involved? What about that Collins fellow?"

"The evidence suggests Tucker suffocated Liz with the pillow and injected himself with insulin."

"That doesn't make sense. The needle would have stayed with him." Monnin set her phone aside. "And he definitely didn't beat or injure himself postmortem."

"Right, but if the person who beat him up also shot him with insulin, he would have taken the syringe with him. If the syringe comes back clean, no prints at all, then maybe my theory is wrong. But if it comes back with Tucker's prints, we know the beater didn't do it." She now knew Collins left the video for the authorities to see. She stood up. "Thank you."

"We could still get the guy for desecrating a corpse." Monnin tightened her ponytail, her agitated movements irritating.

Olivia didn't say anything. The detectives would soon hear from their superior to close the case as murder-suicide and drop it.

Before she forgot, she needed to check in with Deanna on her deep dive on Javier. As Olivia walked out of the station, she took her phone out and started scrolling for the number. Before she had a chance to hit the call button, an incoming call vibrated from an unknown number. After a moment of hesitation, she swiped to answer.

"Tell your people to hit the orphanage now!"

CHAPTER 64

BUNKER

ANA

Ana walked into the bunker with Ortiz and Kyle. The metallic clang of the heavy door shutting behind them reverberated through the space. Inside, a palpable urgency thrummed in the air. Fr. Phil and Fr. Jeremy had decided to head to Lorraine's Kitchen to be with Lorraine and Kate, offering them comfort and prayers.

As Ana stepped further into the room, the largest screen on the wall drew her focus where it displayed a live feed of Grace, Sean, and Connor, all bound and looking frightened. Her heart clenched, but she pushed her emotions aside, focusing on the task.

"How is it that no one knows where this is?" Her voice cut through the room. She scanned the footage for anything to reveal their location. With plain, undecorated walls and scant lighting, nothing stood out. But something was familiar about the setting, something she should recognize.

"Oh, come on, you should know. The tunnel system is like a maze." Kyle punched a wall, his frustration evident.

"Quiet!" Alex commanded, frowning as his fingers tapped on the keyboard. On another screen, different lines of codes began streaming through.

Eva, standing nearby, asked, "What are you doing?"

"Checking for a hidden map of the tunnels."

"Look!" Kyle pointed to Grace on the screen. "Alex, can you zoom in?"

"I should be able to do it." Alex tapped some keys."That's probably it without sacrificing clarity."

Ana saw what Kyle noticed. "Grace's hand. Four and a fist. What does that mean?"

"Four zero?" Max suggested.

"Four something," Eva said.

Dylan frowned. "Maybe it's for, not four. For something?"

"I got it." Lily held her phone up. "It's ASL for the number four and the letter *A*."

"Smart girl!" Ortiz grinned.

"Wow, I didn't even know she knew ASL." Alex's eyes widened.

"Your sister is full of surprises." Kyle patted Alex's shoulder. "Now, did you find a map?"

"We don't need a map. It has to be the orphanage. Where else would they have a room number?" Ana was ready to go.

Max spoke up. "I agree. The nuns operated a school there alongside the orphanage. The rooms have numbers."

"Let's go! We'll take you there." She went out, followed by Ortiz and the rest of the gang.

CHAPTER 65

TASK FORCE OFFICE

RON

R on paced the squad room, his booted steps echoing off the tiles. He glanced at the wall clock, the hands moving agonizingly slowly. The entire afternoon had been a test of his patience, waiting for updates from Ana and Kyle about Grace's situation. He knew Ana's capabilities and trusted her to find Grace and the boy, but the sting operation scheduled for later today left him no choice but to keep his team on task.

Ron halted his pacing to face his team gathered around the screen in the squad room, the usual activity buzz livening the air. "Update," he commanded.

The first to speak, Tanner tossed aside a stylus pen. "Everything is ready for the sting. We'll just be there to monitor and serve as backup." He pulled up a detailed map of the print shop on the screen. "There are two main exits, one at the front and one at the back. We've got both covered, along with a couple of side windows that could potentially be used as escape routes."

Ron nodded. "Good. We need to be thorough. No loose

ends." He turned to Hernandez. "Did you check with the Federales?"

Hernandez straightened up. "Yes, boss. According to what they know, the Perez family is experiencing some internal problems. My source told me his competitors are insulated enough not to worry about him turning himself in. You know how it is—most of them have people in their pockets. He thought it was more likely someone inside his family."

Ron rubbed his chin, the day's stubble grating—or had he not shaved this morning? Coffee had been his only focus this morning. "He doesn't really have any living family anymore. Hugo doesn't sound like a good suspect. Who else could it be?"

Before Hernandez could respond, Deanna raised a hand, her eyes gleaming. "I know why he's turning himself in. Or at least I think I do. He's got terminal cancer. And you'd never guess who his ex-wife is. Cristina Navarro."

Ron arched an eyebrow. "Never heard of her."

Hernandez let out a low whistle. "No way! She's a famous artist."

Tanner's smirk at their computer geek erased the wariness usually smarting in the rugged man's eyes. "I didn't know you were into art."

"That's not all," Deanna continued. "Navarro has a sister—Lucia Jimenez."

The words hung in the air, their implications unspoken yet surely reverberating through the minds of those present. But there was no time for contemplation as the door burst open, admitting Agent Davis. Her arrival snapped the team back on task.

"All set?" Davis asked.

Ron exchanged a glance with his senior agent, Tanner, who gave a curt nod. "Yes, ma'am."

Stylus pen in hand again, Tanner proceeded to outline the positions, marking up the on-screen map and detailing where their unmarked van would park and the vantage points for monitoring the situation.

After nodding her approval, Davis briefed them on a few last-minute intelligence updates, her words clipped and precise. Then, with a final run-through of the operation's choreography, they geared up—checking weapons, radios, and body armor with practiced efficiency. Adrenaline thrummed through Ron's veins, and surely those of his team, as the gravity of the mission settled upon them. It was time.

CHAPTER 66

ON THE ROAD

OLIVIA

Olivia processed the caller's words. The possibility that Collins was involved in Grace's abduction sent a chill down her spine. She hadn't been privy to the case details, but Ron's team was actively searching for the missing girl. Ana and Kyle were likely involved in the search efforts as well.

Squelching a sense of urgency, Olivia climbed into her car, slid out her phone, and dialed Ron's number, ready to share the crucial new information. The call went straight to voicemail. Undeterred, she tried Ana's number next. To the same result.

Frustration mounting, Olivia scrolled through her contacts to Simon's number. She hit the call button, and after a few rings, he answered.

"Hey, it's me," she said. "I just received a call. Grace is at the orphanage. I'm heading out to the estate right now. In case Ron or Ana calls, let them know to get there as soon as possible."

"Of course," Simon replied. "Do you want me to go with you?"

Her heart warmed, but he lacked the training and experience to handle a potentially dangerous situation.

"No, it's okay. I'll call once I know more. Love you."

Olivia sped toward the estate, her foot pressing on the accelerator. Fragmentary details about the abduction flashed through her mind, pieces of a puzzle she desperately tried to fit together. The Perez family was somehow linked to the crime, with the abductor leveraging Grace's safety to coerce Jorge Perez into compliance. The team also suspected an inside job, someone with intimate knowledge of the family's affairs.

Collins's employment at Hugo Perez's gallery took on a new significance. Could his position have provided him with the access and information necessary to orchestrate the abduction? Yet, the connection between Grace's kidnapping and the plot to assassinate the prime minister remained elusive, a missing link Olivia couldn't quite grasp.

As she navigated the winding roads, she gasped at a startling realization. Collins's employer was still a mystery, a crucial piece of information that could tie everything together. Could this unknown entity be the person who had pressured Perez to remain silent, to refrain from turning himself in?

Her frustration mounted as she acknowledged the gaping holes in her understanding. She needed to speak with Collins, to extract the truth from him and fill in the missing puzzle pieces. Without a complete picture, she was a fly trying to navigate a convoluted web of deceit and danger.

CHAPTER 67

BUNKER

ANA

Ana's heart raced as she rushed toward the van, focused on one goal: Reaching Grace as quickly as possible. "We need to get there now!"

Before she could take another step, Ortiz's firm hand grasped her arm, stopping her. "We don't have the key. I already radioed the guards. One is driving a UTV here. A van isn't gonna do it."

As if on cue, an approaching vehicle caught her attention, and a utility terrain vehicle (UTV) lumbered toward them, its engine revving.

"We won't all fit." She glanced back at the group gathered behind her.

Ortiz released his grip. "This one can fit four. I say you, me, Kyle go in the UTV. The rest can either hoof it or stay here. You guys are Feds, and I'm trained."

Ana nodded, but her gaze lingered on Eva. "Eva should come. She's one of us."

The group's attention shifted to the approaching UTV, its presence sparking a flurry of comments and excitement. Ana wasted no time, hopping onto the vehicle as the driver stepped down.

"Kyle, Eva, Ortiz will go with me." She raised her voice above the chatter. "The rest of you can either stay here or meet us there."

Dylan turned a questioning look on Ortiz. "Dante, why do we have just one UTV?"

Ortiz shrugged, a hint of a smile quirking his bristly mustache. "You're asking me, boss? You can always buy another one."

As the group prepared to depart, Alex approached the UTV. "I want to go with you guys." He held up both hands. "She's my sister."

Eva placed a comforting hand on Alex's shoulder. "We'll get her back."

Ana's heart ached for him, understanding the desperation and fear he must be feeling. But they needed to move fast, and the UTV had limited space. "Alex, I promise you we will do everything in our power to bring Grace home safely. But right now, we need to go. Every second counts."

Alex hesitated, his eyes searching Ana's face. Then he stepped back from the UTV. "Please, bring my sister back," he whispered, his voice barely audible above the rumbling engine.

Ana gave him a reassuring nod before turning her attention to the mission. She settled into the UTV, gripping the frame. Ortiz took the driver's seat and focused on the path ahead.

With him at the wheel, the UTV surged forward, leaving a trail of dust in its wake. Ana, Kyle, and Eva held on. Surely, all their hearts pounded as they sped toward their destination and Ana's thoughts raced faster than the machine. Just what might they find at the orphanage? With time of the essence, she prayed they'd reach Grace before any harm came to her.

CHAPTER 68

PRINT SHOP

RON

Ron stepped out of the unmarked van. The print shop, a nondescript building with a faded sign, stood a block from them. Hard to imagine it hid a sinister operation within those walls.

"All right, team." He kept his voice low and steady.

"Hawk is already inside. We need to be ready to move in at a moment's notice."

His team nodded in unison. Agent Davis stood nearby, her focus on the print shop entrance.

Ron checked his earpiece, ensuring the communication line was open. So did Davis. Hawk had infiltrated the operation, posing as a potential buyer for the counterfeit bills. He was set to instigate the transaction that would provide them with evidence to make the arrests.

"Hawk, do you copy?" Davis spoke into her mic.

"Loud and clear." Hawk's voice crackled through the earpiece. "I'm about to enter the print shop. The meeting is set to start in five minutes."

"We've got your back," Davis assured him. "Just give us the signal, and we'll be there."

The team took their positions, blending into the shadows of the nearby buildings while Ron got back into the van. His attention never left the print shop entrance, his hand resting on his gun holster.

Minutes ticked by, each second feeling like an eternity. So much could go wrong. Undercover operations were always unpredictable.

Then Hawk's voice broke through the silence. "I have visual confirmation of the counterfeit bills. The suspects are here, and the transaction is about to take place."

Ron relayed the information to his team. "Everyone, get ready to move in on my command."

From the monitor in their van, Ron saw the action live. Inside the print shop, Hawk stood face-to-face with the counterfeiters. Stacks of bills were laid out on the table before him.

"Looks like we have a deal." Hawk reached for the briefcase filled with the agreed-upon payment.

Just as his fingers touched the handle, the door burst open, and Ron's team swarmed in. "FBI! Nobody move!"

Chaos erupted as the suspects scrambled to escape, but Ron's well-prepared team subdued them, focusing on capturing a low-level member of the operation.

Moments later, it was over. Ron stepped out of the van, approached the suspect, a young man with fear in his eyes. "Listen, kid. We've got you dead to rights. But if you cooperate and help us get to the top guy, we can make things easier for you."

Davis joined Ron, a satisfied smirk creasing her lips. "Good work, Ron. This is a significant step in taking down the whole operation."

He bobbed his head, turning his attention back to his team. "Secure the evidence and take the suspects into custody."

His goal would be to flip the kid, a low-level player. Once

the kid realized what kind of trouble he was in, he'd surely roll over.

CHAPTER 69

BUNKER

DYLAN

Dylan's heart raced as he focused on the live feed. The goon in the room was taunting his victims, waving the gun menacingly, and then pulling back. The fear and tension were palpable even through the screen. Alex and Max were transfixed by the monitor, unable to look away from their loved ones.

Dylan leaned closer to Lily, his voice barely a whisper. "The bad guy is busy. I'm gonna check out the room."

Lily glanced at the screen, mouth muttering something, presumably a prayer, then back at Dylan. "I'm going with you. Let's leave Cedric and Ronnie here with Max."

"No, we'd better take them," Dylan insisted. "They'll help us find our way back here, just in case."

Lily nodded, and they ventured out with the dogs. The bunker corridors were dimly lit and eerily silent, every sound amplified in the oppressive stillness.

"Hey, did you see Alex and Eva?" Lily touched his arm.

He frowned. "Of course, I saw them."

"No, I mean, did you see how they act around each other? Oh, come on, he likes her. And I think the feeling is mutual."

Images of Alex and Eva in the garden flashed in his mind. "Oh, cool."

Lily continued to chitchat about what she thought about the two, but after several wrong turns, she asked, "Are you sure we can get there from here?"

"I think so. Last night, we went in from the restaurant entrance. We just need to think about what's on the surface." Dylan replied. He knew the general direction they needed to head to find the room.

His confidence wavered as they navigated the labyrinthine passageways. The bunker was a maze, designed to confuse and mislead intruders. But he was determined. After all, Ana and Ortiz managed to find a way out without retracing their steps to the restaurant. If they could do it, so could he.

After what felt like an eternity of twists and turns, Lily's voice broke the silence. "Finally!"

They stood before a nondescript section of wall, indistinguishable from the rest of the bunker. "Dante said the switch was hidden in the wall." Dylan ran his hands over the cold, smooth surface.

Lily gripped his arm. "Wait, but how do we get back out? We need to find a way to stop the door from closing."

"Good point." He frowned at the wall. "Let's find the mechanism first. We can figure out the rest once we know how it works."

They continued searching, feeling for any irregularities in the wall. Cedric and Ronnie sniffed around. Then Dylan's fingers brushed against a slight indentation. He pressed it, and a section of the wall slid open with a soft mechanical hiss.

"Got it." He gave a fist pump. "I'm going to grab something sturdy inside to hold the door. You hold it for now."

Lily stood in the doorway. "Hurry!"

He scanned the room and settled on a board on a bookshelf. The door was closing. Lily was trying to hold it back. "Come in!" Then he wedged the board between the door and the doorjamb.

"Stay!" He ordered the dogs he'd left outside. If they needed to get help, he would send them to find Max.

"This looks like a storage room," Lily commented.

"Let's search everything. Maybe we'll find the map here or the cipher key." He began checking the top of the shelves and other likely hiding places while Lily looked below.

"Nothing!" She tossed a scrap of garbage on the floor. "Why are the strange codes out there on the wall but nothing in here?"

"I don't know. Maybe it's just a coincidence." Dylan huffed and forked his fingers through his hair, unwilling to admit defeat. "Wait a minute. The switch was hidden, right? Maybe the map's hidden too. Let's check the walls."

Lily's face lit up. They started touching the walls, knocking on them, pushing them, but nothing happened. Dejected, Dylan sat on the floor.

"I wonder why this is here." Lily grabbed an old doll from a shelf. "I used to have dolls like this, but I was more into stuffed animals."

He hopped to his feet and eyed the ancient, ragged doll. "This one is stuffed. It's probably one of those that sings or talks when you squeeze it." He squeezed it.

"You silly." She slapped his arm. "I'm sure the battery is dead."

Dylan felt the battery compartment. Instead of a rectangular box, he felt something different. He opened the seams. Then his mouth dropped and his eyes widened.

CHAPTER 70

TUNNELS/ORPHANAGE

OLIVIA

Olivia followed the signs to the closed orphanage, her body tense. As she approached the vacant lot, a car parked haphazardly in the middle of the empty space drew her focus. Simon's car. What was he doing here?

She hopped out. Just as she began to move toward the orphanage, Simon emerged from his vehicle.

"I just got here," he called out, striding toward her with purposeful steps.

She hurried to meet him. "What are you doing here?"

"If Grace is here, I can help," he replied. "Remember, I lived here for a few years. I know the place inside out. They're only remodeling the old library building for the Ghost."

When he started walking toward the entrance, she fell in step beside him. "But it can be dangerous."

"I'll stay out of the way." Simon gave her a reassuring look. "Besides, I've got you and the others." He opened the door for her, the creak echoing in the silent building.

Inside, the orphanage was eerily still, a stark contrast to the lively place it must have once been. Dust motes floated in the slivers of light breaking through the boarded-up windows, casting an ethereal glow on the faded wallpaper and worn floors.

"It was a small school," Simon explained as they walked. "Lower grades were in the basement. There used to be a tunnel down there."

Now Olivia was intrigued. "Where did it go?"

"The chapel. But they closed it just before Fr. Phil came here as a transitional deacon."

She grabbed his arm, stopping him. "We'll take the tour afterward—"

Bang!

Her head snapped toward the sound.

"Was that a gunshot?" Simon stopped, his face tightening.

"Yes, go back to the car!" She was already moving toward the source of the noise.

ANA

As the UTV rumbled through the dense foliage, the tension in the air was palpable. The path was bumpy, and every jolt an echo of their mission's urgency. Ana leaned forward as if she could spur the machine faster, her gaze fixed on the trail ahead.

"I don't want to alert him we're coming," she said over the engine's roar. "Let's park this by the hatch opening. We'll go down there the same way."

Ortiz, gripping the wheel, flexed his hold before nodding. "That's smart."

Minutes later, they arrived at the hidden hatch. Once Ortiz shut off the UTV, the surrounding area was eerily quiet, the only sounds being the distant chirping of birds and the rustling leaves. He hopped out, with Kyle following. Together, they lifted the heavy hatch open.

"I'll go first. I know the way. Ortiz can bring up the rear." Ana stepped around the guys and descended into the darkness, the cool air of the underground passage enveloping her. The dim light from above faded, and she pulled out a flashlight, its beam cutting through the gloom. She navigated to the right, her senses heightening.

The passage led her to the hollow wall they found earlier. The wall was now open a crack, and her heart skipped a beat as she peered through the narrow gap, scanning the area beyond. It was empty. She signaled the others to follow.

Kyle and Eva descended next, and Ortiz came down last. Then Ana pointed to the door marked 4A. She gestured to Eva and Ortiz, directing them to the left side, then signaled for Kyle to follow her as they checked the right.

She nearly held her breath, the air so thick with anticipation it clogged her airways. Every step seemed to echo in the silence, amplifying their presence. But who had opened the wall? Where were they now?

Then she felt it—a presence—and held up a fist to signal the others to stop. Her back against the wall in the corner, she listened. There, a faint sound. After a glance at Kyle, she turned the corner, stuck her hand with the gun out, and yelled, "Federal agent!" Only to find the other person hopping into her view, yelling the same.

"Olivia!"

"Ana!" They lowered their weapons. How and where had she come from? But that conversation could wait.

Together, they entered the room with Kyle and the rest of the team behind her. The scene was not what she had expected. Connor lay on the ground, bleeding from his torso. Sean knelt beside his father, crying, "Daddy!" Grace pressed down on Connor's torso with Sean's shirt. Their captor was on the ground in a pool of his own blood. Ana went to check on the suspect and kicked his gun away. Seeing his sightless eyes, she exhaled. He was dead.

Ortiz took over administering first aid to Connor while Eva radioed for help. Ana didn't want to speculate, but he didn't look good. Seeing the boy crying, she couldn't help praying for the family.

Her gaze finally found Grace, who seemed unharmed. "Are you okay?"

"Yes, thank you!" Grace sprang to her feet, rushed to Ana, and enveloped her in a big hug.

"You all right?" Kyle asked.

Grace broke into a grin. "Now I am. I saw the blinking red light and thought someone might be monitoring it. I hoped someone would see me signal 'four A.' I wasn't even sure if I did it right—"

"Shush. You did." Kyle wrapped her in his arms.

"Olivia, how'd you know to come here?" Ana turned in her direction, only to find her gone. "Where'd she go?"

No one answered. *You can take a girl away from the espionage world, but you can't take that world from her.* Olivia would always move like a ninja.

Ana cleared her throat. "Grace, you want to tell me what happened?"

Grace pulled away from Kyle. "I thought he was gonna kill us after he shot Sean's dad. And then, suddenly, he just collapsed."

"Nobody else was in here?"

She shook her head. "It was so sudden. My ears were still ringing from that gunshot when there was this muffled pop somewhere behind me. And then, he fell."

Ana crouched by the body again. Their captor had fallen backward, so the shot was fired from the door, which was consistent with what Grace said. But who? It couldn't have been Olivia. No matter, Ana owed whoever killed him a big thank you for saving Grace.

CHAPTER 71

TASK FORCE OFFICE

RON

Ron's whole body relaxed when Ana and Kyle reported that Grace was safely rescued. She was scared but unharmed. The boy, Sean, was fine, but his father, Connor, had suffered a gunshot wound. The latest news was that Connor was in surgery. They were all pulling for him to come through. Poor Lorraine and Sean. But Ron didn't have the luxury to ponder too long. Agent Davis was ready for the briefing.

The room was a hive of activity, with agents moving in and out, phones ringing, and urgent conversations filling the air. Ron gathered his team together. He'd told Kyle to stay behind at the estate to coordinate with local authorities and the Marino family. But he'd asked Ana to report back. After all, she was the one intimately familiar with the Perez family.

"What'd I miss?" Ana walked in, her dark bob pulled back in a tight ponytail, eyes sharp and focused. She headed straight to Ron. "Olivia was there, but disappeared before I could ask for more information."

Ron nodded. He understood well how Olivia worked. Whatever she was involved in, it was never for public consumption. Spies! "Gather up. Ana, we'll catch you up in a bit. Agent Davis."

Davis stepped forward. "It was a good sting." She detailed what they seized and recovered, the counterfeit currency, computers, etc. "The guy we caught decided to flip."

The lines of his rugged features more pronounced today, Tanner squeezed his stress ball. "What did he say?"

"Oh, he said plenty. Unfortunately, we still don't have an identity of the Moneyman. He gave us the operation details. So, that's good. We'll follow up."

Hernandez frowned. "How does he not know who hired the print shop?"

"Everything is done electronically. They never met," Davis replied.

Ron pointed at Hernandez. "You and Deanna, follow the money. Find something."

"Yeah, boss."

"I hope you guys have better luck than we do." Davis gathered her things. "I need to get back to the office. If our tech guys find anything from their computers, phones, etc., I'll pass it on." With that, she walked out.

Ron waited till she was off-site before turning to Hernandez and Deanna. "Did you find anything?"

Hernandez had mirrored the computer's hard drive in the aftermath of the sting. Tanner had copied the suspect's phone data. Ron needed the information and didn't have time to wait for the Secret Service to share.

"Agent Davis wasn't lying. Everything was done electronically." Deanna's fingers tapped against her leg, jittering as if dancing on a keyboard. "Whoever hired them is hiding behind layers of proxy servers. It took some time, but I finally traced it to Spain."

"Spain?" Ana muttered.

"Oh, Ana, do you know who Hugo's mother is?" Deanna asked.

"Cristina Navarro. I met her once long ago. She left Papi, if the rumor is true. Why?"

"But do you know who her sister is?"

Now, Ana frowned. "Cristina's sister? No, I didn't even know she had a sister."

"Lucia Jimenez. She lives in Spain, so does Navarro."

"Jimenez. Why does that name sound familiar?"

"That would be the murder of Congressman Javier Jimenez." Tanner tossed his stress ball to his left hand.

Ana gasped. "You're not suggesting..."

Deanna shrugged. "Not suggesting anything. According to what I can find, Lucia Jimenez doesn't have any children."

"Jimenez is a common Spanish name," Hernandez offered. True, but in this business, Ron didn't believe in coincidences. But it would be a mystery for another day. "Deanna, what else did you find out?"

"I couldn't find the exact location. José, did you call?"

Hernandez looked up. "Yeah, I called Legat Madrid. But I needed a warrant for them to investigate."

Ron processed what he had learned so far. "Okay, as best we know, whoever hired them is from Spain. Is that correct?"

"Yes." Hernandez sent some text messages to the screen.

"The international number is going to Spain. I'm guessing it's a burner. And the legat office will need a warrant."

"Anything else?"

Ana cleared her throat. "We still don't know who is behind Grace's abduction."

"Have you contacted Perez?" Ron asked.

"I just told him we got her. But I told him not to tell anyone yet. Given the fact that we still don't know who's behind it, I'm hoping we can use that."

Ron agreed. "Okay, Hernandez, Deanna, follow the money and keep checking the data. Ana, go see the old man.

Tanner, with me. We'll have a chat with the suspects. Let's see who caves first." His phone vibrated just as he gathered his things. Kyle.

"Yes?"

"I'm at the hospital now. Grace and Sean got checked out. They're okay. Connor is still in surgery. Ortiz is getting Dylan and Lily out of the room—"

Ron frowned. "What room?"

"Oh, they went to check something in the room where Grace and everybody went and disappeared."

"Why? What were they looking for?"

"No clue. Alex just said one minute they were with them and the next they were gone. Anyway, they got stuck in there. The board Dylan used to hold the door open broke. Thank goodness the dogs went crazy and somehow found their way back to the bunker to alert Alex and Max. When we heard about it, Ortiz went back to get them out. I think they're on the way here."

Shaking his head, Ron groaned. "Those two! All right, let me know about Connor as soon as you know."

"Will do."

CHAPTER 72

ORLANDO HOSPITAL

DYLAN

Dylan sat in the emergency room lobby, the antiseptic scent mingling with the faint aroma of stale coffee. He patted his breast pocket, feeling the reassuring outline of the skeleton key he'd found hidden in the doll.

"Is that a key?" Lily had asked. And he had fished it out to show her.

Man, life would've been more peaceful if he'd declined his grandmother's invitation. Yet, every time he pondered the question, he reached the same conclusion—the dangers and upheavals were worth it. Reuniting with his maternal grandmother and uncovering his family history was invaluable. Just knowing he had a family was a treasure he wouldn't trade for anything.

Lily's hand settled on his, pulling him from his reverie. "What are you thinking?"

He slid his hand palm-up to grip her tender fingers. "Oh, everything and nothing."

She leaned closer. "Thank goodness Michael was able to do the surgery."

They had come to know Dr. Khoury, or Michael, as he requested to be called some time ago. His wife, Clara, was Olivia's best friend growing up, but a tragic incident had left her with amnesia about two decades ago. In a twist of fate, events brought them together. What was more, Clara was also Eva's aunt. And during an attempt on her life, Clara regained her memory.

"That's all you. You called him."

She shrugged. "Just good timing that he didn't have any other commitment. If you listen to Clara, he's the best. So, anyway, what do you think the key opens?"

Dylan scanned the room, taking in the familiar faces. Sean sat with Lorraine, Kate, and Max, their expressions a mix of worry and hope. Fr. Phil had settled by Dylan's grandmother's side, while Fr. Jeremy offered his support to the rest of the family, praying with them quietly. Kyle hovered around Grace, who looked concerned about Sean. Eva and Alex were sitting together.

"I don't know," Dylan admitted, turning back to Lily. "But I don't think it's just another key."

Lily nodded. "I wonder when we'll know."

A man in scrubs exited the surgical suite, fatigue drawing down his features. Dylan nudged Lily. "Hey, that's him, isn't it?"

Lily focused her gaze on the doctor, squinting. "Yes, let's go ask him."

She began to stand, but Dylan pulled her back down. "Wait. There's something called HIPAA. He's not gonna tell us anything. We're not family. He'll come and talk to Lorraine."

Lily made a face at him. "Do you think he looks sad?"

Dylan glanced at the doctor again, noting the droop in his shoulders and the dark circles under his eyes. "More like tired."

A minute later, a nurse came in. "Connor Murray's family?"

Sean, Lorraine, and her parents stood up, and the nurse smiled. "Please come with me."

CHAPTER 73

THE PEREZ MANSION

ANA

As soon as the door opened, Papi enveloped Ana in a bear hug. Then he released her with a look of concern. "Grace is not harmed?"

She smiled her reassurance. "She's fine. Went to the hospital to get checked out anyway, but got a clean bill of health. A few scrapes, and she's hungry and thirsty. But she's okay."

"Bueno, bueno. Come." He led her to the living room and settled into his armchair.

Ana took a seat on the couch, feeling the comfort of once familiar surroundings. "We caught the two guys who abducted her from the van. They're with the Irishman Gang. We believe they were hired to do the job. Any idea who would do that?"

His shoulders sloped. "It would be the same person who wanted me to turn over everything. I still have no idea. I know you said it was likely an inside job. But I just don't know."

She accepted his uncertainty with a nod. "We haven't ruled out Hugo, but an employee there may shed some light on things. When was the last time you talked to Cristina?"

His nostrils flared as she touched a sore subject. "I don't remember. Not since Julio left and she followed him."

Despite the bitterness in his voice, Ana pressed on, "If she followed him, shouldn't she know where he had gone to? You said he disappeared."

"He did. He went somewhere one summer and then vanished. I believe she was on an art show tour here in the States."

"What about her sister?"

"Lucia? What about her?"

"When was the last time you saw or talked to her?"

"I don't remember. Our kids' births, maybe? I don't know. Decades ago."

She paused, thinking of a different angle. "Did you know Congressman Javier Jimenez from Texas?"

Papi frowned. "I don't think so. We have no reason to deal with anyone from Texas. Does he have anything to do with this?"

"He was murdered. He had a Perez family crest tattoo removed."

His frown deepened into a scowl. "Are you sure it's the family crest? Many crests are similar, especially if they were removed."

"True, it might be a similar one." Despite her agreement, she didn't believe in coincidences in her line of work.

"Do you have a photo of this tattoo?" he asked.

"No, but I can get it easily. Why?"

"I'd like to look at it."

She texted Deanna. Moments later, she showed him the photo on her phone.

He enlarged it and squinted, examining every detail. His eyes widened at one point. He handed the phone back to her. "Princess, do you see it?"

She frowned at the faint outline of the tattoo again. It was the same family crest. "What am I supposed to see?"

"It's faint, but look at the bottom right corner. See the initials?"

She expanded the bottom right corner. Now that she focused on it, she could see two faint letters, or at least, they looked like letters. "I can't tell what the letters are."

He started to rise, then sank back in his chair, and gripped his knees as if holding himself in place. "Do you have a photo of this congressman?"

"Of course." She swiped to a photo from the congressman's website and showed him. "Here."

He looked at it and nodded. "I assume you know this man's age, his height. And now, look at his eyes."

She studied the image and concentrated on the eyes. They reminded her of someone else's, but...

"I'm getting inked today. You have the ring. I've got to match it."

She was preparing to leave that day. That was the last thing he said before kissing her goodbye, as it turned out, for good. Now, she gaped at Papi. "You can't be serious."

The old man shrugged. "Do you know if the congressman had any plastic surgery done?"

CHAPTER 74

CHAPEL, MIRROR ESTATE

OLIVIA

Olivia entered the room back in the tunnels and assessed the scene. Collins must've been there and shot Doyle. It was time to track him down and make him talk. To find out how and if Javier was involved in the assassination plot and how things were connected. To be read in on this op.

Simon told her about the old tunnel leading to the chapel. So, she headed there. Simon thought it was sealed, but things might have changed. The tunnel was narrow and damp, the walls lined with moss and the occasional rat scurrying away from her footsteps. The dripping water echoed eerily, each plop adding to the urgency driving her forward.

She passed an open hatch. Did a shadow move in front of her? Instinctively, she chased after it, her heart thudding in time with her footsteps. The shadow led her through twists and turns until she saw a figure at a door, hitting a brick on the side. The door slid open.

"Collins!" she called out, her voice echoing in the confined space. But he was already through the door.

She copied what he did, and the door slid open for her. She stepped through it into what looked like the chapel's basement. Now the scent of old stone and incense tinted the musty air. Collins was nowhere in sight.

She edged up the narrow stairs, her footsteps barely making a sound on the worn stone steps. As she reached the top, she saw him. Collins was outside, helping some people load what looked like donation items into a truck. The bright sunlight, a stark contrast to the gloomy tunnels, made her squint as her eyes adjusted.

He was good, slipped in the line of volunteers unnoticed.

Olivia sidled up to him, trying to appear casual despite the urgency burning inside her. "We need to talk."

He glanced at her, then back at the people he was helping. "Certainly. Let's help these good folks load up the truck. I think it's shared-food Sunday."

Olivia's jaw clenched, but she picked up a box of canned goods. "Fine, but we talk after."

"Of course." He kept up the charade as if they were old friends catching up. "Just give me a hand with these last boxes." They worked side by side, lifting and carrying the boxes, and Collins interacted with the volunteers, his charm evident in his smile and effortless small talk. With him so at ease, it was hard to reconcile this image with the man she needed answers from.

After they finished with the food truck, she cornered him. "I need to be read in on the op."

He glanced around. "I assume you parked at the orphanage parking lot. Let's head back there. We'll talk on the way. You know, somehow, I knew you'd find me."

She arched an eyebrow. "Sure. Talk. Start with what happened back there."

They started on the path to the orphanage, the quiet of the chapel grounds giving way to the city's distant sounds. Collins took a deep breath. "Doyle went rogue. They weren't supposed to kill anyone, but Doyle was a hothead. I'm sure he was the one who killed Perez's driver. Their job was only to get Grace and keep her here. Safe."

Olivia's steps quickened. "Then what happened?"

Collins sighed. "Doyle spotted someone. Some old witness. I didn't get the whole picture, but he decided to go rogue. He grabbed that fellow and the kid. As soon as he pulled the trigger, I took him down. I was hoping your people would get there soon enough, but... well, you know the rest."

She did know. "Now tell me why you're still here. What is your assignment?"

He stopped walking and booted a small rock further along their path. "The congressman had some important information. What it is, I don't know. Where it is, I don't know. That's why I had him under surveillance. I didn't see a thing. Then, as you know, his chief of staff was shagging his wife. Not only that, Tucker wanted the same thing to sell. The auction already took place. An Iranian won the bid. Tucker was supposed to deliver this intel, but he didn't have it. And, well, their justice system isn't exactly the same as ours." He resumed their trek. "He decided to take the easy way out."

Something wasn't computing. "Why did they kill him? Shouldn't Tucker want him alive to find out where he hid the intel?"

He shrugged. "This is just my theory, or educated guess, from what I observed. Tucker believed he knew where Jimenez hid the intel. Right after they killed him, Tucker went straight to the hotel safe. The wife opened it. He had a look of surprise. The two actually argued. I guess at some point they reached an agreement. I was on the way there then so I didn't see this part until later."

Olivia's eyes narrowed. "What happened after he killed Jimenez?"

Collins kicked the rock aside this time. "Mind you, I wasn't on site. I was using my phone to monitor Jimenez. So, I wasn't there in time to stop the killing. Once I saw what they were about to do, I raced over there. It wasn't easy, but I was prepared, room service uniform handy. They made it to the penthouse via the stairs. Construction workers often left it unlocked—"

"Did they know you were after them?"

He shook his head. "No, I saw them on the security feed. You can check with the hotel. And before you ask, I hacked into it. When I got there, they had already done what they did. I, or my cover, had to answer to my employer. So, I staged the scene but left the incriminating evidence, like the syringe, behind for your bright detectives to connect the dots."

"Okay." She'd have to check with Spaulding to make sure the prints from the syringe matched Tucker's. "Let me understand. The congressman had some vital intel. You don't know what it is. So how did MI6 figure it had something to do with the assassination?"

Collins slowed, his expression serious. "Right, we received a tip. When you get a tip like that, you don't write it off as a prank without investigating. I'm sure your agencies have similar protocols. When we dug deeper, we started hearing your congressman's name everywhere. So, here I am."

"If I'm understanding this correctly, the intel could have nothing to do with the assassination plot. I can't see the Iranian would pay for something like this. Maybe a formula for a bioweapon, but a plot?" It wasn't adding up.

"You're absolutely right. The congressman could have separate intel. One worth a lot to our mutual enemies. Another is about the plot."

The parking lot was in sight. Simon was still sitting in his car, patiently waiting. She stopped walking, trying to get her thoughts together. Something was still missing. "Okay. Who hired you, your cover?"

"I don't know. Everything is done online."

"But you must have an idea."

He hesitated. "The only thing I know is the client is based in Spain."

Spain? Could Rafael Montoya be involved? "And this client hired you to capture Grace?"

"Yes, to blackmail old man Perez and to retrieve the intel from the congressman. The pay is phenomenal."

She stood there, the Grace-Perez connection established. "Your client's goal is to stop Perez from turning himself in, correct?"

"As far as I know."

"How did your client know about Grace? It's not public knowledge."

He shrugged. "Not a clue. That part doesn't involve my mission."

She drew in a slow breath, taking in the facts as well. "Do you think your client was the one behind the assassination plot? Think with me. Your client has to be close to the Perez family. How else would he know about Grace? And if your client was behind the assassination plot and Jimenez somehow obtained that information, wouldn't he want that back?"

He closed his eyes for a moment. "Yes, but how would he know the congressman had that information?"

"We're missing something."

"I agree. That's why I have someone working on that end. In Spain. Someone you know."

CHAPTER 75

TASK FORCE OFFICE

KYLE

After hearing the doctor's verdict, Kyle was preparing to take Grace home when Alex stepped in. "I'll take her home and stay with her."

"I don't need you guys to babysit me," Grace protested.

"This isn't up for debate, little sis," Alex replied in a firm, big-brother tone. "Mom wants you home. You heard her on the phone."

Grace sighed. "Okay, okay, you win." She squeezed Kyle's hand. "Thank you."

"Just doing my job. I'll see you." Kyle let go of her hand and stood back as Alex led her away.

Once home, Kyle took a quick shower before heading back to the task force office. It was late afternoon, and he doubted many people would be around on a Sunday. But as he pushed open the door, a lively jumble of voices, all emanating from the direction of Hernandez's desk, led him in.

Curiosity piqued, Kyle sauntered toward the commotion where Tanner, Deanna, and Hernandez clustered around a laptop.

They fell silent upon noticing him, a hush descending, only to be shattered by Deanna's laughter. "It's just Kyle. Go on!" She waved off the sudden quiet.

Kyle, thoroughly intrigued, squeezed in between Deanna and Tanner, a quizzical eyebrow raised. "What's going on?" His gaze flicked between his colleagues and the laptop screen, which Hernandez clicked to resume what had been paused.

On the screen was a young woman, her demeanor and stride echoing that of a seasoned runway model, her image captivating even in the grainy video playback. The narration was in Spanish.

"Did you catch any of that?" His curiosity spiked as he leaned in to get a better look at the young model.

"You don't know who this is?" Tanner crossed his arms, looking Kyle up and down as if he were some kind of suspect.

Kyle studied the model closely. She looked eerily like Grace, but it couldn't be. And then he knew. "Ana!" he exclaimed. "I had no idea she was a model."

"She was more than that," Deanna chimed in, her voice carrying a note of respect. She nudged Hernandez. "Tell him, José."

The screen shifted to another scene, this time showing Ana in a different light, seated opposite a man in what appeared to be an intimate interview setting. Kyle's understanding of Spanish was rudimentary.

"What are they saying?" He waved to Hernandez for answers.

"According to this interview," Hernandez began, "Ana was offered a significant contract to star in a TV series."

"Seriously?"

"There's more." Deanna tapped Hernandez's shoulder, signaling him to continue. With another click, the screen transitioned from the intimate interview setting to a starkly different scene: a news article, dense with text in Spanish. Its headline alone hinted at a dramatic narrative turn.

"This says she broke her contract and walked away after just one filming session."

Kyle's brow furrowed. "Why?"

When everyone looked at him, Hernandez raised both hands and waved them. "It doesn't say."

Tanner, who had been bouncing his squeeze ball while watching the screen, tossed it to his left hand. "I wonder what would've made her walk away from rising stardom. In South America, but still."

Kyle wondered the same.

Before any further speculation could be voiced, a hush fell over the group. Deanna's sharp "Shush!" sliced through the room. They all turned, straightening as they spotted his dad.

In a flurry of motion, Hernandez snapped the laptop shut, the screen's glow extinguishing as their huddled group dispersed. They scattered, returning to their desks or finding reasons to busy themselves elsewhere.

OLIVIA

After her talk with Collins, Olivia made her way to the task force office. The late Sunday afternoon cast long shadows across the nearly deserted parking lot. She checked her phone, confirming Deanna's earlier message that she was available. With a deep breath, Olivia pushed open the glass doors and headed straight to the lab, her heels clicking against the polished floor.

The lab was an organized chaos with all kinds of equipment now dormant, but a humming screen on one wall facing Deanna's workstation was alert and connected to a couple of computers. Deanna finished a call and hung up. Her face broke into a wide grin, and she offered a cheery wave. "Hey, Jane Bond."

Olivia raised an eyebrow, a smile tugging at her lips. She had no idea when Deanna had started calling her that. "Bond, Jane Bond." She did her best imitation of the iconic phrase. "What have you found out about Javier?"

The forensic expert grabbed her tablet. "Let's go up to the squad room. Ron wants an update, so save me from repeating myself." She motioned for Olivia to follow her.

Moments later, they walked into the squad room just as Ana entered from the opposite direction. The usual hum of activity greeted them as the team gravitated toward the large screen at the center. Olivia glanced around, noting the sense of urgency.

"Olivia, where'd you go earlier at the orphanage? You, like, disappeared." Ana thudded her belongings onto her desk.

Olivia hesitated. "I was chasing, um, a source."

Ana raised her eyebrows, but before she could probe further, Ron quirked a thumb at Olivia, his expression expectant. "I trust you'll give us an update."

"I will. After Deanna's report on Javier." As she spoke, Olivia couldn't help but notice the subtle glances the guys were casting toward Ana. There was a curious, almost uneasy atmosphere, and Ana herself seemed distracted, her gaze distant.

Ron, apparently picking up on the tension, addressed Deanna. "Report, then."

Deanna swiped her tablet, sending a flurry of documents to the big screen. "Jimenez didn't have any social media history before he ran for Congress. There's virtually nothing on him before then."

Olivia frowned. "What about his parents? I heard his mother had some kind of business."

Deanna shrugged, her fingers flying over the tablet. "He didn't list his parents' information on his campaign website, and I couldn't find anything official. His birth certificate listed Cristina Jimenez as his mother and no father. I dug into Cristina Jimenez, but no Cristina Jimenez in the US has a son his name and age."

This was getting weird. It was a hunch, but Olivia had nothing else to go on. "Could his mother be a foreign national?" Deanna stared at nowhere. "I never thought about that. That could totally explain it. But then again, it'd take a while to search the world."

"Only the Spanish-speaking countries."

"That still leaves practically the whole of South America and Mexico and Spain."

"How about just Spain?"

Before Deanna responded, Tanner caught the squeeze ball he was playing with and slapped it onto the nearest desk. "I find it interesting that Hugo's mother's name is Cristina Navarro with a sister, Lucia Jimenez. And this congressman listed Cristina Jimenez as his mother. Boss, do we believe in coincidence?"

ANA

The more Ana listened, the more convinced she became that Papi's suspicion was correct. "Did the ME report come in yet?"

Ron checked his phone, his expression one of mild distraction. "It did. I haven't had a chance to look at it yet." He squinted at the screen, then patted his pockets for his reading glasses without success. He extended his arms all the way out to see the screen better.

Kyle stepped forward, holding out his hand. "Allow me."

Ron handed his son the phone, and Kyle scanned the report, his eyes widening. "Well, this is interesting. The congressman had plastic surgery." A deep frown etched across his forehead. "I don't understand all these medical terms. Looks like several procedures."

Deanna snatched the phone. "I'm sending it to myself so I can get the translations." She tapped a few keys, then returned the phone to Ron. Moving to her tablet, she began deciphering the report. "Okay, he had a nose job, chin and jaw work, and facial fillers. Oh, man, he practically changed his entire face."

"Now, that begs the question. Why?" Tanner tossed his squeeze ball up and caught it, his brow furrowing.

"Usually, it means you want a whole new identity," Hernandez speculated.

Time to save them the trouble of further guessing. "I know who he was," Ana declared. "Javier Jimenez was Julio Perez."

A stunned silence followed, the room heavy with unspoken thoughts. Ana broke it, her voice steady as she explained the tattoo. "Deanna, could you put the tattoo on the screen and enlarge the lower right corner?"

Deanna nodded, pulled up the image, and zoomed in. Ana used a laser pointer to highlight the initials. "When I went to talk to Perez, he recognized it and asked me about it, but I didn't want to believe it. You see, it's JP. They gave me the ring—don't look so surprised, I know you guys figured it out. It was my ring. Anyway, I would have had my initials engraved on it if I hadn't left. Julio added the initials to his tattoo."

The silence deepened, the weight of her revelation sinking in.

Olivia, almost always the first to recover, crossed her arms. "Let me get this straight. Javier was Julio Perez. Grace's biological father. And his mother is Cristina Navarro."

Ana's nod confirmed Olivia's statement. "Yes, that's right."

Olivia's lips curved into a knowing smile. "Now it makes sense."

The lines on Ron's forehead crunched deeper. "What makes sense?"

Olivia stepped forward from behind Tanner. "Don't you see? Perez wants to turn himself in. Someone doesn't want him to. My source was hired by this someone to take Grace and use her as leverage. He doesn't know who his client is, but he figures they're based in Spain. He was also tasked with retrieving something from Jimenez. My guess is this something has to do with the Perez family business. And perhaps something else. But it's only my speculation."

"Who's your source?"

At Ron's question, Olivia lowered her arms and raised her chin. "MI6. It seems whoever is behind this whole thing is in Spain."

"But what would this person gain by keeping Perez in business? He's dying, so someone would take over anyway."

Olivia waved to Ana. "Do you know who would take over in the event of his death?"

Ana shook his head. "Seems he hasn't given it too much thought. Back in the day, Julio would have been the one to take over. But then, he left, or he became Jimenez. And Hugo doesn't want it. That's my sense anyway."

"What about his ex-wife, Navarro? They're divorced, aren't they?"

"I don't know." In a frustrated gesture, Ana pulled her pony-tail loose and fingered through her flattened curls. "Deanna, do you know?"

"Sorry to disappoint. I checked Jorge Perez. It looks like they were married outside of the US. Finding that would take a while. And if they divorce outside of the US, same thing."

"It's possible they were married in Spain." Ana rebanded her hair. "I never knew. It sounds like what we need might be in Spain."

Tanner stood up straight. "Boss, do we get to go to Spain? I'm in."

Hernandez snorted. "You don't speak the language." He jabbed a thumb at his chest. "If anyone goes, it's me."

Ana wasn't about to let them take over. "This is personal to me. I'm going."

Ron gestured with his hands to calm them down. "Nobody is

going. I don't have the budget for that. We'll alert Legat Madrid."

The boys groaned while Olivia smirked at them, a maternal gleam in her eyes. "MI6 has someone working in Spain. But you should alert your legat office to coordinate. I'll update you as soon as I know more."

CHAPTER 76
ORLANDO HOSPITAL/MIRROR ESTATE

DYLAN

Dylan waited with Lily, their gazes frequently darting toward the corridor. Lorraine and her parents followed the nurse to a private room where Michael would deliver the news. Lorraine had insisted Sean stay in the waiting room, shielding him from any potential bad news. Grace coaxed the boy to stay with her, offering soothing words.

Grace's parents made it to the hospital, and Alex introduced everyone in quick succession. They appeared mostly concerned about Grace who explained that Ana helped save her, but she had to go back to work. Then the priests gathered the small group—Grace, her parents, Sean, Alex, Kyle, Lily, and Dylan and his grandmother—in a heartfelt prayer, the soft murmur of their voices blending with the antiseptic hum of the hospital. The tension in the room remained palpable, everyone holding their breath as they waited.

Finally, the door to the private room opened, and Lorraine and her parents emerged, their postures more relaxed. Tears gleamed in Lorraine's eyes, and Dylan's heart dropped. Before he could stop her, Lily ran to Michael. "It's okay. You can... tell them," Lorraine told the doctor.

Michael nodded, taking a deep breath. "He's fortunate. The bullet missed his heart by millimeters. He's in recovery and will be transferred to the ICU later. The next few days will be critical. I did all I could. Now it's up to him. And God. I wish I had better news."

"Thank you!" Lily hugged him.

Disengaging, he smiled. "Say hi to your mom. Clara is excited to be the matron of honor. She's planning to shop with you guys."

As he spoke, a nurse approached and touched his arm to get his attention. "Excuse me," the nurse said. "Dr. Khoury, Dr. Jennings would like a word."

Michael excused himself and left.

An hour later, Dylan and Lily returned to the estate, Lily having gone home to fetch a change of clothes. They found Tommy already there, waiting for them. "It's nice of you to offer them a free hotel stay," Lily said.

Dylan shrugged and rummaged in his fridge while taking their drink orders. "Least I can do. Saves them some commuting time. If I know Max, he'll be back here tomorrow."

As they settled in around the patio table on the spacious balcony off Dylan's room, Tommy caught up on the latest news. "So, Lorraine's Kitchen is closed, then?"

Dylan cracked open his Duvel beer and tipped it toward Tommy. "Tell me if you like it. Max was trying to get me hooked on this imported stuff. And as for the restaurant, I don't think so. Lorraine has a sous chef and an assistant manager to help keep things running."

Tommy propped his feet up on the aluminum railing, gazing out at the expansive view. "I never get sick of this view." He took a long pull of the Duvel. "It's, uh, strong. I'm sticking to Bud Light."

Lily set her LaCroix berry water aside—the brand Dylan kept around just for her—then rose, and hung on the railing, overlooking the lush landscape. "It is nice, but nothing beats the view from a high-rise. The ICC still has the tallest building in Hong Kong. One hundred and eighteen floors."

Tommy's eyes widened. "Oh my! One eighteen!" He slurped at the froth coming off his beer as he jostled it. "What's ICC?"

"International Commerce Center."

Dylan reached into his pocket and pulled out the old, tarnished key. "Here's what we found."

Tommy's feet slammed to the wood deck as he sat up and leaned in to examine the key. "This is an ancient key. The key your mom gave you isn't this skeleton type."

"I know." Dylan turned it over in his hands. "So, I wonder what this unlocks. Maybe the rumor has some merit. The alleged treasure was buried a few generations ago. Maybe these are the kind of keys they used back then."

"Well, you guys said you were in a room with the symbols or codes that are on the map. Did you find anything? Like the cipher?" Tommy downed his beer.

Lily retrieved her berry water and sampled a tingly sip. "No, that room was more like a storage closet. Oh, you've got to go down there one day. You'd be amazed by all the hidden doors and secret passages. I felt like I was in a movie."

"That doesn't make sense. They hid this key in a toy, but they didn't hide the cipher there?"

Dylan opened another can of beer. "We searched everywhere. So, let's speculate. Let's say this key opens another box, just an older one. My mom gave me the key to open the box she and my dad buried. So, maybe this key opens another box my ancestors buried. Whether it's gold or other treasures, I don't know."

"We're back to square one. We need that cipher. Or at least the other half of the map would be good." Tommy disappeared inside, coming out with a bottle of water.

No one spoke as they considered the situation.

Then Tommy snapped his fingers. "I wonder if we can get one of those ground-penetrating radar devices you see on TV to scan the earth?"

"But we'd still need to know the area to scan," Lily countered.

Dylan took a swig of his beer. "We should thoroughly search the tunnels. We need to know all the trapdoors, hidden doors, everything."

Lily traced a line of condensation on her bottle, then pointed it at Dylan. "Get Alex back here to examine the system. He said it was impressive, and he's an expert at coding and codes and such. Maybe he can find a map or a way to map it."

Dylan cocked his head to one side, a smile curving his lips. "Actually, I think he'll be back without me asking. I overheard him and Eva. I suspect he might become a regular guest here."

Lily grinned. "So, you noticed too."

"What's going on? Who's Alex? Wait, Grace's brother, right? What about him and Eva?" Tommy asked.

"You'll see," Lily said with a knowing smile, the mystery deepening around them.

CHAPTER 77

COLLINS'S APARTMENT

OLIVIA

The unremarkable apartment building blended seamlessly into the cityscape. Olivia stepped into the modest lobby and took the elevator up to the eighth floor. She knocked on the door marked 8B. As the door opened, a sharp remark greeted her.

"I hope you didn't tell your FBI buddies."

She edged past Collins, the scent of freshly brewed coffee mingling with the faint smell of cleaning supplies. "Not my first rodeo. I only told them things related to Javier. Now, who's your contact?"

The sparsely furnished apartment appeared almost clinical with nothing personal to give away any hint of Collins's personality. While a single bedroom remained visible through a partially open door, the open-plan kitchen blended into a small dining area, and the living room contained just a sofa and a coffee table. Collins waved her over to a laptop open on the dining table, the screen glowing.

"She's here," he announced to someone on the screen.

Olivia moved closer, the wooden floor creaking under her boots. A familiar face appeared on-screen, though altered by time and hardship.

"Hello, stranger. Rumors were floating around that you were out of the game."

She smiled. "Now this is a surprise, Raven! Your intel saved me and Shadow Shot in Paris."

Raven's appearance had changed. Her once full cheeks were now hollow, her long black hair cut short. She looked ill but maintained a jovial demeanor. Sensing Olivia's concern, Raven glanced at Collins. "You didn't tell her?"

Collins cleared his throat. "Didn't have a chance. So, what you heard about the love of my life..."

Olivia's gaze darted between Raven and Collins, her jaw dropping before she broke into a grin. "Good one. Every lie is based on truth. You didn't die, but you must have been captured. They didn't disavow you, did they?"

Raven sighed. "They had to. I escaped, but don't worry. They basically shuffled me to another outfit, doing the same thing."

Olivia didn't want to guess how she escaped, but she could surmise Raven had suffered at the hands of her captors. "I'm glad you're fine. So, what have you got?"

"Are you still Phoenix? Are you back in the game?" Raven inquired, turning serious.

"No, not in the field anymore. A consultant with the Bureau. And forget who Phoenix is and call me Olivia."

"Will do." Raven's expression hardened. "Montoya doesn't know anything. He just pockets the money. I did a check of all his electronic communications and isolated one number. It's the same number as the one who called Falcon."

Olivia nodded, almost holding her breath against the implications. "Can you find out about Cristina Navarro and her sister, Lucia Jimenez? I just discovered that Navarro's son, Julio, who was said to have disappeared, resurfaced as Javier Jimenez."

"So, there's the connection." Collins snapped his fingers. "Luv, one or both of them could be behind this."

"Think with me." Olivia almost started pacing, but no, she needed to keep in Raven's sight line. "Your client wants something from Javier. He or she also wants Perez not to turn himself in."

"Hugo is not the one. I can tell you that," Collins said. "He just wants his art and gallery. Your buddies might have traced the IP back to the gallery, and that would be me."

"You hired the Irishman Gang?" Everything in Olivia stilled. She didn't like this idea.

"Oh no. I inherited the two idiots. I used the network to communicate with my client."

That connected with what she heard from the task force. But... "There's someone else. Someone else logged in from the network to hire the Irishman Gang."

"Really?" Collins's expression remained blank, but he must be thinking of possibilities. "There's someone, but let's focus on figuring out who would want Perez to hold onto his business for now."

"Someone who would benefit from it, I'll say," Raven suggested. "FYI, I checked Perez's will. He just filed a new one. He's leaving his estate to Hugo and his granddaughter. Nothing about the wife. So, assuming Hugo and Grace want nothing to do with his business, then his wife could potentially contest the will and make a claim for the business."

Olivia ran through what Simon told her about his conversation with Javier. Something Javier said about his family business still bugged her. Ana had said Julio would have inherited the business had he not disappeared. "I've got a wild idea."

"Let's hear it."

She shook the cobweb out of her mind. "It's all conjecture right now. What if Julio shows up? What would happen?"

Collins stifled a laugh. "He was a US congressman. I don't

think he had any intention of running a money-laundering busi-ness. Besides, why did he go through all that trouble to assume another identity if his goal was to run the business?"

"I know. But what if someone pressured him to do something?"

"Like what?"

"He hinted to Simon he might follow his footsteps to resign."

"Really?" Collins and Raven shared a look. "So, he would have been in contact with someone in the family or at least someone who had access to the family business."

All while they were talking, Raven had been typing. Now she said, "You might be onto something. I was checking the gallery's phone records, thanks to Falcon. One of the phone numbers traced back to Barcelona."

"But why are they using the gallery? Are they using it without Hugo's knowledge?" Olivia asked.

"Most definitely. Hugo has no interest in managing the gallery. He is into art and gallery. He relies on his old man's business manager to take care of things."

"Who's his business manager?"

"Mario."

CHAPTER 78

GRACE'S APARTMENT

GRACE

Finally, Grace was home. Even her modest furnishings seemed to welcome her back, as if the very walls and furniture were relieved to have her return. It felt like a home eager to embrace its long-lost daughter.

Alex flopped down on the couch, exhaustion evident in his posture. "Please don't get abducted again. Or receive any more threatening notes."

"Hey, it's not like I asked for these things," she retorted with a wry smile. She caught a whiff of her sweat and grimaced. "Yuck. I'm taking a shower."

On her way to her room, she paused. "I heard you were watching us. Did you see who shot the guy?"

"We were focusing on you. And I punched in on you guys, so we couldn't see who shot him. But I did rewind it and check. Thought it was Ana or Olivia, but I just saw a gloved hand with a gun sticking out the side of the door. Ana doesn't know who did it?"

"No, but she said she should thank the person who did it." She continued to her room.

Several minutes later, she emerged from the bathroom, refreshed in a T-shirt and shorts. Standing by the hamper, she patted down the pockets of her dirty pants to ensure no tissue paper was left behind. After several episodes of unwanted confetti in the washer and dryer, she had learned her lesson. Her hand brushed against something. She pulled out two pieces of paper and remembered—the strange symbols. Sean had handed her the map when they were pounding on the door to the chapel. The symbols or codes intrigued her. They resembled musical notes, but she knew they weren't. With a shrug, she tucked the papers into the drawer of her bedside table. She'd deal with them later.

As she returned to the living room, Alex spoke on the phone in the kitchen. His tone gave her pause—it was the voice he used when talking to a girl. Who was he speaking to now? She heard him mention Connor and the estate. Oh, Eva! Now that she thought about it, her brother and Eva had looked pretty cozy in the hospital waiting room.

Alex turned around, saw her, and ended the call. "Want something to eat? We can order pizza." He tapped on his phone, probably opening a delivery app. "By the way, Dylan offered me a gig."

"What do you mean? You have a cushy job." Grace took his phone, punched in her selection, and handed it back.

"He asked me to go back to the bunker and work with the systems to find or build a map of the tunnels. I work from home, so it's easy enough for me to operate from the estate."

"That was Dylan on the phone?" She couldn't imagine Alex talking to Dylan that way.

"No, that was Eva. Dylan texted me."

Speaking of computer systems—what about the piece of

paper she found? She hurried to her room, retrieved it, and gave it to Alex. "Do you know what these are? Codes?"

He examined the paper and frowned. "I've never seen anything like this. Computer codes are typically zeros and ones or words like HTML, header, etc. These look like ancient letters or symbols. You know, like Roman numerals. The X stands for ten, that sort of thing. What is this?"

"I found it in that room in the tunnel. The one with the strange symbols on the walls."

He tapped in his choice for pizza. "That place is something else. Parts of it's like the catacombs, and other sections look straight out of a movie. Then there's the state-of-the-art computer room."

So, not computer codes. She was about to put the paper back in her room when Alex took a picture of it. "What are you doing?"

"I'm going to do some research. Maybe something in that computer system matches these symbols."

CHAPTER 79

DINER/TASK FORCE OFFICE

RON

Ron sat in the cozy diner, the hum of chatter and clinking silverware creating a backdrop to his thoughts. He stirred his coffee as he glanced across the table at Spaulding, who was devouring the order he'd called his usual—eggs and bacon. Ron had opted for avocado toast, its green vibrant against the worn-out brown tabletop.

"You closed your case." Ron broke the silence. He took a sip of his coffee, savoring the warmth that spread through him. "So, why this breakfast invite?"

"Oh, nothing." Spaulding then took a hefty bite of his eggs. "All right, you're right. Regarding the congressman's murder, thanks to the video, it's closed. The video has been authenticated. And Tucker and Jimenez's wife were ruled as a murder-suicide. Everything checked out. The syringe with his prints, the cotton fiber in her nose. Then word came down to close the case."

Ron frowned and cut a corner off his toast. "Tucker and Jimenez's wife? I didn't hear about that."

Spaulding raised his eyebrows, pushing his plate away. "Strange. I thought Olivia would have told you. Sam Tucker, Jimenez's chief of staff, and his wife. He overdosed on insulin, self-administered, after suffocating the wife. They were having an affair. Whoever staged the scene was kind enough to leave us the syringe. Tucker's prints were all over it, and forensics found cotton fibers in Jimenez's wife's nose. The pillow was also conveniently placed by her side. But something isn't right. Tucker couldn't have beaten himself up. What gives? Olivia is hiding something."

Ron tapped lightly on the edge of his cup. Olivia mentioned MI6 as her source and someone with enough clout to get the police to close the case without tying up loose ends. It smelled like a cover-up, and if he had to guess, MI6 had something to do with it. "Honestly, I don't know," he admitted. "As for Olivia, join the club. She's just as tight-lipped around us."

After breakfast, Ron made his way to the task force office. He couldn't shake the feeling that the supposed murder-suicide was intricately connected to their current investigation. Olivia, as usual, was holding back information. He was lost in thought when Tanner poked his head into his office.

"Ready for the briefing, boss?"

Right. Ron stood and headed out to the squad room. His team looked more alert after a night's rest. He took a moment to address them, his gaze steady. "Before we start, there's no change in Connor's condition right now. Keep up your good thoughts and prayers."

He then beckoned Ana. "Why don't you go first? Now that we know Jimenez was Julio, have you found anything else?"

Ana nodded, her expression serious. "I talked to Perez again. He admitted he would have let Julio take over. If Julio was the same person I knew, he wouldn't have wanted it. Perez also said he didn't have much contact with Cristina or Lucia."

Deanna raised her hand like she was back in school. "Well,

now that I knew where to look, I found something about Cristina and Lucia. They're from a crime family too. Small time, but still. Their father, Juan Navarro, was a small-time crook, got caught in a bank heist as a getaway driver. Did his time."

Hernandez added, "I've read reports from their local police in Barcelona and Madrid. Juan Navarro's name is mentioned as a suspect in a few counterfeit currency seizures. But he was never indicted. He died last year."

"Who took over?" Ron finally broke the silence.

Hernandez and Deanna exchanged a glance. "We don't know," Hernandez admitted.

Kyle, who had been quiet until now, spoke up. "Any chance his daughters took over?"

Deanna shrugged. "It's possible. Cristina is an established artist. It could be a front. Lucia acts as Cristina's business manager."

Tanner, catching his squeeze ball, chimed in, "Maybe instead of looking for a Moneyman, we should be looking for a Moneywoman."

Arms crossed, Ron braced himself against the desk behind him. "Why would the Secret Service think the Perez family is involved?"

Kyle leaned forward. "Probably because they're not looking internationally. I'll bet the answer lies in Spain."

Ron shot his son a stern look. "I told you we don't have the budget for that. Tanner, did you alert Legat Madrid?"

"Yeah, boss."

"What'd they say?"

He hunched his shoulder. "Nothing. Said they'd look into it."

"Let me know as soon as they have something."

"You got it, boss."

The minute the briefing was over, Ana sidled up to him.

"He wants me to arrange a meeting with Grace."

He snapped his head toward her, eyes wide. "Perez wants to meet Grace?"

"Yes, which means I'll have to tell her about Julio and his family."

He almost reached to touch her arm, to offer this resilient woman some support somehow. Wouldn't be appropriate. He stepped back, physically and emotionally. "She deserves to know. But do you think she'll be receptive?"

Ana hugged her arms across her chest, her head ducked, and the toe of one boot scraping across the tiles. "She didn't seek me out. Circumstances got us together. And we've gotten along pretty well. So, there's hope she'll be just as open to her birth father's family."

"Good luck." He offered a supportive smile. That he could do, right?

"Just to give you a heads-up. This will all come to light when we file the reports. OPR will likely come after me." She looked him in the eye. "I'll face whatever comes."

He closed his eyes for a second. Once the Office of Professional Responsibility got involved, it always left a stain. Their investigation could destroy a good agent's career. And Ana was a great agent.

"It'll be all right," he told her.

"I hope so." Head high, she walked away.

He pulled out his phone to call Simon. Even though Simon left the senate a few months ago, he still had a lot of influential friends on the Hill. Besides, Simon worked with Ana before.

CHAPTER 80

MARINO HOTEL

LILY

After an exhausting weekend, Lily struggled to find the energy to start the new week. With a deep breath, she entered the grand hotel, her footsteps echoing in the elegant lobby as she made her way to her office. The polished marble floors and crystal chandeliers spoke of a bygone era of opulence, yet they did little to lift her spirits.

As usual, Dylan and Tommy were already there, waiting for her arrival. The soft hum of early morning activity provided a soothing backdrop as she approached.

"Did you guys sleep at all?" She cocked her head, taking in their disheveled appearance.

Tommy, leaning against the doorjamb, flashed a grin. "I did. Don't know about him." He slapped Dylan's arm. "You should have stayed, Lily. I can never get sick of being pampered at the estate." His words carried a hint of mischief, reminding her of the luxurious amenities they enjoyed over the weekend.

Lily dropped her belongings on the desk and joined them, ready for their usual morning ritual of sharing coffee before diving into the day's tasks. The office, with its warm, inviting décor and its large windows overlooking the city, had become a haven of productivity for them.

Dylan's eyes met hers, and a gentle smile curved his lips. "You look tired."

"It was a tiring weekend," she admitted, her mind wandering to the weekend whirlwind. "So much has happened. Oh, any word on Connor?"

Dylan dropped his hand to the small of her back, escorting her to their favorite table, his expression somber. "Last I heard, he hasn't woken up yet."

As they settled into the comfortable chairs, Lily broached the subject on her mind. "I think your best bet is to play your aunt's game. She may just have the map and/or the cipher."

"I don't know. I still think she's the one who updated the bunker. Who else knows about it? Who else has the financial resources to do that? And you know, the last time, she was telling me there was another something, but she got cut off by Olivia coming in."

"Another tunnel?" Tommy stirred his coffee. "Now you know."

"She also mentioned other people were looking for the treasures."

Lily brought her latte to her mouth, not drinking yet, just inhaling the invigorating aroma. Man, that smelled good. "Didn't Fr. Phil tell you these were rumors?"

"Rumors are what prompt people to look for treasures. Lots of treasure hunters out there." Tommy finished his coffee. He always drank too fast. Lily resisted the urge to chastise him for not enjoying life more fully. She savored her first sip, then lowered her cup to the table. "But nobody would know about the bunker and the tunnels."

"Other than the one who financed it." Dylan sipped his cup of espresso. "And it very well could be my aunt."

"But would she tell anyone else?"

"No, but she might farm out the job since she's a guest of the federal government."

"You're thinking your aunt would hire the Irishman Gang to look for the treasures?" Tommy gawked at that.

Dylan finished his espresso and set the empty cup on the table. "Oh, well, just a thought."

They continued their conversation while Lily finished her drink. Then they parted ways, each heading to their respective offices. Lily settled into her chair. The sunlight streaming through the large windows cast a warm glow on her desk. A runner entered, carrying a beautiful flower bouquet. He presented the vibrant blooms to her. "For you, Miss Roth."

"Oh, thank you!" she exclaimed, surprised by the stunning arrangement of lilies, roses, and tulips, their bright colors a stark contrast to her serious thoughts. But who could have sent them? Besides, what would be the occasion?

Curiosity piqued, she reached for the card nestled among the flowers. "Happy Birthday!"

Her frown deepened. It wasn't her birthday, and yet the card was addressed specifically to her. Intrigued, she opened the card, expecting to find a simple message.

Instead, a memory card was taped within, accompanied by a cryptic note.

CHAPTER 81

GRACE'S APARTMENT

ANA

Ana procrastinated about talking to Grace. After all, Grace was likely teaching at this hour. Ana paced the task force office, her gaze flitting to the wall clock. She couldn't put it off much longer. She stopped by the window, looking out at the cityscape, trying to steady her nerves. With a deep breath, she finally picked up the phone, intending to leave a voicemail. But Grace answered on the second ring.

"Oh, you're not at school?" Ana asked, caught off guard.

"No." Grace sounded tired yet relieved. "Alex made me take the day off, and I kind of agree it was a good call. It was an exhausting weekend."

Suppressing guilt pangs, Ana pushed on. "Yes, it was. So, how did you sleep? No nightmares?"

"No nightmares." Grace's tone lightened a bit. "Fits and starts, but I slept, thanks. I was thinking of going to the hospital to check on Sean and Connor."

Ana couldn't delay any longer. She took a deep breath,

steadying herself. "I was wondering if I could stop by for a bit. There's something important you should know."

About an hour later, they sat at Grace's kitchen table. The aroma of fresh coffee permeated the cozy kitchen, and soft late morning light streamed through the windows. Alex was at her desk in the adjoining room, earplugs in, engrossed in his work.

Ana had just finished telling Grace about Julio and Jorge Perez. Grace hadn't said a word. But was her silence a sign of processing or shock? Unsure, Ana watched Grace's face intently, noticing the subtle shifts in her expression as she absorbed the information.

Finally, Grace broke the silence. "So, Julio was my birth father. And for reasons unknown, he disappeared and resurfaced as Javier Jimenez, a US congressman from Texas. And he was recently murdered. His father, my grandfather, is dying from cancer and is the head of a crime family. Did I leave anything out?"

Ana took a deep breath, avoiding some details about Grace's abduction. "Pretty much covers it. Except your grandfather would like to meet you. How do you feel about that? You can take your time, and you don't have to meet him."

Grace looked around the room. The ticking clock seemed louder, each second amplifying the portents of their conversation. Then she whispered, "Is he scary? Like, evil?"

Ana almost laughed, shaking her head. "Papi—everyone calls him Papi—is not scary or evil. He looks normal and weak now."

"Do you know why he wants to meet me now?"

Papi had been keeping tabs on them. Why he waited till now to seek a reconciliation, she couldn't say. He was dying, and he planned to turn himself in. Perhaps that was the reason. She looked at Grace, everything in her softening. "Well, he's dying, so he probably doesn't want to go before meeting his only grandchild."

Grace took a deep breath, her eyes reflecting an apprehensive curiosity. Her hand caressed her cross pendant. Finally, she nodded. "Okay, I'd like to meet him."

CHAPTER 82

MIRAGE FINE ARTS

COLLINS

After a grueling night of meeting with Olivia and Raven, Collins had to slip back into his undercover persona and head to work. The fatigue weighed on him, but he couldn't show any signs of exhaustion. He navigated the early morning traffic with practiced ease, blending into the flow of commuters.

Upon arriving at the gallery, he straightened his tie, checked his reflection in the glass, then made his way to the back office. The receptionist, a young woman with sharp eyes and a permanent look of slight panic, greeted him with a nod.

"Morning," she whispered. "Mario is here. He's in the boss's office and looks intense."

"Oh?" Collins raised an eyebrow. Hugo wasn't even supposed to be in until later. What did Mario want? Collins forced a casual demeanor as he continued down the hallway.

He reached his desk, a nondescript workspace cluttered with papers and innocuous personal items that helped maintain his cover. He unlocked a drawer, the familiar click of the lock a comforting sound, and activated the listening device. Slipping the earbuds into his ears, he tuned into the bug he'd planted in Hugo's office.

Mario's voice came through, speaking in rapid Spanish. Collins's years of undercover work had made him fluent.

"I don't know how, but they found her... That's not what I heard. Somebody named Doyle... Are you sure? But she's... It wasn't my fault. How was I supposed to know he would get himself killed?... Okay."

Hmm. Mario was clearly involved, an insider feeding information to someone. Collins texted Olivia an update. Then messaged Raven to check the sisters' phones. They were getting close to discovering the mastermind behind it all.

Approaching footsteps jolted him back to the present. He stashed the earbuds, closed and locked the drawer, and faced the intruder.

Mario emerged from Hugo's office, his expression a mask of casual indifference. "Hey, morning. When is Hugo coming in?"

Collins shrugged, keeping his features neutral. "He's the boss. He usually comes in just before the gallery opens. Anything I can help you with?"

"Nah, I just came in to check the books. It seems all is in order." The big man headed out, his heavy footsteps echoing down the hall.

Collins frowned. Mario was the business manager, but he didn't handle the books. They had a bookkeeper and an accounting firm on retainer for that. Could Mario be siphoning cash somewhere else? If so, the auditors would have caught it, wouldn't they? Financial stuff wasn't Collins's forte.

To find out more, he logged in to the system using the bookkeeper's credentials. That much, he knew how to do. The glow of the computer screen illuminated his desk as he navigated the financial records. He downloaded all the files, the process taking longer than he'd like, each passing second heightening his tension.

Once he had the data, he prepared to send it to Olivia and Raven. The two of them could uncover if Mario was up to more than just being an inside traitor.

CHAPTER 83

ON THE ROAD/ORLANDO HOSPITAL

FR. PHIL

After morning Mass, Fr. Phil watched the few regular daily Mass goers leave. Some shook hands with him and others waved. The morning light filtered through the stained glass windows, casting colorful patterns on the worn pews. He made his way to the sacristy, where he checked his calendar. Nothing urgent. A tug at his heart reminded him to visit the hospital and check on Connor.

Outside, the crisp morning air greeted him. Birds chirped in the nearby trees, their songs mingling with the distant hum of traffic. As he walked to his car in the parking lot, hurried footsteps made him turn.

Jeremy jogged to catch up. "Phil, are you going to the hospital?"

"Yes." Fr. Phil unlocked his car doors.

"Mind if I join you?" The young priest headed to the passenger side. "I don't have anything scheduled until this afternoon."

"Not at all." Fr. Phil settled into the driver's seat and started the car. Once Jeremy was buckled in, Fr. Phil pulled out of the parking lot, the engine's purr adding to the morning's tranquility.

The easy camaraderie of two men dedicated to their faith highlighted the drive. They discussed parish business, their flock's needs, and the upcoming events requiring their attention. The city rolled by outside the windows, a blend of familiar sights and sounds.

"So, how did you like your first week as an associate pastor?" Fr. Phil glanced at Jeremy as they stopped at a traffic light.

"Oh, it was exciting." Jeremy chuckled. "I thought my marine days were over. I mean, I wasn't at the shooting, but neither was I expecting one in a small chapel parish like ours."

Fr. Phil smiled, his chest swelling. "That's good to hear. You never know when your skills will come in handy." After a beat, he added with a wink, "We're secret keepers. Remember that, my young padawan."

Jeremy laughed. "Yes, Master Obi-Wan."

Fr. Phil's thoughts drifted to the countless secrets he had been privy to over the years, some shared in confidence, others discovered by happenstance. These weren't even the ones people revealed during confessions. Thankfully, by the grace of God, he rarely remembered anything from the confessionals. But one particular secret had been on his mind since he learned the Ghost would be living on the estate grounds. As her move-in date approached, he'd better take action.

The cityscape gave way to the outskirts as they exited the freeway. The hospital loomed ahead, a stark contrast to the serene drive. Jeremy asked in jest, "Thinking about those secrets?"

You don't know how right you are! "Kind of, but I'm also concerned about Connor. He was just a kid when he showed up. I've watched him grow up."

They steered into the hospital parking lot, the conversation fading as their focus shifted to the visit ahead. He parked, and they got out and headed to the hospital entrance. The automatic hospital doors whooshed open, and they stepped into the sterile smell of antiseptic and the quiet urgency of a place always on the brink of crisis.

Fr. Phil led the way. Nurses and doctors moved about, their expressions betraying exhaustion and determination. At Connor's room, Fr. Phil paused and took a deep breath before pushing the door open.

CONNOR

All these voices in his head—Connor became aware of them gradually. At first, they were just noise, indistinct and overlapping, like a distant radio struggling to find a clear signal. He couldn't make sense of them. Did he die? He tried to open his eyes, but his eyelids felt so heavy. It was easier to drift off into the comforting darkness.

The next time he was aware of any noise, it was a child's voice.

"Daddy! Did you just move your hand? Are you waking up?"

That was Sean. How wonderful! The last thing he remembered was the gun moving toward his son, and he had begged the Lord to spare the boy.

"Look, Daddy is smiling!"

A few voices were talking at once. There was a lot of commotion. Maybe he needed more sleep. But then a hand touched his. "Honey, can you hear us?" Lorraine's voice came now, gentle and soothing. He felt her hand in his and managed to squeeze it, a small but significant gesture.

"Oh, he's waking up! He just squeezed my hand," Lorraine exclaimed, her voice breaking with emotion.

"Daddy, open your eyes! We're all here. Fr. Phil and Fr. Jeremy came to visit," Sean continued, his small hands shaking him.

Lorraine squeezed his hand again. "Fr. Jeremy gave you an anointing before you went into surgery, and Fr. Phil just did it again."

"Daddy, Grandpa wants us to call him as soon as you wake up, and Grandma went to get a change of clothes for us. Dylan let us stay at the hotel. Grace stopped by." Sean rattled off everything Connor missed. Then Sean's small hands shook him again, more insistently this time. "Daddy, wake up!"

"Sean, may I take a look at your daddy?" a calm, authoritative voice asked. Connor couldn't place it. Then someone lifted his eyelids one by one, and a bright light shone into his eyes. A doctor.

"How is he, Doctor?" Lorraine asked.

The doctor was speaking with Lorraine in a hushed tone. Connor didn't quite understand. Why couldn't he open his eyes? He told himself to relax, begged God to help, then tried again. Finally, he did it, blinking against the harsh light. He struggled to focus, his vision blurry. "Sean," he choked out.

"Daddy!" Sean's face appeared in his vision, a wide smile lighting up his face. "He's awake."

"Yes, he is," the doctor confirmed with a reassuring smile. "He's awake."

Connor's vision cleared, and he took in the room, the sterile white walls softened by his family's presence. Lorraine was by his side, her eyes red from crying but alight with love and relief. Sean stood next to her, his small hand still gripping Connor's arm. Fr. Phil and Fr. Jeremy stood a few steps back.

"Welcome back, Connor," Fr. Phil said. "We've been praying for you."

Connor tried to speak again, his throat dry and sore. Lorraine brought a cup of water to his lips, helping him take a sip. The cool liquid soothed his throat, and he managed a smile.

"Thank you," he whispered, his eyes meeting Lorraine's. He turned to Sean, his heart swelling. "I'm so glad you're safe." Tears still streamed down Sean's face. "I was so scared, Daddy. But you're okay now."

Connor reached out, pulling his son into an embrace.

"I'm okay," he reassured him, though his voice was thick with emotion. "Thanks to all of you."

Lorraine leaned in and kissed his forehead. "We've been right here, Connor."

Fr. Jeremy stepped forward. "Your strength and the love of your family have brought you through this, Connor. And God's grace, of course."

A profound peace warmed Connor, despite the pain and fatigue. "Thank you, all of you," he whispered, the effort of speaking leaving him winded. He paused to catch his breath, then managed to ask, "Doyle?"

"He's gone," Sean reported. "Agent Ruiz or Ms. Tso or both shot him. Grace was holding me and wouldn't let me look, but I heard it."

Connor breathed easier, his tense shoulders relaxing. A weight he had carried for years finally eased off his chest. With the relief so overwhelming, a tear escaped down his cheek. His family was safe, and the nightmare was over.

CHAPTER 84

TASK FORCE OFFICE

OLIVIA

After Collins texted her, Olivia went straight to the task force office. The message's implications had her heart pounding. She headed downstairs to the lab to find Deanna. As she moved through the hallways, her steps quick and determined, she ran right into Ron coming from the opposite direction.

"Oh, here you are. I believe you've got something to report." He narrowed his eyes.

Olivia hesitated, calculating the best course of action. "I have a lead on who's behind the abduction. But I need the phone records of a number." She resumed her pace toward the lab.

He fell into step. "What do you have?"

"My source said Hugo's business manager, Mario, made a call to a number in Spain. It sounds suspicious." She entered the lab.

The door slid close behind them, the lines on his forehead deepening. "MI6 is tapping his phone line?"

"No." She shook her head. "He just happened to overhear Mario's side of the conversation."

Deanna looked up from her workstation. "Morning, guys. How can I help?"

"I need the phone records for a specific number." She handed Deanna a slip of paper with the number Collins had provided, then waved at Ron. "I trust he'll have someone get a warrant."

Deanna nodded, her fingers already flying over the keyboard. "Give me a minute."

"So you're suggesting this Mario could be the inside man who tipped off someone about Grace's relationship to Perez?" Olivia sat on the edge of a desk. "I'm not sure how it all fits, but he's involved in some way."

Ron folded his arms, almost blocking the doorway. "Tell me how MI6 is involved in this. And why haven't you mentioned the congressman's wife and his chief of staff's murders?"

She pushed off the desk. She couldn't avoid it any longer, could she? "I need to get you authorized before I can tell you everything." She stepped out of the lab and called Jay. After going through the stringent security protocol, she was patched through.

"Jay, it's Olivia. We have a situation." She then summarized the recent developments and the need for authorization to brief Ron fully.

After a pause, Jay gave the okay. "Just the relevant parts. No assassination plot or auction detail."

When Olivia returned to the lab, Deanna had pulled up the list of phone numbers on the screen. "Any specific phone numbers you're looking for?" she asked as Olivia reentered.

"Yes, calls made this morning to Spain. Highlight all the times he called this number and any other numbers with the same country code."

Deanna, irritatingly chipper today, hummed as her fingers worked. Then she rolled back her chair and swiveled it. "There are only three calls, all to the same number."

"Can you check who that number belongs to?"

Deanna's upbeat humming stopped. "You're pushing it. Theoretically, I can, but it'll take time."

Time was something they didn't have. "All right, thanks." Olivia would have to get Raven on it later. For now, she motioned for Ron to follow her out of the lab. "I can read you in. Let's go to your office."

They strode through the busy corridors, bypassed the squad room, and headed to his office.

Ron closed the door behind them, sank into his chair, and locked his hands in his lap. "All right, report."

After a deep breath, she relayed everything she knew. "The MI6 operative we're dealing with poses as a contract killer or fixer. Through Montoya, he's been hired to stop Perez from turning himself in. That's the client's end goal."

Ron leaned back in his chair, his frown deepening. "The client's goal." Fingers still meshed, he opened his palms and pointed his thumbs at her. "What about MI6? How do they fit in?"

Jay's words rang in her ears. "Now, this is the part that will remain classified. Sorry."

He stared at her as if that would make her spill her guts. "Okay. Did the MI6 agent hire Doyle and the Irishman Gang to intercept Grace's first abduction?"

"No, I think Mario answered the Irishman Gang ad. Falcon, his code name, only inherited Doyle's involvement. This isn't typical for MI6. They don't outsource like that, and if they do, they use their own vetted people. I'm guessing Falcon needed to play his part."

Ron rasped his palms together. "Okay. Did he kill Tucker and the wife?"

"No, that is murder-suicide. Scene was staged for a reason, but no, he didn't kill them."

He hunched forward, elbows on his knees, chin braced on his clasped hands. "Anything else I need to know?"

"That's all for now. If I find out more, I'll let you know."

"We need to confirm Mario hired the Irishman Gang."

"It's being taken care of." She fished out her vibrating phone and read Raven's text.

CHAPTER 85

THE ROTH RESIDENCE/MARINO HOTEL

SIMON

Simon sat in his study, meticulously preparing for his final discussion with Ms. Carol about his potentially leading the Marino Foundation. The morning sun spilled through the large window, casting a warm, golden glow across the room, but his focus was almost entirely on his notes.

His phone buzzed on the desk, breaking his concentration. The caller ID showed Lily. Uh-oh. She almost never called unless she was in trouble. Kids only texted these days. He swiped to answer.

"Yes, dear?" Somehow, he kept his voice calm and reassuring.

"Dad, something came for you. At least it says it's for you."

Simon raised his eyebrows. "Are you at work?"

"Yes, that's why it's so strange."

Intrigued, he pushed aside his notes. "Okay, what is it? Why did you get it?"

"I got this bouquet of flowers with a Happy Birthday card. As you know, it's not my birthday. But I opened the card. Maybe it was a mistake. There's this tiny memory card, similar to an SD card, taped inside with a message that says, 'Ask your dad when we met.' Do you know what it means?"

Simon didn't answer right away. Several things ran through his mind. As a former ranking member in the Senate Intelligence Committee, he was familiar with intelligence operations. At least the concept of it. This type of cryptic note had intelligence all over it. But who would send such a note to Lily?

"Dad? You there?"

"Yeah, yeah, keep it safe. I'm on my way." He ended the call, and his finger hovered over the call icon. Should he let Olivia know? If it turned out to be intelligence-related stuff, she'd be more qualified to handle it. No. He slid his phone into his breast pocket. He'd check it out first. Maybe it was nothing.

About twenty minutes later, he arrived at the hotel. He knew how to get to the office building where Lily worked. The cheerful young receptionist greeted him with a bright smile. "Good morning, Senator."

"Good morning." He returned her smile. "I know where her office is."

He proceeded toward Lily's office. As he approached, Lily glanced up from a phone call, saw him, and pointed to the chair across from her desk. The bouquet graced the windowsill. Instead of sitting, he walked over to examine the lilies, roses, and tulips. They were ordinary flowers, but his instincts told him they carried hidden messages.

Lily ended her phone call and swiveled her chair his way. "Yeah, that's the bouquet. But here's the card." She opened a drawer and retrieved the card.

He took the card with gloved hands. "Just in case, I don't want to add my prints to the already contaminated envelope." He opened the card, revealing the SD card and the cryptic note.

"Do you want me to try to play it?" She held out a hand.

"Sure." He started to hand it over. Then drew it back. "Wait, no. In case it has some virus, I'd better have your mom check this out. You don't want any virus on your computer."

"Okay." Her delicate brow creased. "What do you think it is? Who sent it? Why send it to me?"

"I don't know." He examined the card again. "The Floral Emporium. Isn't that the hotel flower shop?"

"Yeah, it's one of the retail shops, atrium level." She reached for her phone. "You want me to call and find out who ordered it?"

"Let me do the snooping." He winked. "You know what your mom would say."

Lily rolled her eyes but smiled. "'Let her do it. It's just a phone call.'" She already had the directory up on her screen and was dialing the flower shop.

"Good morning, yes, it's Lily from Private Select Program. I received a bouquet this morning. Everything is fine. They are beautiful. Do you happen to know who ordered it? I was just wondering if it was Dylan. I'll hold." She smirked at Simon.

"Yes, room 1202. Got it, thanks. I'll have to tell him he's got competition from this secret admirer."

Hanging up, she beamed her triumph. "The congressman sent this—or his wife, which I really doubt. That's the room he was staying in."

CHAPTER 86

PARK

OLIVIA

O livia's phone buzzed, pulling her attention away from her notes. A text flashed across the screen.

RAVEN

Phone belongs to Lucia Jimenez. Will update when she's in custody.

Olivia texted Raven back a thumbs-up emoji before turning to Ron.

"I gotta go." She stood up and made her way out.

Sometime later, she found herself in a serene park. She sat on a weathered stone bench, surrounded by the scent of blooming flowers and the distant sounds of children playing. The warm air carried a gentle breeze, and leaves rustled in the trees overhead.

Collins approached from the opposite direction, his posture casual as he sat next to her, facing the other way. They both acted as if they were strangers, immersed in their own worlds. She held her phone up, pretending to scroll through messages, while he had earbuds in, seemingly engrossed in whatever was on his screen.

"What do you know?" she asked quietly, her lips barely moving.

He didn't turn his head, his focus fixed on his phone. "Once Raven has Lucia, we'll know if she's acting alone or if in cahoots with her sister. By the way, Cristina is on the way here."

Olivia frowned. "She's coming to see Perez?"

"Allegedly to visit the gallery displaying her artwork for an upcoming auction."

Her mind flashed back to something in Ana's report. "Hugo did say he hired you based on recommendations from his mother. Did you know that?"

Collins turned his head slightly, just enough to glance at her from the corner of his eye. "News to me. You know how it is. They give you a cover and you take it. No questions asked."

Olivia bobbed her head, understanding the unspoken rules of their world. Yet, it all felt too coincidental. "Any chance Cristina is your employer?"

He shrugged, a gesture almost imperceptible. "Let's wait till Raven has Lucia. We'll know more then."

Olivia mentally went through everything she knew again to put the puzzle pieces together. It seemed logical that whoever hired Collins was behind this whole thing. Assuming Mario was the one in the employ of Collins's client, Mario had to know who this person was. He was on the phone with him or her. Collins never had direct contact with this person. Perhaps they could get Mario to reveal who the client was.

She voiced this out.

After a pause, Collins said, "Sounds good, but we'd have to do it covertly. We don't have anything for a warrant by your country's standard."

She was aware of that. *This is a covert op. Different rules!* "I'm good with it."

"All right, leave it to me." He then ran his idea by her, detailing how they could pressure Mario into revealing the client's identity. They discussed it, tweaking the plan and considering the pitfalls.

Then Collins stood up and stretched as if he were just another parkgoer. "I'll make the necessary arrangements. Be ready."

Olivia nodded, already shifting to the next steps. "I will be."

Collins walked away, his movements unhurried. She waited another five minutes, during which Raven sent a new text message. She had Lucia.

CHAPTER 87

TASK FORCE OFFICE

SIMON

Even after Lily told him who might have sent him the chip, Simon couldn't shake the need for confirmation. He made his way down to the flower shop, a quaint store tucked between a bakery and a bookstore. The bell above the door chimed as he entered, and the humid air carried the heady scent of roses and lilies. The salesperson, a young woman with a friendly smile, looked up from arranging a bouquet.

He approached her, trying to appear casual. "Excuse me. My daughter, Lily, called a few minutes ago."

"Oh yes, Senator. How can I help?"

"Do you remember anything about the person who ordered the bouquet?"

Her brow furrowed in concentration. "Er, Hispanic or Middle Eastern, man. That's about all I remember. Sorry."

Simon smiled. "No worries. Thanks."

He glanced around the store, scanning the corners and ceiling for a camera. None were in sight. With a sigh, he turned to leave.

The bell chimed again as he stepped back onto the bustling street.

Even without a detailed description, he was more convinced it was Javier since the saleslady remembered a Hispanic man. Other than Olivia, who was busy with her own investigation, he didn't trust anyone else except Ron.

Thanks to his consultant status, Simon still had access to the task force office. As he navigated through the crowded streets, the afternoon sun was still high, casting short shadows on the pavement as he hurried to his destination.

When he entered the building, something felt off. Tension—even more than usual—charged the atmosphere, and a palpable energy seemed to hang in the air. Tanner brushed by him, offering a nod of greeting before rushing off. Simon spotted Ron standing by Hernandez's desk, deep in conversation.

He made his way over, quickening his pace. "Got a minute?"

Ron looked up, his expression strained. "Not really. What is it?"

With the busyness around him, Simon hesitated. He couldn't bother them during whatever crisis they were handling. "Any chance you could spare Deanna for a few minutes?"

Ron glanced around before jerking his thumb toward the door. "Yeah, she should be in the lab."

"Thanks." Simon headed in that direction.

The lab buzzed, as usual a hive of activity, but he found Deanna at her standing desk, focused on two screens, her hands flying over the keyboard.

"Hi there!"

Deanna almost jumped, turning around so quickly her hand knocked against her desk. "Oh, hi, Senator!"

"Sorry, I didn't mean to startle you."

She shrugged it off, a faint smile appearing. "It's okay. May I help you?"

He stepped forward and showed her the chip in a plastic bag.

"I'm just wondering if you could scan or somehow determine if this is safe to open."

Deanna took the bag and examined the chip. "What made you think it might be infected?"

"It's just the way it came to me. It was sent to Lily on a pretext."

"Oh, that's odd. Let's have a look," she chirped.

She plugged the chip into one of her contraptions, a sophisticated piece of equipment that hummed as it whirred to life. An icon appeared on the screen almost immediately.

"It's harmless." She released it and plopped it into his outstretched hand. "Encrypted though. Do you have a password?"

CHAPTER 88

MIRAGE FINE ARTS

OLIVIA

Olivia sat at a corner table in the coffee shop, her attention fixed on the gallery across the street. The glass panels allowed her an unobstructed view of the entrance, and she sipped her iced latte, feeling the cool liquid slide down her throat. Her fingers drummed on the table. It would've been better to have a partner stake out the other end of the street, but she was alone. Collins had assured her everything would go smoothly, so she had no choice but to trust him.

She didn't have to wait long. Her phone buzzed, and she checked the screen. It was Collins.

"Package secured. Meet me where we met last night."

Olivia tossed the remainder of her coffee into the trash can and hurried out to her car. The urgency in Collins's message was clear. She drove with purpose. Just what might they learn from Mario?

Soon, she stopped outside Collins's apartment building. She hesitated before shutting off the ignition. She couldn't let Mario see her face. From her trunk, she pulled out a small bag she'd packed for just this purpose. Not the face mask— she needed something less conspicuous. She opted for the wig and makeup.

Several minutes later, her new look in place, she approached Collins's door. She knocked in the predetermined sequence: three short raps, a pause, then two more. The door opened a crack, and Collins scrutinized her before letting her in. He was wearing a face mask.

Mario sat bound to a chair in the living room, his eyes wild. All the blinds were drawn, casting the room in a dusky light.

"Who are you people? Do you know who I work for? You're dead—dead, I'm telling you!" Mario shouted, his voice echoing off the walls.

Olivia and Collins ignored him. Instead, they sat at the desk in the corner, communicating through texts. They'd planned their strategy, intending to break Mario's defiance and make him talk.

Mario continued his tirade, cursing them and threatening them. Olivia watched him, noting the twitch of his eye, the clench of his jaw, the signs his bravado might soon crack.

Once Mario had stewed enough, Collins stood and approached him. Olivia moved to the side, her focus never leaving Mario's face.

"You can stop with the threats, Mario." Collins leaned in closer, his voice low and menacing. "We know who you work for."

Mario's gaze darted to Olivia, then back to Collins. "You won't get anything from me."

Collins smirked. "You think we don't know? Let me show you something." He pulled out Mario's phone and displayed his recent call logs. "You've been making a lot of calls to Spain. Specifically, to someone very close to Perez."

Mario's bravado faltered for a split second—a momentary flicker in his eyes.

"You recognize this, don't you?" Collins thrust the screen closer.

Mario's jaw flexed. "You're bluffing."

Collins's smirk widened. "Am I? What do you think Perez would say if he found out you were responsible for his granddaughter's abduction?"

Subtle tells edged into Mario's demeanor: a tremor in his hands, the sweat beginning to bead on his forehead. He was breaking.

"You don't know what you're talking about." But Mario's protest now lacked his earlier conviction.

Collins pressed on. "Do you really want to take that chance? Perez won't just kill you, Mario. He'll make you suffer. But, if you cooperate, maybe we can protect you."

Mario's shoulders sagged. He looked between Olivia and Collins, maybe realizing he had no other option.

"Fine," he muttered. "What do you want to know?"

Collins exchanged a glance with Olivia, their plan falling into place. He turned back to Mario. "Start by telling us everything you know about your boss."

CHAPTER 89

THE PEREZ MANSION

GRACE

Grace's fingers drummed on the armrest, her gaze flitting between Ana and the mansion ahead. Her heart raced and sweat slicked her palms. The old mansion loomed before them. Despite its age, the place portrayed a vibrant grandeur, a testament to its storied past.

Ana parked, got out, and turned to look at her. "Coming?"

Grace took a deep breath to steady her nerves and opened the door. She stepped out, and the gravel crunched beneath her sneakers. From the outside, the mansion wasn't nearly as magnificent as the Mirror Estate, but it was still grand, much better and bigger than the modest house she grew up in. Its ivy-clad walls and ornate windows hinted at the elegance within.

As they approached the front door, it creaked open. Standing before them was a frail old man—square jaw, prominent chin, and thinning gray hair. His once strong frame had been diminished by age, but his eyes still held a spark. He must've been a handsome man, the kind who commanded attention.

"Grace, I'm so glad you came." He offered a smile, his voice warm and welcoming despite its slight tremor. "Come in, please. Princess, thank you for bringing her."

Grace's heart continued to race as she stepped inside. Ana followed closely. The interior offered a blend of opulence and history. Ceilings adorned with intricate moldings towered over polished wooden floors that gleamed under the soft lighting. Antique furniture and tasteful decorations graced the rooms, each piece hinting at a bygone era.

"It's good to see you," Grace managed to say.

Ana placed a reassuring hand on her shoulder, giving her an encouraging smile. "We're here together."

The old man led Grace and Ana further into the house, his steps slow but steady. "This must be overwhelming for you," he said. "But I've been waiting for this moment for a long time."

Grace nodded. They entered a spacious living room where a fire crackled in the hearth, casting a comforting glow.

"Please, have a seat." He gestured to a plush armchair near the fire. "Can I get you something to drink? Tea, coffee?"

Grace shook her head, still trying to process everything. "No, thank you." She sat and clasped her hands in her lap to stop them from trembling.

Ana sat beside her, her presence steadying Grace's nerves.

ANA

As far as Ana could tell, Grace was curious to meet her biological grandfather. Still, unspoken questions hovered around the hesitant smiles. Grace's eyes sparkled, but the tremor in her hands betrayed the significance of the moment for her.

Before the two got too familiar, Ana scanned the room. It was just the three of them in the room. "Where's Mario? Isn't he your bodyguard?"

Papi scoffed, a hint of amusement in his eyes. "No, he's our business manager. For convenience, he works out of here. Look at me." He waved to his frail frame. "I don't need a bodyguard anymore."

"Why don't I let you two get acquainted? I'll look around." She caught Grace's eye, and her daughter nodded.

With Grace now engaged in conversation with Papi, Ana sought any clues about whoever was behind Grace's abduction. She made a show of strolling toward the lawn, admiring the vibrant flowers and trimmed hedges. But once out of sight, she doubled back and slipped into the house through the patio door.

She donned a pair of gloves and began her search in Mario's office. She checked the usual places—drawers, cabinets, under the desk. Nothing suspicious revealed itself at first glance. However, one drawer was locked. After ensuring no one was nearby, she picked the lock and extracted the sole item within—a single notebook. Her heart thudding, she flipped through the pages. A ledger of some sort, it displayed columns of dates, amounts, and notes written in code. She slid out her phone and snapped pictures of the pages, capturing every detail.

A couple of the codes were easy to decipher. Her breath caught. Mario must've been the inside man. He'd discovered Grace's existence about a year ago and sold that information for a significant sum. Ana's fingers trembled as she turned the pages, absorbing the implications.

Then she came across the latest entry—"Queen returns." She paused at the strange words. What did it mean?

Ana restored everything to its original place before slipping back out to the living room through the garden. She stepped in at the same time Papi looked up and gasped.

"It's been ages! This must be our granddaughter. And, Princess, it's been far too long. Now, come over to Papi's side slowly."

CHAPTER 90

SPAIN

RAVEN

In the gloomy windowless room, Raven approached Lucia Jimenez, her footsteps padding on the concrete floor. The flickering light overhead cast eerie shadows on the walls, heightening the tension in the air. Lucia sat in a metal chair, her hands trembling, eyes wide with fear. Raven scrutinized her, her instincts on high alert. Either Lucia was an exceptional actress, or something was very wrong. It didn't add up—a brilliant mastermind capable of orchestrating Perez's granddaughter's abduction shouldn't appear so timid.

Raven flashed her Interpol credentials. "Señora Jimenez, we just want to ask you a few questions."

Lucia nodded, her face pale, lips pressed into a thin line. Raven took a seat across from her, laying out a list of phone calls Lucia allegedly made, along with the evidence tracing the IP to her Barcelona home.

"Wait, let me see." Lucia reached out, her hand shaking, her voice whispering.

Raven handed over the list. Lucia studied it, her brow

furrowing with each line she read. "You took my phone. Please, check my calendar. You'll see I was in Paris on one of those dates. Depending on the time of day, the only time I was alone was when I slept."

"You could have rerouted your phone to make it appear it was in Spain."

For the first time since Lucia was taken, she scoffed. "I wouldn't know how even if I wanted to."

Raven cursed. She should've dug deeper before bringing Lucia in. Could Navarro have been tech savvy enough to set this up?

"One moment." Raven slid out her phone and accessed the date Lucia mentioned, cross-referencing it with travel records. The calls were made from Spain according to the cell tower. Her memory told her there was no bouncing back and forth. Lucia was telling the truth.

Raven shot a text to Olivia and Shane.

RAVEN

Lucia is innocent. Navarro set her up. Digging deeper now.

She followed up on the other dates listed, delving into travel records, phone logs, and digital footprints for any inconsistencies or clues to reveal Navarro's involvement.

Lucia twisted her fingers together. "I swear, I have nothing to do with whatever you're investigating."

An Interpol alert flashed on Raven's screen. The two sisters were registered owners of Holding Mediterráneo, SA—a company intricately tied to the Moneyman operation. Could this woman be that skilled of an actress?

Raven steeled her gaze as she leaned forward. "Explain why you and your sister are listed as owners of Holding Mediterráneo, SA. What exactly does the company do?"

Lucia's eyebrows knitted together. "I don't understand. I've never heard of it. I have no knowledge of my sister's business dealings. I only manage her art business."

Raven straightened her stance, her fingers flying over her tablet's keyboard. Minutes stretched as she pieced together the digital trail. Navarro had been meticulous, but not infallible. Discrepancies emerged—anomalies in the IP addresses, time stamps that didn't quite match up. She forwarded the new evidence to Olivia and Shane.

"Where is your sister now?"

"She's going to America. Said she had some business to take care of."

Not good. Raven texted Olivia and Shane right away. If she had to guess, Navarro was headed to Florida, but why? She had no idea.

CHAPTER 91

TASK FORCE OFFICE

RON

Ron and his team gathered around the screen for the briefing. Deanna was absent, still in the lab assisting Simon, but she wouldn't have any new information to report. The tests they were running required time and patience. Ana was out in the field, escorting Grace on a visit to Perez where she hoped to dig up any leads. The absence of a few key players didn't diminish the gravity.

Tanner broke the silence, his voice steady, but excitement brightened his usually wary eyes. "Agent Davis has some good news." He pressed a button on the remote. The screen flickered and split into two, one-half displaying an email, the other showing a live feed of Agent Davis.

The Secret Service agent appeared, her expression serious yet confident. "Our tech found the money trail." Her voice resonated through the room. "They traced it to an offshore account. I've forwarded the details to you guys."

Hernandez's fingers flew over the keyboard, pulling up the

email Davis had sent. The text appeared on the left side of the screen, while Davis's live feed remained on the right.

Ron scanned the email, his brow furrowing as he processed the information. "It's a holding company," he murmured, more to himself than anyone else.

"Yes," Davis confirmed. "And it is registered in Spain, which makes it harder to trace the ownership. But we got lucky. Interpol has been investigating this company, and they're willing to share intel. The registered owners are Lucia Jimenez and Cristina Navarro."

A collective murmur ran through the room. Heads turned, eyes widened. Kyle, always quick to connect the dots, spoke up. "They're Hugo's aunt and mother."

"Yes, indeed," Davis replied. "So perhaps the Perez family is involved somehow."

Ron dipped his chin. "They're both in Spain. We'll alert our legat."

"We also alerted Interpol," Davis added. "Do you have anything to share?"

Nobody piped up, so he shook his head.

"Okay, then." She swiveled to someone off the screen and swung back. "Sorry, gotta go."

She clicked off.

"Hernandez, dig deeper into this holding company. See if you can find any connections Interpol might have missed. Tanner, get in touch with Legat Madrid. We need eyes on the ground."

Hernandez nodded, already turning back to his laptop while Tanner picked up his phone to make the necessary calls.

Ron's phone buzzed. He was going to decline, but Olivia's contact number flashed. He excused himself and swiped to answer. "Cristina Navarro is in town. Tell Ana."

"She's not here. I think she's with Grace."

"Can you ping her phone?"

Ron was already motioning for Hernandez to do so. "Yes, Hernandez... She's at the Perez address."

"Thanks." Olivia hung up.

Ron tried calling Ana, but only got her voicemail. He had a bad feeling about this. He leaned toward Hernandez. "I bet Perez has security cameras. Can you check?"

The young agent glanced at him before typing furiously. Moments later, he pointed to the screen, and Kyle muttered a curse under his breath. While there were no cameras inside the house, several covered the exterior. One showed the front door, another the garage.

On the screen, a woman matching Navarro's description stepped inside. Her body language was tense, and Ron sensed her intentions were far from good. What was worse was the reflection on a window. She was holding what looked like a gun.

"Can you zoom in?" He pointed to the reflection.

Hernandez did.

"We need to go. Grace is there," Kyle said.

Ron inclined his head. "Grab your gear."

CHAPTER 92

THE PEREZ MANSION

ANA

Ana's pulse thrummed in her ears as she assessed the situation. Grace and Papi were at gunpoint, and the cold gleam of Cristina Navarro's weapon left her no choice. She sidled up to Papi, her movements deliberate and slow to avoid any sudden reactions from Cristina.

"Put your weapon on the floor and kick it over here," Cristina commanded, her voice as steely as the gun she held.

Ana hesitated for a second, then placed her gun on the floor, and kicked it toward Cristina. The weapon skittered across the wooden floor, coming to a stop at Cristina's feet.

Ana risked a glance at Grace. Despite the fear in her eyes, Grace's expression was defiant. Her chin was set, and a spark flared in her gaze.

"I don't believe you're my grandmother. If you were, you wouldn't be pointing a gun at me."

Cristina's eyes narrowed, and her lips twisted into a cruel smile. "You have a lot to learn about our family history."

Ana had to take control of the situation. In her mind, the

puzzle pieces began to fall together, but the whole picture was still elusive. "You're the one behind it all. Mario is your inside man. So being an artist is just a cover?"

Cristina smirked, her eyes gleaming. "Art is my passion, but *this* is business. Family business. Princess, this is something even you don't know. My family's enterprise helped Jorge build his. So, it's only fair for him to return what belongs to my family."

Cristina's family? Hadn't Deanna mentioned that Juan Navarro was a small-time crook? That didn't align with what Cristina was saying. "I thought Juan Navarro was a nobody."

Cristina's smirk widened. "Juan serves my father. Carlos Mendoza was my real father."

Carlos Mendoza—the name struck like a thunderbolt. He was infamous, the head of a major crime family. Everything clicked into place, yet new questions emerged.

OLIVIA

As soon as Olivia heard Ana was at the Perez address, she headed there. On the way, she updated Collins, who offered to be her backup. She appreciated the offer but told him to keep his cover. Ron and his team would arrive soon.

Parking a block away, Olivia used the tree cover and neighboring houses to approach the Perez residence. Adrenaline sluiced through her as she moved stealthily. Reaching the side of the house, she peered through the glass patio door.

Cristina had Grace, Ana, and an older man—likely Jorge Perez—at gunpoint. Ana's weapon lay discarded on the floor, and tension claimed Ana's posture as she tried to engage Cristina in conversation.

Olivia pulled out her phone and started recording, hoping to capture any useful information. Cristina's words answered some of Olivia's lingering questions. The web of deceit and family ties was more complex than she'd imagined.

Ana continued to engage Cristina, trying to buy time. "Why did Julio become Javier Jimenez? Did he know about Carlos Mendoza?"

The woman's expression didn't change. "Oh, he knew. He knew all right. He tried to run away from his heritage. But I knew I could get through to him. He would have done as I asked if his cheating wife and her lover hadn't killed him."

On hearing this, Olivia frowned. That wasn't what she understood from Collins. Then, again, Collins still hadn't found Javier's intel. Perhaps that would answer the question. However, a more pressing matter was whether she should intervene now or wait for Ron. She trusted Ana to take care of herself if given the opportunity. However, there were two other people. If only she could get Ana's attention...

ANA

Ana kept Cristina and her gun in her vision, every muscle in her body tense. Papi, standing by her side, took a deep breath and stepped forward. "Cristina, why don't you and I talk this out? You have nothing against our grandchild. It's me and my business you're after."

He began to saunter toward Cristina, his movements slow and deliberate. Ana's focus followed his every step as his hand behind his back made subtle gestures toward the patio. She risked a glance in that direction. Oh! Olivia was there and signaling her.

Ana gave a slight nod to acknowledge Olivia. Papi was already providing a distraction, and soon an opportunity would arise to take control. Her primary concern was ensuring Grace's safety.

Cristina's focus locked on Papi, suspicion narrowing her gaze. "Stay where you are, Jorge. This isn't just about you. It's about restoring what my family lost."

Papi kept moving. "Cristina, we can work something out. There's no need for violence. Let Grace and Ana go. This is between us."

Papi's gaze flicked toward Grace, and Ana understood. She shifted, positioning herself to shield Grace if things went south, calculating the best moment to act.

Cristina's attention wavered, her grip on the gun tightening. "You think you can talk your way out of this?"

Papi took another step closer. "I never wanted any of this, Cristina. We can make amends, but not like this. Let's put the gun down and talk."

Ana's taut muscles tensed. Olivia inched closer to the patio door, ready to make her move. With the tension so palpable, each second stretched into an eternity.

Cristina's gaze darted between Papi and Ana, uncertainty slackening her expression. "Stay where you are!"

Olivia burst through the patio door, her gun trained on Cristina. "Drop the weapon, Cristina! It's over!"

Ana lunged sideways, grabbed Grace, and pulled her to the floor, shielding her with her body. Papi took advantage of Cristina's distraction and tackled her, but he was too weak to wrestle the gun from her.

Cristina screamed and aimed at Papi.

A shot rang out.

Ana held Grace down.

Sirens whirred closer and closer.

Grace screamed.

Olivia checked Cristina's pulse. "She's alive." Then she helped Papi up.

Ron and his team burst open the door with their guns out.

"A little late! We're all good." Olivia then briefed Ron. Ana followed with her own report.

As the paramedics arrived, Ana flagged one down to check on Papi while the other tended to the wounded Cristina.

CHAPTER 93

TASK FORCE OFFICE

SIMON

Simon froze. Password? What was the password? "I can try to crack it, but it'll take some time," Deanna's earlier words still rang in his ears. He flipped the chip in his palm again. Just what crucial information had Javier encrypted on it? Why the secrecy? Why hadn't he just handed it over at the hotel lobby bar? The flower delivery nagged him, bringing with it a possible clue.

He pulled out his phone and called Lily. After a few rings, she answered, and papers rustled in her background.

"What message came with the flowers?" he asked.

"Ask your dad when we met. Why? Did you open it? What is it?"

"I haven't opened it yet. But I'm thinking that's a clue to the password. Will let you know. Thanks, dear."

Ending the call, he passed the chip to Deanna, who peered at him with a raised eyebrow. "We met at freshman orientation when we were first elected to Congress." He then told her to try the year.

Deanna typed quickly. After a moment, she shook her head. "Nope, six digits."

Simon frowned. "Try adding the month."

Deanna's fingers danced across the keyboard again. Another pause, then a shake of her head. "Nope. Do you have the exact date?"

Simon rubbed his temples, searching his memory. The first date of orientation had to be it. He rattled off the date to Deanna, hoping it was right.

Deanna entered the date, and her eyes widened. "Oh, wow! Eyes only, Senator." She pointed to the screen.

Simon stared at the screen on the wall. The names of the documents and files confirmed it—he had hit the mother lode. "All right, so I can just insert that into my laptop and use that password to open all these, correct?"

Deanna carefully removed the SD card from her computer and handed it back to him. "Yes, sir."

Simon's fingers closed over the card. Then he gestured toward her desk in the back office. "Do you mind if I read it at your desk back there?"

"Not at all. I'm out here working anyway." Her attention already shifted back to her screen.

Simon made his way to the back office. He settled into Deanna's chair, the desk a quiet refuge from the bustling lab. After signing in with his consultant's login, he inserted the SD card and typed in the password. A plethora of files cluttered the screen, more than he could sort through in one sitting.

He began browsing, skimming titles and keywords until one file caught his eye—SIMON.README. His curiosity piqued, he clicked on it. The file opened to reveal a note from Javier.

After reading it, he logged off, retrieved the card, then went to look for Ron. But the squad room was empty, and Ron wasn't in his office. He called Ron and got his voicemail. He did the next best thing by calling Olivia.

"Not a good time," she said by way of greeting.

"I have Javier's intel. Cristina Navarro is behind everything."

In the pause, he thought she had hung up, but then she came back on. "We have her. Did he have evidence?"

"You have her. She's here? Where are you?" Commotion clamored in her background.

"Yes, Jorge Perez's house. Long story. Did he give you any evidence?"

"I didn't get to see them all. But there are a lot of files and photos. Ledgers and phone logs and such."

"All right, where are you?"

"Task force office."

"Stay there. I'll be there once I'm done here."

"Is that Ron's voice I hear?"

"Yes, I'll let him know."

CHAPTER 94

TASK FORCE OFFICE

RON

When they wrapped everything up, it was almost 5 p.m. Fatigue settled in Ron's bones as he and his team headed back to the task force office for the debrief. It had been a long and grueling weekend, and all he wanted was to finish and send everyone home.

When they entered the office, Olivia was already there with Simon, both looking unusually tense.

"Ron, you should see this first before your team's debrief."

Spurred on by her urgency, he led them to his office.

"I'll need to use your computer." Olivia nudged his desk chair aside and leaned over his computer.

Ron stepped aside as she inserted an SD card into his computer and typed in a password. She sent the files to the screen on the wall, and a series of documents and folders appeared.

"Okay, what am I looking at?" He slid into his chair and scanned the screen once Olivia moved away, not recognizing the significance.

Simon stepped forward. "Javier sent this to me via Lily. His note explains it."

When Ron waited for him to elaborate, Simon pointed to a document on the screen labeled SIMON.README.

Simon,

If you're reading this, I've met some unfortunate end. The documents and files are self-explanatory, but here's a bit of background.

I was born Julio Perez—Jorge Perez is my father. And that's only half of it. My mother, Cristina Navarro, is from a powerful crime family in Spain. As a naive young man, I allowed my mother to convince me to change my name and appearance. Something I didn't know at the time—she has been grooming me for this moment.

Before you question, I never betrayed our country or revealed any secrets. I've gathered all the relevant communications between her and me and others, as well as some other pertinent documents. I was supposed to hand this over to a designated agent from the MI6, but before he made contact, I received threats.

So, I took the precaution to give you this, trusting that you will get it to the right person. By the way, I had no idea she had such an ambitious plan.

Thank you.

Javier

The note from Javier was open alongside a multitude of files and folders on his monitor. Ron leaned back in his chair, scanning the text while debating the next steps.

"Should I dive into this now or brief the team first?" he muttered to himself, tapping his fingers on the desk.

Olivia, standing near the door, leaned against the jamb. "By the way, one file is restricted. I have to get it back to my contact and my superior."

Ron had long since grown accustomed to the layers of secrecy that came with Olivia's CIA affiliation. "As long as it has nothing to do with our current case, that's fine. But before you go, tie it all up for me, please."

Olivia did.

CHAPTER 95

TASK FORCE OFFICE/CAFÉ

OLIVIA

Olivia stepped out of the task force office, the cool evening air providing a calming contrast to her heated thoughts. Beside her, Simon matched her pace, studying her. They walked in silence, each absorbed in their thoughts.

"What are you thinking?" Simon broke the silence.

"Javier said he received threats. But from whom?" She couldn't shake the feeling that all wasn't as it seemed.

They stopped by his car, the streetlights casting long shadows on the pavement. She turned to him, searching his eyes for reassurance. He leaned in, and she kissed him goodbye, their moment of intimacy brief but comforting.

"I know you will figure it out." He fingered a tress away from her face, then cupped his palm to her cheek. "Be safe." She nodded, smiling as she continued toward her car. Sliding into the driver's seat, she took a deep breath. She pulled out her phone and dialed Jay's number, her fingers tapping as it rang.

"Jay, it's Olivia. I need to update you on the situation and bounce some ideas off you."

"Go ahead." His voice crackled through the speaker.

"I think Falcon is here to do a job, but the MI6 may have other agendas they don't want us to know about."

Jay paused, the silence on the line almost palpable. "Have you read the files?"

"Not thoroughly. One of them did catch my eye. It's a document about a quantum stealth suit. I think a prototype is being developed. If it works, it'll make clandestine activities much easier."

Jay remained silent for a minute, obviously processing the information. "This is what they're after. Send me the files through the secured line. Give him only the file he was tasked to find."

Olivia agreed, understanding the gravity. "Got it. I'll send them right away."

She hung up, accessed the secured line on her laptop, and transferred the necessary files to Jay. Her head pounded. Just imagine the implications of the quantum stealth suit, the potential it held, and the danger it posed if it fell into the wrong hands! The transfer complete, she sat back.

Only one more detail to confirm. Perhaps Collins would provide the answer. Shortly later, she met up with him in a discreet café, the hum of quiet conversations providing a comforting background noise. She handed him a small, encrypted drive containing the one file he was tasked with finding.

"Have you read it?" Collins palmed the drive.

"Yes." She took a sip of water. "The plot turns out to be a long-term plan. No immediate threat. But there is an outline of her plan. Now you can thwart it. By the way, we have Navarro."

Collins's face lit up. "That's fantastic!"

"And Mario?"

"I sent him to your FBI as a gift." He winked. "There's nothing else in the drive?"

"Just a private note to Simon." She shrugged.

He looked disappointed but nodded. "Oh, well. Raven found enough evidence on the Mendoza family for Interpol to make arrests."

"I'll call that a win." She raised her water glass.

He touched her glass with his coffee mug. "It was good working with you."

"One more question. You were monitoring Javier. Did you see who threatened him?"

He smiled. "Nothing escapes you. I believe you have something called 'pleading the fifth.'"

She smirked. "I thought as much."

"And I assume your government is holding onto something." He put some cash on the table. "On me."

"No comment."

The two countries were allies, but they still each liked to keep certain things to themselves. Both understood that.

"By the way, sending your daughter and her wealthy boyfriend to the gallery would have been a better move. Your senator is too well-known."

He had obviously done his homework, but she wasn't going to drag Lily into the world of deceit. "Leave her out of our world." She stood up. "You're gonna leave the gallery?"

"Not for me to decide." He got up.

CHAPTER 96

ORLANDO HOSPITAL

ANA

When they wrapped things up at the Perez mansion, Ana took Grace to the hospital to check on Papi. The drive was quiet. She glanced over at Grace, who sat subdued in the passenger seat, her glazed eyes fixed on the passing scenery.

"I'm sorry your birth family isn't picture-perfect." Ana broke the silence.

Grace sighed, her shoulders sagging. "I didn't expect it to be. But several weeks ago, I found out you, my birth mother, were a federal agent. And now, I know my birth father's side of the family is a mob of criminals. It's just so, so messed up."

Ana's heart ached for the girl. "Well, as far as I know, Hugo, your uncle, is not involved in the business. He owns an art gallery."

Grace nodded. "Will I meet him?"

"I'm sure it'll happen."

After a beat, Grace said, "Thank you—thank you for giving me the good genes."

"Believe me, I'm no saint. And you didn't get all of it from me. You got your musical talent from Julio. And I just learned he wasn't a bad person either. He resisted his mother's coercion and planned to turn her in. In fact, he left his collection of evidence for the authorities."

Grace blinked doe-wide eyes at her. "He did?"

Ana dipped her chin. "Yes, he did. He wanted to do the right thing, even if it meant going against his family."

Minutes later, they arrived at the hospital. Ana parked, and they made their way inside. She flashed her credentials at the reception desk, and they were directed to Papi's room.

GRACE

Even though she only just met this man, he wasn't as scary or evil as Grace had imagined. In the short time they talked, Papi, as he insisted she call him, was genuinely interested in her. He confessed he had "stalked" her. So, it was him at the Christmas program last year! And he had secretly visited her apartment to see how she was living.

"What did the doctor say?" Ana asked.

"I'm fine. No broken bones," Papi replied.

Someone rushed in. "Papi, you okay?" The distinguished-looking middle-aged man hurried to Papi's bed.

"Relax, Hugo. Stop fussing over me. Meet your niece, Grace. She's got Julio's musical talent."

The man looked over at her and then Ana. "Princess, I can see you in her."

"I haven't been Princess for ages," Ana said.

Hugo approached Grace. Without warning, he hugged her and kissed her on the cheek. "Welcome home, Grace!"

CHAPTER 97

TASK FORCE OFFICE

RON

After Olivia and Simon left, Ron sat at his desk, organizing his thoughts before heading out to the squad room. The quiet hum of the office provided a brief moment of clarity. He checked the clock and took a deep breath, preparing for the debriefing.

As he walked into the squad room, the team gathered around the large screen, as usual.

"All right, let's make it quick so we can all go home."

Tanner stepped forward, a stack of documents in hand. "Olivia sent me a bunch of documents from her source in Spain. It's got everything we need to prosecute the Moneyman—or in this case, Moneywoman. I updated Agent Davis and forwarded the files to her. So, as we all know now, Cristina Navarro is the Moneywoman. She's behind Grace's abduction."

"How's she behind it?" Kyle asked.

"She's the congressman's mother. As we discovered, the congressman was actually Julio Perez. She didn't want Jorge Perez to turn himself in—usually, it means he would have to turn over his business dealings and files. Her inside man, Mario, tipped her to the old man's plan to, quote, unquote, invite Grace to meet him. She orchestrated the whole abduction."

"But she was in Spain, no?" Hernandez folded his arms, leaning back against his desk.

Ana rushed in then, her breath slightly labored from hurrying. She must have heard the last bit. "Yes, she was, but she contracted it out through Rafael Montoya. Shane Collins is the hired gun."

Ron put it together. "Mario is the inside man. He feeds the information to Cristina. From the documents, call logs, and dates, Interpol determines that Mario hired the Irishman Gang on the dark web. Then Collins came on the job."

"So, he inherited the Irishman Gang?" Kyle asked.

Ron nodded. "According to the call logs and texts, that would be the case."

"Are they all in custody?" Hernandez asked.

Tanner waved the documents still in hand. "Cristina is, but a few agencies, including ours and Interpol, are fighting to keep her. Mario is in our custody. Collins is not. I understand he's an undercover agent. I got all this from Olivia."

Ana's eyes went wide. "Collins is FBI?"

"No, he's MI6," Ron corrected.

Ana frowned. "MI6? What's their interest?"

"Above my pay grade. All we need to know is Cristina is the Moneyman—or woman. She's behind Grace's abduction. Even though she didn't kill Perez's man, she's ultimately responsible. And is Jorge Perez still planning to turn himself in?"

Ana's frown relaxed into a soft smile. "He's prepared to. His attorney will accompany him."

"That's good. He'll turn over all his operation details, correct?"

"That's my understanding."

"Great!" Ron sighed as the weight lifted off his shoulders. "Looks like we've covered everything."

"What about the congressman's murder?" Kyle asked.

"Where have you been?" Deanna playfully punched his shoulder. "His wife and the chief of staff killed him. And then, they killed themselves. Karma."

"All right, good work. Go home!" Ron clapped his hands.

CHAPTER 98
FEDERAL DETENTION CENTER

DYLAN

Dylan walked into the visiting room with Olivia, his steps slapping against the tiled floor. The Ghost was already seated, her posture relaxed yet commanding.

Olivia sat across from the Ghost. "We got the Moneyman, well, Moneywoman."

The Ghost nodded, the faintest smile curving her placid lips. "Good to hear you got Cristina."

Olivia smirked. "So you knew who the Moneywoman was. And you neglected to tell us."

"Oh, what's the fun in that?" The Ghost's tone was light, almost teasing. "Now, I'd like to talk to my nephew in private."

Olivia's expression hardened, her eyes narrowing. "Next time, you need to give us a name and everything you know about the person."

"Yeah, yeah." The Ghost waved dismissively, the gesture rattling the chain holding her hands. "Hopefully, I'll be at my new accommodation then."

Olivia's gaze didn't waver. "Five minutes." She stood up, her movements sharp and controlled, and walked out the door, the tension lingering in her wake.

Once Olivia walked out, Dylan spoke. "We found the tunnels, the bunker, and the computer room."

"Fantastic!" The Ghost's eyes lit up. "Guard it. That woman, Cristina, had designs on the treasures. Why do you think she had that girl taken to the bunker?"

He frowned. "How'd you know about that?"

The Ghost leaned forward and dropped her voice to a conspiratorial whisper. "One thing you need to know is that I have eyes and ears everywhere."

No matter what, he wasn't going to tell her about the key he found. "I don't know where the treasures are. Unless you have a map, I can't help you."

He waited with bated breath for her answer. It would tell him if she had the map or knew where it was.

She sat back on her chair. "When the time comes, I'll let you know."

CHAPTER 99

LORRAINE'S KITCHEN

CONNOR

Sick of the hospital food, Connor wanted to go home. Today was the day! Lorraine and Sean arrived to pick him up, balloons in hand and smiles on their faces. The nurse handed Lorraine all the discharge paperwork and instructions for home care. Connor had already thanked Dr. Khoury when he came to check on him one more time before signing the discharge papers.

"Come to Lorraine's Kitchen anytime. Eat on the house!" Connor had offered the doctor.

Dr. Khoury had laughed. "We might just do that. Take care now!"

During the relaxing ride back to Mirror Estate, relief washed over Connor in waves, building as they pulled into the familiar lot.

In Lorraine's Kitchen, the whole family and friends erupted in cheers. "Welcome home!" Everyone cheered, and he scanned the familiar faces: his in-laws, Dylan, Lily, Ortiz, Eva, and even Ms. Carol, Fr. Phil, and Fr. Jeremy. Longtime employees joined in the celebration, their smiles genuine and heartfelt.

Connor thanked everyone for their prayers and help. As he moved through the crowd, shaking hands and exchanging hugs, a profound gratitude warmed him.

"Now you can really put the past behind you," Fr. Phil said quietly when they had a moment alone.

Connor grinned, looking across the room at his son, who was chatting with Dylan and Lily. "I watched my parents' murders so many years ago. In that room, when I was shot, I was praying for Sean to be spared, and then I worried history would repeat itself and Sean would have to live like I did."

The priest placed a comforting hand on Connor's shoulder. "But God had other plans."

Connor nodded beneath the weight of that hand and words. "Yes, He did. And for that, I'm forever grateful."

FEDERAL DETENTION CENTER

FR. PHIL

Later that day, Fr. Phil entered the private visiting room. He had never been to this prison before, but the atmosphere was all too familiar. His decision bore down on him. He didn't take this step lightly. After many hours of prayers and contemplations, he believed he'd set on the right course of action.

The door across the room clanked open. A guard led Marge in, her wrists shackled to her waist. The guard secured her to the table, the chains clinking in the silence.

"Holler if she gives you any trouble, Father." The guard then banged the door closed.

Fr. Phil watched Marge for a moment, noting the tension in her shoulders and the guarded look in her eyes. She met his gaze.

Eyes wide with fear, she asked, "What's wrong? Did something happen to—"

"As far as I know, nothing happened. Everybody is fine. But we need to talk." He pulled out the chair opposite her and sat.

Shadowed Secret, the next gripping installment in the Mirror Estate series, is available on Amazon and Kindle Unlimited. Grab it now!

In case you miss it, here's where you can download book 4, *Tangled Secrets*, or any previous books you've missed.

THANK YOU!

Thank you for diving into *Hidden Secrets*! Writing this story has been such a wild ride and knowing that you've spent time with the cast means the world to me.

I hope you loved reading it as much as I loved writing it. If you'd be so kind as to leave a review on Amazon and/or Goodreads to share your impressions with others, I would greatly appreciate it. Your insights will help other readers find the book.

BONUS SCENES

BONUS SCENE 1

NEW JERSEY

CARTER

The sun hung low in the sky, casting a golden hue over the suburban neighborhood. The cool evening air carried the scent of freshly cut grass, a telltale sign of the season. Fifteen-year-old Carter's sneakers squeaked against the blacktop as he shot hoops with his buddies. The basketball, worn from countless games, thudded against the pavement before sailing smoothly through the rusty rim. Laughter and shouts reverberated as they jostled each other, enjoying the last minutes before Mrs. Reynolds, CJ's mom, came home from work.

The familiar rumble of her car turning into the driveway caused the boys to pause. "Uh-oh, here comes Mom." CJ chuckled.

Carter and the others exchanged knowing looks. Mrs. Reynolds was nice but believed in "work before play." They gathered their things as she stepped out of the car, her professional attire contrasting with the boys' casual outfits.

"Hey, Mrs. Reynolds," Carter called out, trying to sound

cheerful. She smiled at them, though weariness tinged her affectionate expression. "Hey, boys. You know the rules."

"Yep, we were just leaving." Carter hopped onto his bike. He glanced back at his friends with a grin and then pedaled off toward home, just a few blocks away.

The rhythmic hum of his bike tires against the pavement filled his ears as he coasted down the quiet streets, the evening sun casting long shadows around him. The breeze tugged at his hair, and the familiar sight of his house brought a sense of peace. That peace shattered when he rode up the driveway and saw the new mirror his dad had installed.

The round mirror, designed to help with backing out of the garage, reflected a scene that sent a cold chill down Carter's spine. He saw a man, his face partially obscured by a hat, pointing a gun at his parents. Panic set in as he watched, frozen, and then his dad yelled, "Run!"

A pair of muffled pops broke the silence, and Carter's heart sank as his parents fell to the ground like rag dolls. The man in the mirror turned, his eyes cold and piercing, meeting Carter's terrified gaze.

Carter's shock transformed into a primal urge to flee. He turned his bike around with a desperate jerk and pedaled toward the nearest neighbor he knew had a gun.

BONUS SCENE 2

PARIS

OLIVIA

Olivia adjusted her sunglasses, scanning the area for the hundredth time. The Eiffel Tower loomed in the distance, its lights just beginning to twinkle as dusk settled over Paris. Across from her, Shadow Shot absently stirred his black coffee, but she knew his casual demeanor masked the same hypervigilance she felt.

"Target's fifteen minutes late," she murmured, her lips barely moving.

Shadow Shot gave an almost imperceptible nod. "I don't like this. Something's off."

A waiter approached, menu in hand. As he turned to arrange nearby chairs, Olivia caught a glimpse of a concealed weapon beneath his apron. Her hand instinctively moved toward her own hidden firearm.

"We're blown," Shadow Shot whispered urgently. She followed his gaze to the street where two men in dark suits had appeared, moving with purpose toward the café.

Olivia's fingers tightened around her espresso cup, her

knuckles whitening. Her eyes darted from exit to exit, mapping escape routes in her mind. She shifted in her seat, muscles coiling like springs ready to launch her into action. Just as she was about to signal Shadow Shot, a lilting voice cut through their comms. "Changing the game, darlings." Olivia's shoulders tensed at the crisp British accent of Raven, their MI6 liaison. "Sorry for the late notice, but our mutual friends decided to spice things up."

"Raven? What's going on?" Olivia whispered.

"No time for pleasantries. Pont des Arts, five minutes. Look for someone 'feeding the pigeons'. That's your new contact." Raven's voice was cool, professional. "Oh, and there's a lovely little exit through Le Petit Café's kitchen. You might need it. The staff there owes me a favor."

Shadow Shot's eyebrows shot up. "How did you—"

"Questions later, mate. Tick tock."

Olivia locked eyes with her partner. In one fluid motion, they upended their table as gunshots erupted. She winced at the screams filling the air as café patrons scrambled for cover.

"Go, go!" he yelled, providing covering fire as she sprinted for the kitchen. They burst through the swinging doors, startling a young chef who yelped and dropped a pan of croissants.

"Pardon, monsieur," Olivia said, flashing a quick smile as they raced past. "Merci, Raven," she added under her breath, grateful for the intel.

They emerged onto a narrow alley leading to the Seine. She could hear the sound of pursuit not far behind.

"Think you can make that?" Shadow Shot nodded toward a passing tourist boat.

Olivia grinned, adrenaline pumping. "Wanna bet?"

They sprinted along the riverbank, leapt, and landed with a thud on the boat's deck. She muttered a quick apology to the shocked tourists as they raced to the other side.

Minutes later, breathless and disheveled, they arrived at Pont des Arts. Olivia's eyes darted around the iconic bridge, crowded with couples attaching love locks and street performers entertaining for euros.

"There," Shadow Shot nodded subtly. She spotted a middle-aged man tossing breadcrumbs to a cluster of pigeons.

She approached casually, her heart still racing. "Lovely evening for feeding the pigeons," she said, the code phrase feeling clumsy on her tongue.

The man stiffened almost imperceptibly, then slowly reached into his coat. For a moment, Olivia tensed, but he simply withdrew a small package wrapped in brown paper.

"They do get hungry this time of year," he replied, pressing the package into her hand as he passed.

Mission accomplished, they melted into the Parisian night, the weight of the flash drive heavy in her pocket.

Back at their safe house, as Shadow Shot secured their prize, Olivia's phone buzzed with a text.

RAVEN

Glad to see you didn't take a swim in the Seine. Dinner's on me next time.

Olivia smiled, shaking her head. Their British friend had come through again. In this game of international espionage, she was grateful to have friends in high places—even if they did have a flair for the dramatic.

SHADOWED SECRET

A Thriller

BOOK 6
SNEAK PEEK

PROLOGUE

VATICAN

PHIL

The grand splendor of St. Peter's Basilica loomed behind them, its intricate façade bathed in golden afternoon light. The ceremony had been overwhelming—the Gregorian chants, the solemn laying on of hands, the lingering fragrance of sacred chrism oil. Now, standing outside in St. Peter's Square, Phil Shagley touched the diagonal white stole draped across his chest, the mark of his new role as a transitional deacon.

Around him, groups of newly ordained deacons and priests stood with their families, posing for photos, offering blessings. A murmur of conversation mixed with the footsteps echoing across the stone pavement. The peace he felt in those sacred moments inside was already fading. Maybe it was the memories of his SEAL days, the ones that always crept up when things got quiet.

"Deacon Phil." Fr. Michael Donovan, his mentor, approached with measured steps. Walking beside him was a tall younger man with a bright expression. Fr. Stanislaw Novak, a newly ordained priest from Poland.

Phil nodded his greeting, then addressed Fr. Donovan. "Thank you for being here, Father."

Fr. Donovan clasped Phil's hand. "Of course, Phil. I wouldn't miss this for the world." Warmth smoothed his voice, but beneath it lay something else, an unspoken weight. "I'm proud of you."

Fr. Novak shook Phil's hand. "Congratulations, Deacon Shagley."

They exchanged pleasantries, speaking of the beauty of the basilica, the solemnity of the ceremony, and the uncertainty of the road ahead. The square overflowed with jubilant commotion —clergy and seminarians congratulating one another, family members embracing their sons who had taken the next step toward the priesthood. Then Novak excused himself, moving toward a group of fellow priests and guests gathered near the basilica's steps.

Fr. Donovan's expression shifted. The warmth remained, but the lightheartedness faded. His gaze held something deeper, something that pulled Phil's attention like a long-forgotten instinct.

"I heard about Leon Roche," Fr. Donovan said. "I'm sorry, Phil."

Phil stiffened. He hadn't expected his mentor to bring up his stepfather's death, let alone know about it.

"You knew?" Phil whispered. At Donovan's nod, Phil exhaled. His gaze drifted across the square, past the towering columns framing St. Peter's Basilica. "They gave me leave for the funeral. Then I had to come straight back here."

During his pause, the din of the square intruded on the silence between them.

"I understand Mickey is at St. Ann's Orphanage now."

"St. Ann's?" Phil's head snapped up. "No, that can't be right. Mickey was supposed to be with an elderly aunt. That's where he went after the funeral."

"Well, 'elderly' is the operative word. My sources told me she had a stroke and is now in a care facility. She can't take care of a teenager. Mickey's been at St. Ann's for a couple of years now."

A hollowness carved itself way into his chest. They had never been too close, not with the twelve-year gap between them. And Mickey was still just a kid when Phil left for the service. "I didn't know. Why didn't he tell me?"

"Mickey's been through a lot. I imagine he didn't want to burden you while you were in formation. But he needs you, Phil. More than ever now."

"I should have been there for him. I should have—"

"You did what you had to do," Fr. Donovan interrupted. "Anyway, that's not why I'm telling you this."

Phil lifted his gaze, waiting.

His mentor edged closer. "I wanted to talk to you about an opportunity."

Phil tensed. He knew that tone.

"You've been here in Rome for a while now, and you must be thinking about what comes next," the priest continued. "I've spoken with some people, and there's a possibility for you to be placed somewhere closer to Mickey. Fr. Bob, the pastor at the chapel parish on Mirror Estate, is nearing retirement."

Phil narrowed his eyes. "Okay…?"

"The chapel parish is connected to St. Ann's Orphanage." Donovan let that sink in. "It would give you a chance to be close to Mickey, to keep an eye on him. But there's more to it."

"What do you mean?"

Fr. Donovan scanned the bustling square, then signaled him to follow.

As Phil trailed the priest, they approached a narrow stone passageway near the basilica, partially concealed by an ornate archway. A discreet but authoritative sign affixed to the wall beside it displayed lettering etched into aged brass: Accesso Riservato—Solo Personale Autorizzato.

Phil understood it meant "Restricted Access—Authorized Personnel Only." But his mentor barely spared it a glance as he pushed open the wooden door and led Phil into the dimly lit corridor. The hustle and murmur of St. Peter's Square faded behind them.

Only then did Fr. Donovan turn to him. "The Church has… certain needs in that area. People with your experience, both military and spiritual, are rare. I'm not asking you to pick up where you left off, but I am asking you to be aware. Vatican Intelligence has interests there and believes you'd be uniquely suited to assist them. Quietly."

Phil's pulse quickened. He left the SEALs for a reason. God called him to be a priest. And yet… he still maintained his training regimen as much as possible.

"What are you suggesting? For me to serve as a priest and… what? An operative?"

"Yes, in a way only you can."

He rubbed the back of his neck and dipped his head, his blood rushing. *Lord, is this what you want for me?* Even as the thought appeared, he was at peace. When he looked up again, he already knew his answer.

"When do I leave?"

Fr. Donovan gripped Phil's shoulder. "Relax. This is not an order. You'll be notified of your transitional deacon assignment like everyone else. And we'll be in touch."

Phil glanced at the basilica behind them.

Apparently, the life he thought he left behind wasn't done with him yet.

CHAPTER 1

CHAPEL, MIRROR ESTATE

PRESENT DAY

PHIL

Phil thudded closed his leather-bound notebook, marking the conclusion of the final meeting with Olivia Tso and Simon Roth before their nuptials. The years had etched subtle lines around their eyes—crow's feet framing Olivia's bright almond-shaped eyes and deeper creases marking Simon's distinguished face beneath his salt-and-pepper hair. Though both were in their middle years, Olivia's petite, athletic frame and Simon's trim, average-height figure spoke to their vitality.

"Well, that's it!" He clasped his hands. "You've made it through all the sessions. And you're still together."

Simon chuckled. "We are definitely getting married."

She smiled at her fiancé. "We'd better."

Phil got their attention back. "The rehearsal is the day before the wedding. I hope there's no last-minute changes."

She shook her head. "We're good. We'll be here. Hard to believe it's only two weeks away."

"Here's to new beginnings." Simon clasped her hand in an affectionate squeeze. "You should show him your medal."

"Right." She reached for the necklace and pulled out the medal hanging from it. "I'm sure you're familiar with this medal."

Phil took one look at the famous Medal of the Immaculate Conception and nodded. "The Miraculous Medal. It looks heavier than any I've seen."

"It is. My best friend, Marie—a nun, by the way—gave it to me years ago. She has one too. Her grandfather, after witnessing a bullet deflect off his friend's Miraculous Medal, had one crafted from repurposed military-grade steel. He believed it saved his life when it later deflected a bullet meant for him."

Phil smiled. "I've read countless similar testimonies, illnesses cured, accidents averted. Remember it's not the medal itself, but the power comes from God."

She slid her necklace back. "So, Father, how has the parish been lately? The holidays are always a whirlwind, but anything new as we enter the new year?"

He scratched his chin. "The same, for the most part. We had an enormous turnout for all the Christmas Masses, as always. It was good to see so many faces, even if some are what we call 'C&E folks,' only showing up at Christmas and Easter. But they're part of the flock too."

"Of course," Simon agreed. "It's wonderful that they have a place they can return to, even if it's not as frequently as you might like."

Phil inclined his head. "Well said. And, of course, Fr. Jeremy's been a blessing to have around. He took some time off to visit his family. Will be back any day now."

"Are you thinking about retiring?" Olivia glanced at the wall clock.

"I'm not quite at the mandatory retirement age yet, but it's on the horizon. It's good to have Fr. Jeremy around, so I can take a break now and then. And you? Still keeping busy at work?"

To most people, she was a consultant with an elite FBI task force, though he knew she was still an intelligence operative.

"You could say that. Nothing exciting. Mostly paperwork and consulting with other agencies these days. But I manage."

"We haven't had a lot of excitement since the Ghost's move. Come to think of it, she's been rather quiet." Simon drew his fiancée's hand into his lap. "She's still giving you names, isn't she?"

"Yeah, but nobody exciting."

Marge Beaumont, aka the Ghost, a notorious criminal, had made a perplexing deal with the government since her capture about a year and a half ago. She agreed to help an elite FBI task force apprehend those on the most wanted list. In return, she would stay on the Mirror Estate grounds instead of the supermax.

Phil remained quiet. At the beginning of last year, he visited the Ghost at the Federation Detention Center.

"Remember your promise?" he asked.

A pallor crept across her features, her breath catching as her eyes went wide, darkened by something only she could see. "Yes, of course."

He narrowed his eyes. "Not what I've been hearing."

She scoffed. "I have an image to maintain. Everything is going according to plan."

"I heard you gave the order to put Grace and Kyle on a hit list."

"Absolutely not!" Those darkened eyes flashed. "It was Rook's doing. I only wanted to find out who was responsible for Jade's death. As it turned out, their parents are."

He took a deep breath and muttered a silent prayer. Ah, secrets. So many secrets. He couldn't reveal to her Jade,

Olivia's legend, wasn't dead. "The agents had to do what they had to do, but their children had nothing to do with it. Most importantly, this is not the way to salvation."

Her defiant posture didn't waver, nor did she respond.

"Listen." He leaned forward. "Soon, you'll be living on the Mirror Estate grounds. Don't even think about escaping or reneging on your promise. Any funny business, I guarantee Vatican would hear about it, and then you know what would happen."

"Father!"

Olivia's voice brought him out of his reverie. He refocused on the couple before he stood up. "I should let you two go. If I don't see you before rehearsal, enjoy your week, both of you."

He led them to the door of the parish office. The warm afternoon air met him, heavy with Florida humidity and a lingering pine scent from the holiday season. They nearly collided with Jeremy, who hustled up the path, hands tucked into his coat pockets, head down.

The young priest beamed when he saw them. "Hey, Olivia, Simon, ready for your big day?"

Simon nodded while Olivia said, "Yes. How was your visit home?"

"Wonderful, thank you. It was nice to be with family. But I'm glad to be back."

They shared goodbyes, handshakes, and well-wishes before Olivia and Simon strolled down the path.

Jeremy waved them off with a grin, then stepped closer to Phil. "Anything I should know about?"

He shook his head. "Everything is good."

Phil's gaze drifted toward the chapel. A lone figure sat in one of the pews, head bowed, hands clasped. Something about the man seemed familiar, though Phil couldn't place him. The chapel's subdued lighting cast the man in shadow, but the briefest flash of white at his collar confirmed it—a clerical collar, like his own.

Odd. It wasn't unusual to see another priest visit the chapel, but something about this one made him pause. A vague, unsettled feeling prickled at the back of his neck.

He waved Jeremy on. "You go ahead. I'm going to check on something."

The young priest continued on his way, leaving Phil to edge closer to the chapel.

"Sorry, Father, are you going in?" Leo, the longtime custodian, stopped on the chapel door's other side, a toolbox in hand. "I can come back."

"Ah, yes, the loose hinge." Phil had reported that. He frowned. The man was gone. "No, go ahead. Thank you."

He walked toward his office, his mind racing through years of faces, names, encounters. Had he seen the man before, or was it his imagination? Or perhaps, something else?

ABOUT THE AUTHOR

S.F. Baumgartner writes fast-paced Christian suspense thrillers. Book 1 of her Mirror Estate series, Living Secrets, was selected as one of the Top Picks in the thriller category at Killer Nashville, 2024. Her love for writing comes second only to her love of reading.

When she's not busy writing about complex characters, secretive operatives, and relentless agents, she spends her time binge-watching crime TV shows, such as NCIS, or playing with her cats. If you enjoy James Patterson's style—specifically short chapters—you'll love her Mirror Estate series.

To be the first to know about any sales, promotions, and new releases, sign up for our monthly newsletter. By subscribing, you'll stay informed about all the latest happenings and never miss an opportunity to explore this captivating world.

ALSO BY
S.F. BAUMGARTNER

Mirror Estates series

Buried Secrets, book 1

Living Secrets, book 2

Forgotten Secret, book 3

Tangled Secrets, book 4

Hidden Secrets, book 5

Shadowed Secret, book 6

Stolen Secrets, book 7

Box Set (Books 1-4)

KC & Orlando Prime series

Christmas Murders, a prequel

Fatal Invitation, book 1

ACKNOWLEDGMENTS

Publishing a novel is not a solo endeavor, and I'm deeply grateful to those who made this book possible.

A heartfelt thanks to Deirdre Lockhart at Brilliant Cut Editing, Kelsey Darling and Chelsea Lauren from Represent Publishing for their invaluable guidance and support. To the team at 100Covers.com, your stunning cover design perfectly captured the heart of this story.

I also want to thank the amazing beta and ARC readers—your feedback and enthusiasm were crucial in refining this novel.

To my family, your unwavering support has been my greatest strength. And finally, to you, dear readers—this book is for you. Enjoy the journey!

www.ingramcontent.com/pod-product-compliance
Lightning Source LLC
Chambersburg PA
CBHW032117310726
48972CB00001B/250